Reva

a novel

First paperback edition July 2020

Cover design by Estella
Interior design by Elementi.Studio
Author photo by Shrinath Keskar

ISBN 978-1-7354273-3-1 (paperback)
ISBN 978-1-7354273-3-2 (hardback)
ISBN 978-1-7354273-3-3 (ebook)

For more information, contact:
Cox&Quito Publishing
Campbell, CA
coxandquitopublishing@gmail.com

"As the creeper that girdles the tree trunk
The Law runneth forward and back

For the strength of the Pack is the Wolf
And the strength of the Wolf is the Pack"

From 'The Law of the Jungle'
by Rudyard Kipling

This book is dedicated to my Pack.

Chapter 1

The last of the monsoon clouds had finally succumbed to the brilliance of the September sun. Yet Reva sensed a storm lingering in the gray and gloom of Miss Tytler's gaze as it followed her around the classroom that sun-drenched morning.

A year had passed since Reva's mother, Aai, had died. The century had turned. And without Aai to hold her hand, so had Reva's life. Reva wondered if she still looked as broken as she felt. Was her teacher counting the cracks or looking for signs of healing? Reva squirmed. She knew that her only wispy chance of happiness lay somewhere between the bare mud walls of this classroom, with Miss Tytler and all that her white world promised.

Cross-legged on the floor, Reva hunched over her book, trying to drown herself in the pool of braided heads bobbing around her. At fourteen, unquestionably past the perfect age for marriage, she was the oldest and the tallest in her class. No matter what, she stood out.

"Reva." Miss Tytler's voice held her back as the lesson ended, and the girls began putting away the floor mats, the slates, and chalk. Reva waited. Miss Tytler was one of the few people that still mattered.

Miss Tytler wasted no words. In broken Marathi, she came straight to the point. "Reva, *tu shaala kaa sodtey?* Why are you leaving school?"

Bewildered, Reva shook her head.

"*Kai?* What? What did you say, Miss Tytler?"

"Your uncle sent me a message that next week is to be your last. I should be very disturbed if it is. You have two years of lessons left in order to matriculate."

"Kaka is pulling me out of school? There *must* be some mistake. Aai and I had decided I would surely complete school..."

Her mother's name slipped through Reva's guarded lips easily in Miss Tytler's presence. It was barely a year ago that Aai had been sent away to nurse a sick aunt in Bombay where she had caught the black disease herself. In four days, Aai had departed from Reva's world forever without so much as a goodbye, leaving her in shock and utter despair. With Miss Tytler by her side and her schoolwork to gather her mind, Reva had painfully pieced together the fragments of her shattered life.

Reva's hazel eyes glistened for a moment as her grief resurfaced. But the string of thoughts that was beginning to flood her mind was too frightening to entertain the impending tears.

Reva's mother had nurtured a dream of educating her daughter, and despite strong family disapproval, Reva's father had supported the idea. After his untimely death, a powerless Aai had guarded that dream passionately for a decade by playing her only trump card—being the oldest brother's widow who was keeping alive her husband's last wish that his daughter continue to go to school. Reva's education was the only cause that had ever pushed Aai to assume a fierce outspoken manner that had at times frightened as much as reassured Reva. But from where Aai was now, she could not make any demands to honor buried wishes. And Reva was just a child. A girl. Who would listen to her?

With her heart pounding in her ears, Reva walked out of the school yard as calmly as she could until she was out of Miss Tytler's sight. Then, without a moment's hesitation, she broke into a run. She knew that Miss Tytler would never approve of this common native behavior, no matter how urgent the situation. And neither would Kaku, Reva's aunt and guardian.

"Revati!" she could almost hear Kaku now calling her out by her full name, a jab that always found its mark. "Stop behaving like a child. It's no wonder that you are fourteen and still not married. Even the village idiot would not want such a shameless wife!"

Reva had no inclination to be any kind of wife. Her dream was loftier—she would learn to speak English; she would matriculate ... maybe even attend college. She would work in an office where stacks of important papers lined the walls, and the hot humid air felt alive with the clacking of typewriters and the gentle swish of the ceiling *punkhas*. People would listen to her. She would make heads turn with her knowledge, her kindness, and her grace. Just like Miss Tytler.

Reva's dream was also the only way to keep her mother's memory alive as life returned to normalcy at home. Kaku and the other women in the family lamented Aai's death only when it was time to cook the food, or polish the giant idols in the prayer altar, or when frequent gossip sessions had to be interrupted to make fresh tea for visitors and family members alike.

In reality, Aai had been a cook, a nurse, a servant for the family. It had been an unsaid rule that Kaku would visit with the villagers, arrange and attend festivals and celebrations, and engage in the luxuries of well-to-do women while Aai's widowhood was barely tolerated in the confines of her home and the village temple where she would join the locals for an evening of singing *bhajans* in praise of Krishna.

Such sweet talking to God had not done Reva's mother any good. Aai's life had remained hopeless. Her God had not been able to give her what a husband could have—a respectable place in society.

Reva had heard stories from the villagers of the vibrant woman that her mother had been before the shadow of widowhood had overpowered and crippled her. Reva had wished for that woman to resurface someday. But she had also observed how the very same people who outwardly cursed fate for the loss of that spirited woman would not let such a miracle happen. Reva had never ceased to marvel at how Aai had borne her suffering with silence, even an unexplainable contentment.

"I know I work harder than anyone else in this house ... but I get what I need here—a safe home for us so you can go to school," Aai used to say. "Don't worry about me, my dear. You just pay attention to your studies. Miss Tytler is *dev-manoos*, god-like. Learn from her. Finish your schooling. Stand on your own feet. What more can an unfortunate widow like me want?"

As Reva hurried home, Aai's words swirled in her mind like dust clouds that obscured everything in her surroundings.

She crossed through the village and neared the mill, the very last shack on the street, where the line of women waiting to grind the wheat into flour was beginning to form. Reva could feel their eyes following her as they took in the deep flush spreading on her fair complexion and the unruly tendrils breaking loose from her bun, an indisputable evidence of her running. She had no time to make explanations for her sprint to these self-appointed nosy guardians of propriety. She slowed down a little, lest news of her unladylike travel reached Kaku before she did.

A frown started to form across Reva's small forehead and along her eyebrows that arched only slightly at the temples, giving her face a proud look. Would these women ever question and scold the boys for racing each other? The frown etched deeper on her face.

As Reva approached the narrow dirt road that led through the sugar-cane fields to her home, her feet slowed down. At the end of the path, her ancestral *vaada* towered behind a deterring iron gate. For more than a century, this stone mansion, built by her great grandfather, had sheltered the multiple generations of the Lele family—brothers, cousins, uncles, their wives and children. Spacious rooms and connected balconies formed a protective enclave around an open, meticulously clean courtyard. Reva recalled the days when Aai would stand in the courtyard behind the solid wooden door, eyes glued to the entrance, waiting for Reva to come home from school. Reva would run into her arms and inhale the familiar scent of musk incense that was an inseparable part of Aai. In her mother's embrace, Reva had felt as treasured and as safe as a pearl in its oyster.

Reva blinked rapidly as her most fragile memories threatened to spill out. Taking a few deep breaths, she tidied her appearance and stepped into the *vaada*. Her eyes involuntarily traced a path to Sumi's room as they did each time she entered the house; more out of habit now than hope. It had been three years since she had last seen Sumi. Reva missed her cousin who had not only been like a sister but also a best friend. A year older than Reva, Sumi had been 'shown' to a family from a distant village when she was only ten. Sumi had cooked for them, sang for them, walked gracefully around the courtyard and touched the feet of these strangers that had appeared before her. She had said not a word about the book she was reading and the lessons she excelled at in Miss Tytler's class, fearing Kaka's threat to pull her tongue out if she did. Despite her best talents being hidden, the family had approved of Sumi. Two weeks later, a married Sumi had been packed off to her husband's home, and Kaka-Kaku had washed their hands off their daughter forever. Standing in the doorway that morning, Reva could taste Sumi's dread. It left her tongue heavy and her mouth dry.

Reva slipped off her *chappal* and headed to Kaka's study, tripping over the folds of her *loogduh* as she navigated the stairs. Silently, Reva cursed 'the crow' and the *loogduh* that had followed its arrival.

If losing her mother had not been traumatic enough, finding blood on her underclothes soon after had thrown Reva in a panic. Kaku had attempted to explain this horror as a blessing for good marriage prospects. To Reva, it sounded like an additional monthly punishment for being born a girl. Overnight, her childhood had disappeared, as had her comfortable clothes. Her *purkur* had been donated to the temple, and Reva's cupboard had overnight been stocked with the *loogduh*, the traditional nine-yard drape of fabric that girls were expected to wear as soon as 'the crow' started visiting. Since menstruating was not any kind of achievement to be rewarded with new clothes, Kaku had announced that her hand-me-down *loogduh* would suffice, and that her niece should be grateful for the generosity.

Gratitude was the last thought on Reva's mind as she urged her tense body, wrapped in layer upon layer of fabric, towards Kaka's study.

Kaku intercepted her as she reached the doorway. And it was just as well. Had Reva been able to produce any words at all in her uncle's presence, the audacity of questioning him would have landed her in the storeroom with no dinner for a week.

"And where are we rushing to, Revati?" Kaku demanded. "And that too in the wrong direction. The vegetables in the kitchen are not going to chop themselves today, are they?"

Reva ignored the reminder.

"Kaku, Miss Tytler said that I might be leaving school. Why would she say that?" she asked, keeping her voice as respectful as possible.

"Yes, I was going to talk to you about that," Kaku replied.

Reva dreaded the sound of 'that'.

Although Kaka and Kaku had not been unkind to her since Aai's death, Reva questioned their intentions. They would not do anything obvious to jeopardize their saintly reputation in the village. But Reva was a constant reminder of an unpleasant time when Kaka had to squash his opinions and play second fiddle as a show of respect for his elder brother. For the last few years, Kaka had seethed silently as Reva continued to attend school despite his opposition, making their family the subject of hushed conversations in the village that found their way back to Kaku's inquisitive ears. Reva had good reason to fear for herself now. For what she was going to hear.

"Two weeks ago," Kaku started to spin her tale, picking her words carefully, as she paced the length of the corridor outside Kaka's study, "my friend from Rajapur called on us with a wonderful proposal for you. Her sister's husband's brother's son is looking for a wife. The boy is only twenty years older than you. The family owns a big mango business in the city. You will live like a princess. Your birth charts match perfectly. And thank goodness you are fair—that is the only condition of the mother-in-law. She wants a wife as white as a freshly harvested pearl for her precious son."

"But Kaku…!" Reva panicked.

Kaku ignored Reva's distress.

"The family is coming to see you next week. If the elders approve of you, the engagement will be right away. Your going to school after that will not be advisable. It is a conservative family. And did I tell you already? Also very, very rich. That's not all. Your future husband also has a son from his first wife. The poor woman died in childbirth. The son will keep you busy until you have children of your own. I am so happy for you. I have spent sleepless nights wondering who will want to marry a girl like you, so old and cursed with an education. I thank my stars that this proposal came through!" Kaku wiped her fake tears while running a tentative hand over Reva's head.

Marriage! Reva's fear turned to terror. She had always suspected that Kaka and Kaku, hoping to find a match for Reva, had cast their net long before her mother's ashes had turned cold. But a marriage ceremony in the house during the year of mourning was inauspicious. Now, a year later, it could be passed off as a much needed blessing. There was nothing to stop the calamity now.

For a few moments, a pregnant silence filled the hallway. Kaku watched Reva with eyes narrowed, trying to gauge the intensity of her emotions, ready to squash any trace of an outburst.

Reva willed herself to find her voice, now that she could no longer hide behind her mother's.

She took a deep breath and said, her voice shaking, "I don't want to get married, Kaku. I want to go to school. I want to be like Miss Tytler."

"What's that? Miss Tytler?" Kaku spat out the name as she would a piece of raw bitter melon. "That *firang*, that white woman of no caste? No shame. Living alone in her house with all those servants. Even a man-servant!"

Kaku's opinion of Miss Tytler was not news to Reva. But in an effort to stop her aunt's tirade against Miss Tytler, Reva's words spilled out a little more loudly than she intended.

"I want to study, Kaku. I want to work."

Reva's uncharacteristic assertiveness silenced Kaku for a moment, but it also brought Kaka out from the study.

"Enough!" Kaka thundered, leaving no doubt about the outcome of the disagreement. "Revati, you have more education than most girls in the village. You know enough to run a household, raise healthy children, and be a dutiful companion to your husband. This marriage will be good for you, and it will help our family business. What else do you want?"

Reva sensed the hidden warning to remain silent. *Aai would NOT have liked this idea!* her mind screamed, but all that came out was a pathetic cry for her mother.

"Aai!" Reva sobbed into her hands. Aai's memory was her only hope.

Kaka and Kaku exchanged a long look before Kaka continued, "Listen carefully to what I am about to tell you. When your mother fell sick, she wrote me a letter asking me to make sure you had a good future in case she did not make it home. As your guardian, I am following her wishes. When you are settled in a worthy home, my responsibility will be fulfilled, and your Aai will rest in peace. Now tell me, who is acting against her mother's wishes?"

Reva did not believe a word. This marriage was not to safeguard her interest, but to get rid of her in a respectable way and help the family's sugarcane business.

"I want to read Aai's letter," Reva stammered as she stifled a sob, desperate in that moment for a connection with her mother, however disturbing.

"When you are older, and you understand the ways of the world a little better, I will let you read it. Until then, I will take care of it. I have wasted enough time on your silliness now. You are not the first girl to marry, and you won't be the last. Now, do as your Kaku tells you, and get ready for their visit next week. This subject is closed."

Kaka turned and stepped back into his study. Kaku too beat a hasty retreat from what now seemed like a crime scene.

Reva walked in a daze through the courtyard, out the front door, following the dirt path along the long stretch of sugarcane fields. She stumbled on a rock lying in her path; it did little to snap her out of the nightmare that only got darker and scarier with each passing moment.

"Aai! Where are you? I need you," she called out weakly. Reva's vision blurred, her legs gave out, and she crumbled to the ground.

"*Ugi, ugi.* Hush. Don't you cry, my dear. Such a young child. Such a heavy burden. Hush now. Come and sit with me for a bit. Here, eat a carrot. You will feel better."

A familiar voice cut through Reva's fog of hopelessness. She saw Hirkani, the vegetable seller, walking towards her with her basket overflowing with fresh carrots and green bananas and felt a sliver of comfort in her solid presence. She needed a friend, and Hirkani, although a good decade older than Reva, was most definitely her friend.

Reva's first instinct was to hug Hirkani, but she held back. As a high caste Brahmin, Reva was not permitted to hug Hirkani whose caste was much lower in the social hierarchy. Violating that rule would get both of them in trouble, as Reva had learned a few years ago. She waited as Hirkani set her basket of produce down and squatted beside her.

Hirkani was a tall woman. When unraveled to her full height, she was a hand's length taller than Kaka, and the only woman in the village who had to bow at the waist in order to enter the back door of the temple. In a society that favored petiteness, she was an oddity. Hirkani was also a strong woman from the years of relentless walking between villages with a basket full of pumpkins and potatoes on her head. In a society that equated physical strength with dominance, she was intimidating. Some called Hirkani a strange woman. Despite being uneducated, she imparted, in her moments of leisure, saintly nuggets of wisdom that confounded her listeners. Some villagers speculated that Hirkani's forced solitude had provided her with a uniquely profound education.

But Hirkani was also an optimistic woman—she did everything in her power to change her misfortunes. She scrubbed her dark face with lemon everyday hoping to lighten it to the color of wheat. She lined her small, expressive eyes with black *kajal* to make them look bigger, more attractive. She wore a delicate nose ring to coax a fragility from her sturdy nose. And she chewed raw fennel seeds to keep her breath fresh, a secret she had learned from a missionary woman passing through the village.

Her efforts had yielded a satisfactory result. Two years ago, Hirkani had married a simple man who was everything she was not—short in stature, weak from poor health, and very resigned to his fate. Hirkani had proposed that they live together and overcome their loneliness with a handful of children. He had agreed. They had married. The children had followed. The lemon peels had stopped. The *kaajal*, now reduced to a dot on her children's foreheads, served only to ward off the evil eye. And the fennel seeds were mainly a remedy for good digestive health. Hirkani insisted she had never been happier, and Reva believed her. A husband had given her friend something precious that even her God had not. Reva knew that story well.

As Reva followed Hirkani into the quiet of the fields away from the dirt path, she couldn't help thinking how simple Hirkani's world was, where a carrot could be a solution to a problem. But Reva's appetite was dead and so was her future. No more school. No more Miss Tytler.

Miss Tytler ... a plan began forming in her mind.

"Hirkani, Kaka has arranged for my marriage. But I want to study. I don't want to marry. I am going to tell Miss Tytler. I am sure her people can help me. They can make Kaka stop. I can't get married. I CAN'T. You understand that Hirkani, don't you?"

"My child," Hirkani responded softly, "even if your teacher can help you, think about what your life will be like afterwards. The family will not let you be in peace going to school. If you get them in trouble and make them a laughingstock of the village, there will be no place for you in this house. That is our lot as women. Heed my words."

"Then what should I do?" Reva cried out in frustration.

Hirkani looked at her with a calm, steady gaze. "Don't make any hasty decisions when you are angry. The winds have changed. You cannot change their direction, but you can adjust your sails. Remember, even an arrow must be pulled backwards in order to launch it forward to its target. Why don't you at least see the boy? Maybe he is just as handsome and noble as he is rich. A fine match for my beautiful fair princess!"

Hirkani's words made Reva breathe a little easier.

"I miss Aai, Hirkani."

"I know you do, dearie. But your mother is watching over you. Trust in her. Trust in God. Everything will be alright. You'll see. But now I simply must go to sell my vegetables. I will come back in two days. Should I bring some fresh brinjals for you then?"

Reva, attempting a smile, waved goodbye to her friend and started walking back towards the house, each reluctant step a reminder of her nonexistent choices.

Reva had always known that her marriage was inevitable. However, since Sumi's last visit home, Reva had begun to dread the prospect. Reva's joy at seeing her cousin again, a year after her marriage, was replaced by a curious anxiety in just a few hours. Sumi's smile did not reach her eyes which mostly remained downcast. Even though they were only a year apart in age, Sumi appeared more at ease in the company of Kaku and Kaku's friends than when she was with Reva, her childhood confidante. Reva remembered the awkward moments when the soft sizzle of the vegetables cooking in the pot had filled the strange silence in the kitchen where they had sat together. The only assurance that this was the same Sumi who had pranked the village boys and slept in the same bed with Reva was in the fierce hug she gave Reva as soon as she had stepped in her parents' home.

"What is your new home like, Sumi?" Reva had asked on her first day back.

"Very different from this one," Sumi had answered curtly.

"How so?" Reva had persisted.

"It just is," Sumi had remarked before joining the older women in the family.

When they were alone again, Reva had asked, "Do you like your husband, Sumi?"

"Mostly," was all that Sumi had offered.

On another occasion, Reva had wondered aloud to her, "How come you don't ask me about Miss Tytler or school or the books we are reading? You were Miss Tytler's best student you know..."

"I don't even think of school anymore. There is just so much to do at the house. I take care of the prayer room. I cook the morning breakfast. I take my brother-in-law's boys to school. Then I have to help with lunch and clean the kitchen. By the time I have a few moments to myself, it is time to fetch those boys from school and attend to their meals and studies. Mother-in-law says I must know how to care for children, for boys. She says it will soon be time ..." Sumi had stopped mid-sentence.

"Time? Time for what?" Reva had pressed.

Sumi had pretended to hear Kaku calling for her at that very moment and had rushed out of the room. Reva was left baffled. Who was this stranger that had come to visit them? At twelve, Sumi was sounding more like Aai or Kaku or even Hirkani. Where was the cousin, the sister, the friend she had missed so desperately in the last year?

There had been no time to find out. A telegram arrived summoning Sumi back right away. Her mother-in-law was craving the sweet *laadoos* that only Sumi could make for her. Amidst exclamations of how much Sumi was loved and missed in her husband's home, Sumi with her *laadoo*-making hands was once again hastily packed and transported to her in-laws before Reva had a chance to scrape at the shell that Sumi had built around herself and that had poked Reva to no end during her visit.

The evening after Sumi's unexpected departure, Reva had decided that marriage was not the rosy picture the elders painted it out to be. How could it be if there was no possibility of going to school? She was better off staying with her mother. Aai had laughed at her naive comments, but the creases in her mother's forehead were evidence that she too was thinking about what had become of Sumi.

Reva had waited anxiously for her cousin to visit again. But Sumi had never returned. Kaka-Kaku had visited her village a handful of times and returned with the same tired words: "Sumi is so happy in her husband's home that she does not have the time or the desire to visit her poor parents."

Eventually, Reva had stopped asking.

Back in the *vaada*, seeing Kaku busy in the kitchen, Reva felt a moment's relief. At least her mother was finally free from her earthly hardships.

But was she really? Reva had heard of spirits stuck in between worlds because of wishes that remained unfulfilled from their lives on earth. And whatever Kaka might say, Reva knew her mother's one true wish still remained unfulfilled.

Chapter 2

September 1900

"May her soul rest in peace. I came as soon as I heard."

Reva's ears perked. They had a visitor.

Reva had spent the entire afternoon cleaning Gau's barn as she racked her brains for a way out of her predicament. Gau had been gifted to Reva by her father just before he died. Reva and her calf had grown up together. Isolated behind the chicken coop and rarely visited by any other inhabitants of the *vaada*, Gau's barn had been Reva's place of refuge in the last year as she had mourned her mother. It seemed like the best place to find a solution to her current problem. With every firm sweep of the broom that day, she had hoped to find something, anything, that would save her dream.

The groom's family had visited the previous day. Reva had sat motionless with her head bowed under Kaka's stern gaze as the women commented on the pale white color of her feet peeping through the layers of her *loogduh*. When one woman raised Reva's chin to view her face, a gasp of admiration had rippled through the group. Reva had heard another woman call out 'Chandramukhi', as beautiful as the moon. And just like that, the match had been approved. Her fate had been sealed.

In two days, Reva had to quit school. In two weeks, she was to be engaged.

At first, Reva had been consumed by the memory of a girl from the neighboring village who had flung herself into a well after a string of families rejected her as a prospective bride for their sons. It was a possible solution, but deep dark places terrified Reva even more than an imminent marriage. Plus, she needed to be alive to attend school. Being honest about her dream with the bridegroom's family was another option. But when Kaka found out how she had gone behind his back to jeopardize the match, he would probably push her down that village well himself. Running away from home and seeking help from the Christian missionaries was the most plausible solution. But for a girl who had never spent a single night outside the house, that prospect was as traumatic as ending her life.

Two hours later, the barn looked spotless and her future still hopeless.

To make matters worse, that morning, Hirkani had dismissed every plan as impossible, or flawed, or just plain stupid.

"*Pori*, only a fool would take a step forward while standing on a cliff," Hirkani had warned her. Hirkani had an exasperating way of painting precise pictures with her words.

Tired of thinking, Reva's senses switched to high alert when she heard the visitor. She stopped sifting through the wheat and quietly set the winnowing basket on the floor. Then, she tiptoed to the doorway of the storeroom and peeked into the courtyard to see who had come to mourn her mother.

From that angle, she glimpsed a gleaming bald head and a straight back, clad in a very fashionable knee length English coat worn over a pure silk Indian *dhoti*. The visitor was seated on the *divan* alongside the swing on the open porch. At his feet lay a stylish brown bag. Reva had never seen anything quite like it. It looked important ... like something the white people would carry. But, from his speech, it was obvious that the visitor was most certainly of Indian birth. Who was this stranger, and how had he known her mother?

So intent was she in getting a more thorough look that she leaned farther out from the door frame, lost her balance, and landed with a thud, drawing the attention of Kaka and the visitor, who tried hard to hide a smile.

"Come here, Revati," the visitor called. "Do you remember me?"

As Reva walked hesitantly towards the two men, the stranger's eyes crinkled into a smile that made Reva smile back.

Should I remember you? she wondered to herself.

"No, no. Of course not," the visitor answered his own question. "You were very little when I saw you last. Look at you now."

Reva instantly liked this guest with the kind eyes. She glanced at Kaka, who was momentarily busy chastising the servant for bringing them lukewarm water.

"Miss Tytler says that to us all the time. She says we are getting too big for our boots," she replied quickly. Reva was surprised how easily she could converse with this unknown man.

The visitor's smile gave way to a deep laugh that started at the bottom of his stomach and engulfed the body as it made its way upward.

"*Vah! Chaan-chaan!* Brilliant! Now tell me *pori*, who is this Miss Tytler?"

"The most wonderful teacher. She is a *gori*, a white woman, and she runs our school. She is very smart. She knows a lot and talks about big important things," Reva blabbered, encouraged by this interest and warmth, and also by Kaka's turned back.

"Like what, my child?" asked the visitor with the twinkling eyes.

"Like going to college, and working, and helping people. I want to do it all. Just like her."

"*Eeshwar krupa!* God willing!" said the visitor with delight.

Expecting the same old reprimand that she should now be turning her thoughts towards a husband and his home and children, this reaction took Reva by surprise. Unfortunately, Kaka had missed that exchange. Perhaps it would have created a dent in his plans for Reva. But Kaka was now talking in a hushed tone with Kaku. From the unpleasant expression that had settled on Kaku's face, he was most likely instructing her to plan on having a guest for dinner that day.

Reva's eyes turned back to the visitor's bag. The leather looked so soft that it might gather in her hand and yet seemed to have the strength to stand upright on the ground. It was plain, with a simple golden clasp to keep the contents secure. It conveyed an oddly attractive sense of power and promise.

The visitor followed Reva's gaze. "You like my briefcase?"

Reva nodded shyly.

"Not really what little girls like to play with," the visitor remarked softly with a smile, making Reva bristle with indignation at the unfairness of that thought.

The next instant, she forgave the speaker as he reached into the briefcase to pull out a small brown stick. Reva had seen it in Miss Tytler's hand and knew it was a pencil, a tool to write on paper. Miss Tytler had demonstrated for the class, and the children had been fascinated by the blackness and the smoothness of the writing.

"Here. This pencil is for you. You said you wanted to study, and work, and do all those important things. This little pencil will come in very handy. And then perhaps you will remember this old uncle every once in a while too."

Reva's face broke into a smile as she extended her hand. The pencil was plain brown wood with pointed lead poking through. On its side were imprinted the letters Koh-I-Noor.

"My friend from England gave this pencil to me as a gift, but I want you to have it," the visitor offered.

A gift! All the way from the home of the Queen! Miss Tytler had been translating *The Jungle Book* to the class. Perhaps that English writer had used a pencil such as the one she now held in her hand. Reva ran her fingers over the letters K o h I N o o r—tall, bold, and commanding. As her palm curled around the pencil, she felt her spine straighten. She felt a sliver of hope.

"Revati, stop bothering our guest with your nonsense," Kaka's voice cut impatiently through her thoughts. Reva quickly hid the pencil in the folds of her *loogduh* as she realized that Kaka would never approve of this gift.

"Go to Kaku now. She was looking for you. Where have you been the whole afternoon?" Kaka scolded before turning his attention back to the guest.

Reva recognized the command in Kaka's voice and refrained from asking this kind visitor who he was. She hoped she could talk to him again.

Kaku was in the kitchen. A year after Aai's death, Kaku was still like a fish out of water around the stove.

"Where were you, lazy girl? I want you to cook the brinjals for dinner. You can make it like your mother did. I want to make sure your cooking is improved before you go to your in-laws. Otherwise, they will curse us for unloading a clueless lazy girl on them. Now get to work quickly!"

"Who is that outside?" Reva asked, shrugging off Kaku's commentary.

"You don't know him. So just keep your nose on the job that I told you to do."

Before Reva could muster a protest, Kaku continued.

"Good thing you don't know him. Whatever little sense I have managed to shove in that pea-brain of yours will disappear again. I can tell ... just from the way he still speaks ... nothing has changed from the past. He and your father would talk and talk and talk about the foolish plans they had ... what was that group they had started? ... *Pragati Samaj*, or something like it ... to educate they said ... all the villagers ... I knew it would come to nothing. Books don't put food in the cobbler's mouth ... words don't pay for the cleaner's rent ... making *chappal* and cleaning houses feeds and protects them ... this education business should be left to the Brahmin boys ... God has given them the brains and the right to carry forward His important work."

"Kaku, what if the cobbler does not like making *chappal* ... why should he have to do it all his life?" Reva argued. In that moment, she identified with the cobbler.

"Not like? Where does the question of liking or not liking even arise? Oh, I know ... it is exactly this school-business of yours that makes people wander away from the path that God has chosen for them. All nonsense if you ask me ... and those *firangi*, filling your father's head with more white nonsense about reforming our world ... as if we needed that. I knew the whole bunch of them had gone crazy when their *Pragati Samaj* started calling for educating women ... girls, housewives, even widows! That's when I knew that this stupidity had gone too far ... your Kaka always said that ... but who would listen to him, younger in age that he was to your father!"

Kaku stirred the lentils in the pot vigorously as past family disagreements and rebukes arose like sleeping demons in her mind.

"I knew your father had gone against the word of God with his blasphemous activities. Why else would he be called away from this life so early?" Kaku ended with a low blow that made Reva suck in her breath.

But she despaired only for a moment. Aai had explained to Reva how her father's death was caused by his low immunity. Her father had turned a blind eye towards his own health as he worked day and night for those less fortunate. He had succumbed to the flu as had many pious God-fearing people, a sure evidence that God was not as petty or vengeful as the rest of the family made Him out to be.

Reva had missed her father all these years, but mostly as a person who would have filled her mother's days with happiness. For the first time, squatting beside the crackling kitchen stove that evening, Reva mourned the memory of her father for herself. He would never have allowed her present predicament to even take shape under his watchful eye. Her Baba would have not only sent her to school, but even to college. Perhaps she could have helped him with his important work of reforming their village with the help of their English friends.

Kaku's rant was not over. "...Now here is that man again. Why did he have to come here? ... That too a year late. He should have stayed in that little village ... Tarapore ... where he retired after the *Pragati Samaj* went kaput. They say he looks after their family land business now, a very prosperous situation I am told ... should have never strayed from it to begin with if you ask my opinion," Kaku grumbled, still lost in her thoughts that tumbled out like bushels of grain released from jute sacks.

Reva warmed at the idea of having her father's friend in the house. She could understand why their friendship had taken root—they were likeminded and kind and selfless. She put extra attention in preparing the roasted coconut stuffing for the brinjals, and then kept a vigilant eye on the boiling curry, waiting patiently until the oil separated from it. She made sure the tender brinjals were cooked to perfection, still holding their oval shape, but melting in the mouth at first bite. The entire kitchen was drenched in their spicy aroma by the time Kaku sent Reva to announce dinner.

The raised voices in the courtyard slowed Reva's step and stopped her from making herself visible to the men who seemed to be engaged in a heated conversation.

"Revati is getting married? She is just a child!" the visitor exclaimed. Reva could feel her own distress mirrored in his voice.

"She is almost fifteen. My sister-in-law's last request was that she be well settled, and that's just what I am doing." Kaka sounded resolute. Determined.

"That cannot be true," objected the visitor. "Revati's mother and father both believed in educating their daughter. We used to talk about changing times and what that means for our children, especially the girls."

"Revati is my responsibility now," Kaka harshly reminded him. "With all due respect, let me handle my family business. You are our most honored guest, and good hospitality demands that I not argue with an esteemed guest. Let's just proceed now to enjoy the dinner. The food must be ready, and I can see Reva dilly dallying in the shadows. I am sure she was sent to fetch us. Revati! What are you doing, sneaking up on us like a thief? Tell your Kaku that we are ready to eat."

Reva jumped back and hurried into the kitchen, her mind racing at what she had heard. She muttered a quick desperate prayer that her father's friend would persuade Kaka to change his mind. She continued to plead her case to the divine all through dinner, silently forwarding the compliments lavished on her cooking as an offering to the deities.

Dinner done, the men retreated to the courtyard while the women cleaned up the kitchen. The visitor was gone before Reva had the courage or the opportunity to beg him to help her out of her predicament. But what could he do? Kaka had told him, clearly and rudely, to keep his nose out of their family affairs. No self-respecting person would try to intervene after such humiliation. Reva teared up. To be honest, what could anyone do? She was going to be married and that was that.

The following day after school, Reva was surprised to see the very person who had been on her mind the whole morning. The visitor. He was slowly pacing up and down in their open courtyard, hands clasped behind his back. Every once in a while, he ran his hand over his head as if sifting and reaching for an elusive idea. Kaka sat on the stationary swing, watching the man's movements, his anxiety apparent in the creases of his forehead and in the silence hanging around him.

On seeing Reva, the visitor looked at Kaka, as if to demand permission, and then gestured to Reva to walk with him out the front door.

Reva couldn't believe her luck. The Gods had listened to her prayers. Now was her big chance to plead for help. Could there be a shred of hope for her?

"*Pori*, you were hardly five when I saw you last. You were a very smart girl then, and I can see that you are growing into a very bright young lady now. Your mother and father would be very happy."

"Kaka…" started Reva, unsure how to address this man.

"You can call me Appa. Everyone does," he responded with a smile.

"Appa," Reva tried again, liking how comfortably the word rolled off her tongue. "Appa, I don't want to get married. I want to study."

Reva blurted out the words before she lost her nerve.

Appa looked grim. "That is what I want to talk to you about. I have already discussed this matter with your Kaka."

Reva felt the sun beginning to work its magic on her. Although he did not appear to be a bearer of good news, she wanted to believe there was something Appa could do.

"*Pori*," Appa said tentatively, "I have offered my son, Avinash, as a prospective husband for you, and your Kaka has accepted."

Reva was stunned. Speechless.

So Appa rushed on, "But I have made it clear to your uncle that this marriage plan would not proceed until I knew how you felt about it."

He peered anxiously into Reva's face.

"Appa, yesterday, you said girls must study and not rush into marriage. So how can you suggest such a thing now?" Reva finally asked, her dismay apparent.

"Child, I understand your confusion. Listen to me carefully. Your Kaka is determined to get you married, and there is nothing I can say or do to stop him. He is your legal guardian."

"I thought you would help me, Appa. You are Baba's friend. He would want you to," Reva said softly as a tear ran down her cheek followed by another and another. She was surprised at how easily such brazen words came to her lips. But these were desperate times, and Appa did not make her tremble at the sound of her own voice as her Kaka did.

"My dear, I understand that this is not the best solution," Appa explained. "It goes against everything I believe in, too. I have spent most of my life trying to teach villagers to take care of and educate their girls, their women. And now, here I am, proposing something that goes against what I have been teaching. But I have thought and thought about this all of last night. The best I can do, my dear girl, is try to bring a little good out of a bad situation."

Appa placed a hand on Reva's head, trying to calm her agitation.

"I know the family you are getting married into. School would be out of the question, you might not even see the outside of the kitchen and the children's rooms. I cannot let that happen. I will not let that happen. My son Avi, Avinash, is ten years older than you. He has been in London for two years now. He went to take the Civil Service examination there, but then decided to extend his stay to work for some time in the Queen's service. He wants to become an officer in the British government. He is a good boy, a dutiful son, and will do as I bid. Most importantly, he will be occupied overseas for a year or two more. For you, that means an absent husband. You will be married, but only in name. Do you understand what I am saying?"

Appa paused to catch his breath before continuing.

"But as my daughter-in-law, I will see that you go to school. When Avi comes back, you can build your life together when the time is right. But under my roof, you will continue to study as long as you want. I'll see who will dare to oppose my wishes then. So, my child, I want you to think about what I have said. Your father was like a brother to me and your mother was a brave, hard-working woman. I cannot just sit and watch their dream, their daughter, being disposed of in this cruel way. I hope you will see the advantage in this proposal. I will not proceed until I know your feelings about it."

They turned around to head back towards the house.

Appa had appeared in Reva's life less than twenty-four hours ago. Strangely enough, she trusted him more than the uncle she had known for a lifetime. Still, Reva couldn't help wondering—if Kaka was so tied to the promise he claimed he had made to her mother, how could he agree to this strange plan in which the groom himself was a big unknown?

"And Kaka is okay with … this?" Reva stumbled trying to find the right words.

"Don't you worry about that, child. Your Kaka is very happy with this arrangement. I have made it so. At this moment, my concern is only for your future and your well-being."

In a moment of fleeting but utmost clarity, Kaka's change of heart was as transparent as the October sun now beating down relentlessly on Reva's face. Appa was a landowner. A very rich and successful landowner. Kaka's business needed land to grow. Yes, for Kaka's own economic prosperity, this match was one made in an even higher heaven.

A few feet from the front door, Reva turned to Appa and said, "Yes, Appa … I will do as you say."

Appa gently ran his hand over her head and blessed her.

"You are a brave girl. I know these are hard times for you. But this decision is for the best."

Then Appa proceeded towards Kaka's study. Reva stood rooted on her spot. A new village, a new home, a new family. There was no way out of that future. But Appa had offered her the prospect of an absent husband and a trusted promise of school. She would try to be happy.

Chapter 3

Appa's home, Tarapore, was as foreign to Reva as Miss Tytler's England. But later that night, after the excitement of the sudden proposal had settled, Appa talked to Reva about Tarapore. He described his small village, nestled in the Sahyadri mountain ranges, as a piece of heaven on earth. Reva had thought a lot about heaven in the last year.

Then Appa shared with her the legend of the hills.

"A long long time ago," he began, "the hills were so tall, *so* tall that they touched the sky. That was a problem for Surya, the Sun God, as he drove his chariot across the sky."

Appa stretched out his hands in a majestic arch.

"The hills would not back down to let him pass, so the Sun God requested the counsel of a powerful saint who was the Guru, teacher, of the hills. Seeing the Guru approach, the hills bowed. The Guru blessed them and said, 'Stay there, my children, until I return.' But the Guru never returned, and the mountains stay bowed, a mark of humility and respect for knowledge and truth. And those, my dear girl, are the hills on which rests our beautiful village of Tarapore."

Appa concluded the story with a little pat on Reva's head and a proud smile in his twinkling eyes. Reva could not decide which was more delightful—the story or the storyteller.

"If the hills are so beautiful, how come my Baba didn't want to live there when you were friends?" she asked.

"Just as I love the hills where I was born, your father loved the river beside which he was born," Appa patiently responded. His answer made sense to Reva. Appa made sense to Reva.

Appa's father had settled in the hills when the local king had entrusted him the responsibility of exploring that untouched land, and later, of overseeing the development of residences there. He had granted a large portion of that land to Appa's father in return for his services. Appa had been born in the hills and had continued to look after the land that was now leased to the farmers and their families to build their own houses and to cultivate.

A shiver of excitement coursed through Reva's body when Appa told her that their tiny village was also home to the English people who came for a few months each year to take refuge from the hot summer sun of Poona and Bombay. As an expert of the land, Appa's father had helped establish settlements for the English people, aiding and befriending them over the years. The friendship had continued to the present day.

It did not take long for Reva to reason that if her new home was the summer abode of the white people, surely Miss Tytler would have heard of it. She decided to ask Miss Tytler about Tarapore as she reluctantly made her way to her last day of school.

"YOU are getting married? Just like that?!" Miss Tytler exclaimed, rising from her seat like a cornered cobra.

Reva was startled since Miss Tytler's impeccable manners never revealed any intensity of emotion.

But the teacher's disapproval soon turned into a resigned acceptance after Reva had narrated the events that had led her down that path. Miss Tytler had fought for Sumi so she could continue her education a little longer, as she had repeatedly done for other girls in her school. Now, as she saw the same drama playing out, she appeared to have little hope left in her own ability to fight for Reva.

Reva's description of Appa and his promise to continue her education somewhat pacified the good woman. But Reva knew that Miss Tytler was just as sad to see Reva leave as Reva was to say goodbye to her.

"Tarapore?!" Miss Tytler exclaimed when Reva mentioned her new home.

Miss Tytler then pulled out a map in the school room to show Reva where she was going. "How I wish I could go with you! I have heard that the hills are like a beautiful dream in the summer. The trees are forever green and shade bearing. The song of the birds, sweet and delightful to the heart. The gentle breeze like a cool balm on a burning soul."

Miss Tytler sighed and fanned herself with her hand as though the mere memory of hot summers on the plain had made the temperature in the room instantly unbearable.

How lovely Miss Tytler made Tarapore sound! Reva wished she could make her teacher's wish come true and take her along. Miss Tytler's positive reaction to her new home sowed a tiny seed of excitement and hope in Reva's mind.

"And do eat the juicy strawberry they grow there, Reva. I have not had a taste of that sweetness since I left England," Miss Tytler added.

Strawberry. So foreign the word and so unknown the fruit that Reva struggled to remember it the next day as she told Hirkani what she had learned about Tarapore.

"Hirkani, I will get some ... *shut...bar...serbeti*...yes, that's it, *serbeti* for you, when I come to visit."

"So now *you* will be *my* vegetable seller?" Hirkani demanded with mock ridicule. They laughed at the thought, barely easing the sorrow of parting soon.

As Appa got busy with setting the date for the marriage, Kaku's taunts about Reva's incompetence acquired a new focus: her future mother-in-law.

"Make sure you keep your mouth shut in front of your mother-in-law. Speak only when you are spoken to. No woman needs an *agaoo*, an insolent, in her house."

"Appa made you his daughter-in-law out of pity. That will change in a blink if you anger your mother-in-law."

"Walk gracefully in that *loogduh*. Otherwise your mother-in-law will say we unloaded a cripple on them."

"Don't skimp on the sugar when you make your mother-in-law's tea. She will think you came from a pauper's kitchen."

With each comment, Reva's mother-in-law started sounding more like a demon and less like Appa's wife.

Appa had sent his wife, Mai, a message with the news of her son's marriage. From the gossip among the servants, Reva knew that he had not summoned Mai to attend the marriage. Would she be upset, possibly even angry about this arrangement that was planned and executed without her approval? Would such total disregard for her feelings and for her status as the groom's mother affect her judgment of Reva? Would she disapprove of her daughter-in-law before even meeting her?

Reva tried talking to Kaku about these troublesome thoughts.

"That is not your business," Kaku had dismissed the question before warning her, "You just be a dutiful and respectful daughter-in-law. Don't try to act too smart just because you are educated."

Reva had heard stories about her own grandmother who had been feared as a mother-in-law. Aai and Kaku had to move heaven and earth to keep up with her demands, many a times unreasonable ... but always unquestioned. After her father had died, Reva's grandmother had watched over Aai like a hawk, making sure she conformed to a dull life of widowhood and reminding her of what she was missing each and every day. Then Kaku had taken over that mission with a sadistic pleasure. Reva wondered why women behaved antagonistically towards other women? It was bad enough that the men were rude, inconsiderate, and even cruel to them.

As always, Reva had appealed to Hirkani for help. But having met neither her own mother-in-law nor Reva's, all she could offer was some more of her cryptic wisdom.

"If you are going to live in the river, make sure you are friends with the crocodile."

But what if the crocodile is unfriendly, or worse, hungry?

Reva shuddered.

On a warm cloudless day in October, one week after Appa had put forth his bewildering proposal, Reva found herself in the midst of a strange marriage ceremony. The courtyard was decorated with a few lonely banana fronds, and limp garlands of marigold hung on a newly erected canopy. Reva, drowning in the folds of her new bridal *loogduh*, sat under the canopy feeling more like a pumpkin than a person.

Reva wished she had paid attention to Aai's instructions on how to drape the nine yards instead of discarding those lessons in a fit of clowning and giggling. She missed the care and patience with which Aai had explained each step of draping so that the *loogduh* looked graceful and attractive while still allowing the woman to function around the house...unlike Reva's futile attempts since. For the wedding, Kaku had managed to get the stiff, billowing nine yards under some control, but Reva remained fearful of tripping and falling flat on her face during the ceremony.

The solemn gathering of people around her talking in hushed tones made Reva wonder if they were attending a wedding or witnessing a funeral. Although Reva was in no mood to be festive herself, she resented the quiet that only served to amplify her heartbeat and to exhume the terrifying question she had buried under Appa's promises. What was in store for her? Beads of sweat began to occupy the tiny creases on her forehead as she stared into the sacred fire. Tears caused by the smoke and mixed with those rising from her heart gathered in the corner of her eyes. As if on cue, a melancholy strain of the lone *sanai* started in the background, revealing, note by gloomy note, the future that lay ahead for the bride.

There was one element of absurdity in the whole ceremony that Reva clung to desperately as she fought to control her nerves. 'Seated' grandly beside her was the groom, represented by a beautifully decorated coconut! No doubt the fruit was a symbol of good luck and prosperity, but could it really be a valid substitute for a groom? The ancient scriptures had apparently blessed the idea. Reva, on the other hand, remained baffled. A gnawing fear of the unknown kept her urge to giggle at bay as the priest recited verse after verse for a fruitful marriage and all those present referred to the coconut by the name Avinash, treating it as though it was a real person. While Kaka and Kaku raved about the excellent match they had arranged for their niece, Reva silently proclaimed her husband to be a *gota*, a bald, empty head ... a coconut head. Coconut Head was a concept easier to address and ignore than an Avinash.

Since Appa was in a hurry to get back to his home and his work that he had left unattended a little longer than anticipated, the wedding had been performed in haste, a request that Kaka and Kaku were more than willing to accommodate. In less than three hours, a week before her fifteenth birthday, Reva became a married woman. Appa got busy arranging for their journey to Tarapore while Kaka and Kaku turned their back on any matters that concerned Reva. Reva was left mostly to herself as she struggled to come to terms with her new status.

Reva missed Sumi.

"The girl who never wanted to get married sure beat a fast path to the marriage canopy," Sumi would have teased Reva. But Sumi was not around.

"Kaku, Sumi will come for my wedding, won't she?" Reva had asked when the date of the event had been set by the family priest. Her cousin was long overdue for a visit home. Reva had hoped to see Sumi before her departure from Uruli.

"Sumi is so devoted to her home that she cannot find time to visit her poor mother and father," Kaku had replied, the pride in her daughter's adjustment to her situation obvious in the fake grievance. "Maybe you should learn something from her, Reva."

If Reva had not suspected that Kaka and Kaku had essentially sold her off in exchange for a lucrative land transaction, she would have sincerely attempted to miss this house and its inhabitants that had been her family for the last fifteen years. But on the eve of her departure, Reva could not muster any tears, only an endless stream of precious memories that she would never leave behind.

In the courtyard, Reva could hear her younger cousins squealing as they played past their bedtime. Inside her now bare room, Reva stood quietly staring at a large trunk, its oiled and polished teakwood planks carefully held together with shiny brass joints. She ran her hand lovingly over the joints, feeling just as patched-up as the trunk. It had belonged to her father. It had traveled with her mother. Now it was the biggest part of Reva's meagre inheritance. A large clasp mounted on a sun-shaped plate securely guarded Reva's few belongings: Aai's luminous '*kudis*', seven pearls clustered together in flower-shaped ear studs, and a small idol of Krishna, the divine child known as much for his mischief as his wisdom. Rolled in a newspaper and tucked underneath her clothes was the pencil that Appa had gifted her—her very own secret magic wand.

That morning, in a moment of uncharacteristic generosity, Kaku had handed Reva three new *loogduh* as part of her wedding trousseau. A new bride arriving in her mother-in-law's presence with hand-me-downs would reflect badly on the maternal family. But seeing that Reva was marrying into a family with money, Kaku reasoned that there was no need to go overboard with that sentiment. A minimum number would suffice. The new *loogduh* lay unloved and untouched, even dreaded, inside the trunk.

However, it was not really what lay inside the trunk that held Reva's gaze that night. Attached on the top, right in the center, was a label that proclaimed the owner to be '*Saubhagyavati* Revati Tambay'. Overnight, Reva's name had changed. *Tambay.* Overnight, her status had changed. She had become a *Saubhagyavati*, or, the one who was blessed with a husband. *Saubhagyavati* Revati Tambay. Sandwiched between two unfamiliar worlds, she had to remind herself that Reva still existed and was moving closer to her dream.

With a sigh of resignation, Reva shut the trunk and stepped outside into the courtyard, awash with moonlight. It was *Kojagiri Poornima*, the night of the October full moon. When Aai had been alive, she and Reva had indulged in a secret tradition of sneaking into the courtyard long after the rest of the family had gone to bed to get an extra serving of the nourishing and healing rays of this special moon. Aai would tell Reva about the goddess of prosperity, Laxmi, who went from house to house on *Kojagiri* night inquiring, "Who is awake?" Those who responded were blessed generously by the goddess. One year, Aai's blessing had been in the form of a tiny baby girl with skin as white as the moon itself and eyes as bright as its beams—Reva was Aai's own little ray of magical moonlight.

Today Reva turned fifteen. She stood alone under a resplendent October moon. There was no one to talk away the night and no one to make her day special. Except Hirkani.

"Don't look back, my dear. You are not headed that way. And who is to say? Your new name may be your best birthday gift yet."

Hirkani had tried to brighten her mood that morning. And when words had failed, she had handed Reva a small basket of gooseberries— sweet and sour in the same bite. Reva had felt her spirit inflate with each berry she popped in her mouth. It was just as well that Sumi was not around. It would have been harder to leave the village. Appa was going to be with her. Why worry about a non-existent husband? She would go to school again. Soon. Her dream, Aai's dream, would come true.

Reva's departure from the village the following morning turned out to be a bigger event than she had expected. Appa arrived in a *buggy*, a gleaming horse-drawn carriage. A small group of villagers stopped their work to gather around it. They spoke in hushed tones, their faces mirroring their curiosity and awe. The carriage was made of shiny wood with velvet seats and brass details that shone. The two horses, restless and anxious to get going, had all but swallowed the tiny dirt path outside the *vaada*.

The sun had risen fairly high up in the sky when the servants loaded Reva's trunk into the carriage.

As the travelers prepared to take leave, Kaka and Kaku stepped out of the *vaada*. Appa discreetly motioned with his eyes, reminding Reva to seek their blessings before the departure. She complied and touched their feet readily. In a twisted sort of logic, they were, after all, responsible for the adventure and promise that now awaited her.

Appa had requested a companion for Reva on the journey. The woman cried louder in distress at the thought of leaving Uruli for two weeks than Reva, who was leaving forever the only home she had ever known.

But Reva was clinging to Hirkani's wisdom like a lifeline.

"A home is where there are people who love you and care for you," Hirkani had reminded her. "Without them, it is just a pile of stones. Don't let it trip you up or weigh you down."

And as Reva set out on her journey up those lofty hills, she decided she should neither trip up nor be weighed down.

Chapter 4

October 1900

The carriage headed in the direction of Waikan village, the first part of the overnight journey into the hills. As the travelers settled into the rhythm of the road, Reva sneaked a glance at Appa seated diagonally across from her. Despite the long journey ahead, her father-in-law was dressed in a fine brown silk dhoti bordered with delicate gold embroidery, complemented by a neatly pressed beige *bundhgala*, a long sleeved fitting jacket that stopped short just above the knees. He appeared to be lost in thought. Reva wondered if Appa was wishing to undo the events of the past month just as she had been trying to undo the events of the past year. Was his grim face a reflection of his regret?

Appa had telegraphed Coconut Head after Reva accepted the proposal. Had Coconut Head received the message in time? Had he replied? What had he said? Had he been angry, perhaps even furious? As a boy, he was entitled to those feelings.

Avinash. Even though Reva had not seen this man, his name now triggered an innocent curiosity held in check by an amorphous fear and even a hint of awkward shyness. Appa had informed her that Coconut

Head had studied in a school run by the British missionaries close to Tarapore. He spoke English just as well as he spoke Marathi. He had attended college in Bombay before pestering Appa to go to Cambridge for the Civil Services exam two years ago. He dreamed of securing a job as a Civil Services Officer in the British Raj, India's government. He had passed the examination successfully and then accepted an opportunity to stay on and work in the Queen's service abroad.

Educated *and* ambitious, Coconut Head would have gained Aai's approval. There was no doubt that an English-versed husband was an exciting prospect. After all, as Appa's daughter-in-law, she was soon going to be fluent herself. But what in the world would they say to each other? Would her husband be interested in hearing about her school in Uruli? Would he want to hear about the games she had played with Sumi? Would he help her with her studies in her new school? Would he even care? Would he be happy with Appa's choice for him? For a few minutes Reva felt the weight of Appa's burden. As her new life drew closer with each lurch of the carriage, Reva felt inadequate in every respect. Longing for her mother, Reva fought back her tears lest Appa's face turn even more grim.

She gave herself a firm talking to instead.

Just think of school, Reva. Why worry about Coconut Head who is not even expected to come back any time soon? He is just a name.

As Reva's silly nickname for her husband worked its magic on her fears, her imagination transported her into the hills, where there was a school, white people to emulate and befriend, a comfortable home, and most importantly, Appa to guide her. Having grown up fatherless, Reva had, in the past week, wondered if Sumi had always felt as secure with Kaka as Reva now felt when Appa was around. Aai had fought and sacrificed to provide that protection for Reva, but for Appa, it was effortless.

Maybe Hirkani had been right—her birthday this year might have just brought her the best gift yet.

It was nighttime when the carriage finally came to a standstill at the travelers' bungalow in Waikan village that served as gateway to the mountains. Here, the travelers planned to replenish their food and water and then wait for daylight before beginning the journey up the steep and winding mountain tracks.

It was pitch dark outside. The single wick in the oil lantern hanging on the front door barely illuminated three feet around the entrance to the bungalow.

After a day of hearing the carriage squeak and rattle, as Reva's ears adjusted with relief to the silence of the night, she heard the gentle lapping of water against the shore. She closed her eyes and stopped to listen, feeling a strange sense of home.

"The Krishna river is on the other side of this house. If you want, you can walk along the river and visit the temple on its banks before we leave tomorrow morning. It is very beautiful," Appa informed her gently. "But now, make haste. Let's get ourselves inside and rest our tired bones."

Appa sent for the *durwan*, the caretaker, who lived in a little shack behind the bungalow.

The presence of the river calmed Reva. Its name comforted her. Krishna—Aai had been devoted to this deity all her life. And here it was now, the namesake river, snaking around her, calling out to her, keeping close as if on guard. Reva promised herself a visit to the river at dawn. For now, she could see that her companion needed her as she struggled to unload the trunk and knick knacks from the carriage.

Once the travelers and their belongings were safely inside, the *durwan* closed and secured the door to the house.

"... to keep out the wild animals, sister, that might stray from the hills," he explained nonchalantly. "Not the robbers and thieves. We don't have those here—if you don't count the white people, of course..." he mumbled, smiling wryly at a joke Reva did not understand. She shivered at the thought of wild animals and hurried to her room where her companion waited heavy-eyed and yawning.

The next morning, Reva got up early. Her companion helped her with the nine never-ending yards of her stiff *loogduh*, a problem that confronted Reva now on a daily basis. The old softened-with-use hand-me-downs were cumbersome enough, but these new *loogduh* made of a thick silk were even worse. No matter how hard she tried, the blasted thing ballooned around her as if it had a mind of its own. She needed a pair of hands to put the mounds of fabric in place and another pair to hold it down. How did anyone ever get any work done in this monster?

The sun was just rising as Reva stepped outdoors and headed in the direction of the river. As the rays inched lazily over the surrounding hillside, Reva heard the rising notes of the *kokila* and the faint splashing of water coming from behind the thicket of tall *mogra* bushes that perfumed the air around the bungalow. The distant clangs of the temple bell confirmed that she was on the right path. As she squeezed her way past the overgrowth into the clearing beyond, she sucked in her breath and stared at the scene that greeted her.

Two hundred yards away, the land, lined with banyan trees, met the wide river. Village women were descending the steps of the *ghat* into the water to offer prayers to the river deity before filling their pots for their daily household needs. A few of them were gathered together, pots on their head or anchored by their arm at the waist, catching a quick word with their friends and neighbors before getting caught up with the demands of the day.

At the farthest end of the *ghat* stood the temple, a streamlined rectangular stone structure with arches leading into the inner sanctum—the abode of Ganapati, the god to whom the temple was dedicated. Reva had grown up believing in Ganapati's power to remove obstacles. No task, major or minor, had ever commenced in their house without invoking this god and seeking his blessings. Reva felt heartened by the presence of the temple in these foothills as she began her new life. The tall, tapering tower that crowned the inner sanctum of the temple rose majestically emulating the surrounding peaks and reaching unchallenged towards the sky. Reva took it as a sign that Ganapati was directing her into the mountains.

The temple priest had started the morning prayers, echoed by other villagers. The passionate chanting floated on the gentle breeze alongside the river, across the ghat, and towards the bungalow. The words to the prayers that Reva had memorized when she was just a toddler drifted into her entranced ears. Automatically, her lips mouthed them as she stood at a distance, hands now joined in prayer.

'*Sukha karta, dukh harta, varta vighna chi...*'

'Oh, Provider of Joy, Remover of Sadness, Destroyer of Obstacles...'

'*...Nurvi purvi prem krupa jayachi...*'

'Who spreads love everywhere as his blessing..'

The bells clanged in accompaniment and Reva marveled that even from that distance, she could smell the fragrance of the incense as it created a foggy blanket around the Ganapati statue in the inner sanctum.

The river, catching the light of the morning sun, made the villagers on the banks appear as dazzling celestial beings as they made their way towards the sound of the prayers. In the background, the hills soared.

There were tall peaks, rounded tops and flat plateaus as far as her eyes could see. Some parts appeared dry and bare while others were a riot of green. Somewhere in those mountains was her new home. She would have to wait and see which part of the mountain range her life was destined to mirror—the green and fertile, or the dry and barren.

'...*Sankati pavave, nirvani rakshave, survar vandana...*'

"Help us, protect us during bad times, my Salutations to you Oh Lord...'

So enthralled was Reva with her surroundings and so engrossed was she in her chanting that she stood rooted to her spot longer than she had planned.

"Reva *tai*," her companion called impatiently, shaking Reva out of her reverie. "Hurry up. It's time to go."

Seeing Reva's hesitation and her hurried glance towards the temple, the companion insisted, "Don't make Appa wait. He has already asked the *durwan* to load your trunk."

Reva offered a silent apology to Ganapati whose temple had been her unreached destination that morning. But it seemed to her that she had encountered the divine without even stepping into the temple. Would she have found or felt anything different within the four stone walls of the temple that she had not enjoyed from the distance? Reva's eyes were slowly drawn to the vast open sky, now illuminated with a glorious sunrise. She wondered then if she could continue to enjoy Aai's love in the very same way. From a distance.

Reva could have spent the whole morning basking in the peaceful environs of the temple, but she hurried after her companion back to the bungalow. She did not want her idle wishful thinking to keep Appa waiting.

"Appa, you must visit my humble home the next time you stop in Waikan," the *durwan* insisted, as Appa took his leave.

"*Nakki Nakki!* Of course! I have been away from home longer than expected, and I must get back. Otherwise, I would never have lost an opportunity to eat my sister-in-law's *jhunka-bhaakur*."

Reva was surprised. Would a person as rich and refined as Appa ever eat *jhunka-bhaakar*, a poor man's meal in a poor man's house? She got the feeling that Appa had indeed shared the *durwan's* food in the past. Appa's response had pleased the *durwan*, who stepped out of the way nodding his head humbly. Reva marveled at how flexible the walls of social class seemed when Appa was around.

The travelers stepped outside the bungalow. The carriage that had brought them to Waikan was gone. In its place stood a bullock cart drawn by two handsome bulls, their horns painted flaming red, orange, and yellow. Bright vermillion was applied in decorative designs on their foreheads. The animals waited patiently, heads held high and turned slightly towards Appa as if to say, "We're ready for the hills if you are." The richness of the cart, the regality of the bulls, and the height of the surrounding mountains overwhelmed Reva.

"*Arrey*, Maadhu! Always on time!" Appa greeted the driver and motioned for Reva to step into the bullock cart. Her companion settled next to the driver's seat.

Maadhu touched Appa's feet.

"Maadhu, meet our new daughter-in-law, Revati," Appa said, pointing towards Reva. "Reva, this is Maadhu. He and I played together when we were boys. If there is anyone who knows these hills better than me, it can only be Maadhu. I want you to call him Maadhu Kaka. That's what all the children around here call him."

Maadhu Kaka smiled humbly and bowed to Reva, a gesture that made her feel uncomfortable and welcome at the same time. She was not used to having an elder bow to her. It did not feel right, but before she could even think of an appropriate reaction, the men had moved on to more important talk.

"Mai is waiting anxiously for your arrival," Maadhu Kaka said to Appa.

"How is the weather at home, Maadhu?" Appa asked.

"Mostly dry now, but a few stray storms still arrive unannounced, Appa," Maadhu Kaka replied.

"Not that weather. The weather inside the house, Maadhu," Appa said with a forced smile.

"Forgive me Appa, that's big talk for my small mouth. How can I answer that question?" Despite Maadhu Kaka's subtle admonishment of Appa, Reva could sense the close friendship that lay just beyond the impregnable gulf created by their social class.

"Don't worry. I was just teasing," Appa replied with a tender smile. "Let's get started, so we can reach before nightfall."

As the bullock cart made its way slowly up the mountain tracks, the greenery of the surroundings and crispness of the air made Reva watch with wonder as her new home appeared before her eyes one sharp bend at a time. She held her breath and gripped the sides of the cart as the tracks got steeper and the cart rattled under the strain. This heaven on earth that Appa had described was beginning to make her stomach churn. Fortunately, the terrain gradually flattened. Reva saw houses that blended in the landscape and that were unlike any she had ever seen in her village. There were deep shaded porches at the entrances, and Reva could see glimpses of flower gardens and vine covered pergolas in the back. Who lived in these enchanting homes?

As they neared their village, the land seemed to be on fire, as if taking the hint from the receding sun. The dry, hard mountain tracks had given way to soft crimson dirt paths that laid out hoofmarks and wheel tracks like fresh prints on paper. How delightful it would be to walk barefoot on this earth and absorb its color with each step forward, like the color of henna that deepens with each passing hour. Reva promised herself that she would indulge in this silly fantasy soon.

The hint of cold in the mountain air had changed to a definite chill. Reva pulled at one of the woolen shawls lying in the corner of the cart and wrapped it around herself.

Appa smiled. "You will get used to this cool climate very soon. It's what brings our English friends here every summer. And lucky for us, we get to enjoy it all through the year," he said. "You can close your eyes for a little while. It will be another two hours before we arrive home."

Reva shook her head. "I want to see the *serbeti*," she said.

"And what is that?" Appa questioned, his eyebrows drawn together in confusion.

"The red fruit that grows here. Miss Tytler said it is the most beautiful and sweetest thing she has eaten in England. She wished she could come to Tarapore to eat some...I want to see it."

Appa thought for a brief second before starting to laugh.

"*Serbeti!*" he exclaimed, his laughter doubling as he slapped his thigh in delight.

For the first time since they departed, the worry lines on Appa's forehead relaxed, and a warm smile lit up his face.

"It is called a strawberry, my child. You will not see them along the roadside. Not yet. They grow in the fields that belong to our English friends. But I will arrange for you to taste some when they are in season... *Serbeti!* Maadhu, did you hear that?" Appa laughed again, wiping his eyes leisurely.

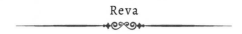
Even though Reva was a trifle embarrassed at her ignorance, Appa's laughter reassured her.

Appa was proving to be the indulgent, caring father she never had. She would soon learn to love the rest of her new family. How could they not love her back?

Chapter 5

October 1900

R eva wished she had stayed awake until the end of their long journey. But the harder she had tried, the heavier her eyelids had become. Reva could not pinpoint the precise moment she had fallen asleep or the exact reason why. Perhaps it was the exhaustion caused by the constant chatter in her mind or the comfort created by Appa's soothing voice as he talked to Maadhu Kaka about the goings-on in their village. Perhaps it was the rhythmic rocking of the cart or the gentle commands of Maadhu Kaka urging the animals uphill. Perhaps it was the fatigue of having traced the path of the sun as it climbed to its highest perch in the sky before beginning its slow descent. Reva had finally succumbed to the approaching darkness and slept a deep dreamless sleep.

She awoke the next morning with a vague recollection of being helped out of the cart the night before, then led up a flight of stairs and laid onto the bed that she found herself on now. As her eyes adjusted to the first flush of dawn creeping into the room through large glass arches on shuttered windows, she was thankful that the rocking and the jolts of the bullock cart had stopped. She was thankful for the thick woolen blanket enveloping her body that had replaced the flimsy shawl from the cart, and for the large four-poster bed that was the most comfortable sleeping arrangement she had ever known. She ran her hands over the bed sheet and took in a deep breath—sun-dried, crisp cotton. The bed linens were snow white and unwrinkled, except for the few creases she had created. As Reva let her gaze venture around the room, she noticed her companion sound asleep in a corner.

The room was three times the size of her old room in the *vaada*, and twice as tall. The edges of the ceiling were intricately carved and a seven-petal flower motif adorned the center, where hung a bell lantern. Reva wondered how she would ever reach up to light it. Crowned with graceful arches, three windows overlooking the hillside lined one side of the wall. A heavy wooden door framed the other, and, for now, protected Reva from the uncertainty that lay beyond. What was the world like on the other side of that door? Was anyone waiting anxiously to meet her? A long chest of drawers ran from the door along the remaining length of the wall and ended in a wide closet with mirrored doors. All of Reva's worldly possessions would likely fit in one of the drawers. She had never seen a palace, but she was convinced that she was waking up in one right now. Although the room had sparse furnishings, each one was solid, rich, and luxurious.

Wide awake and alone in a huge bed, Reva could feel her heart beating in the same uncontrollable way as when Kaku had told her about her impending marriage. Appa was probably in the house somewhere. But so was Mai. Her mother-in-law. The title scared her. She imagined a big woman with expensive clothes, family heirlooms to match, and a smile that never came.

A low growl outside her window snapped Reva out of her thoughts. She leaped out of bed and sprinted for the door, silently cursing her unwieldy *loogduh*. She found herself on a landing that extended on either side and paused to catch her breath. A wide flight of stairs stretched majestically towards the ground floor. Where could she go? A faint sound of feet shuffling downstairs prompted her to head right back into her room, but she stopped herself. Why was she behaving like a common thief? She had every right to be in this house. She was the daughter-in-law of the family. She needed to keep that prickly yet important detail in her mind and not behave like a village idiot. Reva drew in a long breath. Then another. And another. All was quiet again.

Light-footed, she walked towards the stairs slowly. But her feet seemed to have a mind of their own as they picked up speed. Like the rest of the furnishings, the sleek polished bannister spoke volumes about her new family and her new home. If Kaku had been there, her mouth would have dropped permanently at the opulence and the obvious promise of a comfortable life. And yet, Reva could not calm the butterflies beginning to flutter again in her stomach.

At the bottom of the stairs, she found herself in a spacious *divankholi*. Appa and Mai must receive visitors here. The room, as big as the courtyard in her *vaada*, was surrounded by large forbidding doors that Reva dared not explore. Looking up, she could see the landing and the open door to her room. She realized there were at least two more rooms on either side of hers. Who else lived in this mansion? As she stood deliberating her next steps, Reva heard voices through the last door in the corner of the *divankholi*. The door was slightly ajar. As she approached, she heard Appa talking. A woman's voice responded, soft but agitated. Mai.

Reva did not wish to be caught eavesdropping. She turned on her heels and started to scurry away, but the mention of the name 'Avinash' transformed her feet to stone.

"Avinash," Reva whispered, knowing that she was defying tradition by brazenly referring to her husband by his first name. How strange that name felt rolling off her tongue. How indifferent she felt at the sound of it. And yet, how quick her mind had been to register it. What was this person like? Reva had hoped to see a likeness, a portrait, somewhere in the house, but in her limited exploration thus far she had not come across any. She had considered asking Appa about Coconut Head on their way to Tarapore, but then she had refrained. How could she even think of asking shameless questions about her husband to an elder in the family? She would wait and see. There was, after all, no rush to be bothered with him at present.

"...But you should have consulted Avinash first before making such a big decision."

The woman's voice was firm. It commanded attention. However, in the tone, there was also a hint of the familiar diplomacy, a readiness to back off, if necessary. It reminded Reva of the conversations she had overheard between her uncle and aunt at home when Kaku had presented an opinion that was counter to Kaka's.

"I know, Uma. But I had to make a decision before they married off the child into an unsuitable family," Appa replied, his voice calm, pacifying.

If the mention of Coconut Head had immobilized Reva outside Appa's room, this reference to her now provided the justification. How could Reva not overhear the rest of the conversation?

"But why did you have to offer your own son?" Mai tried to reason again.

"Uma, I understand what I have done. This was the only respectable way to save that poor girl..."

"And what about our son? Have you thought about him?"

"Yes, I have. Reva will be a good match for Avi. In a few years." Reva sensed a note of impatience creeping into Appa's voice.

"You really think so? An officer, God willing, and a village simpleton?" Mai's voice was also losing some of its carefully veiled calm.

"Avi is an obedient boy. He will be happy to do as I ask. I have sent him a letter to explain the events. Who knows—the idea of a wife waiting at home might even keep him motivated and focused on his work in that foreign country. Perhaps Uma, you should be thankful—you can rest easy now. Your son most surely will not bring back a *gori* wife, a white woman, who will not care for our traditions and our way of life."

The strained mirth in Appa's voice warmed Reva's heart. He was trying to diffuse the tension, and she loved him more for it. There was no doubt that he was the head of this family. But respect and caring were obviously a mutual obligation in his books.

The conversation confused Reva. Had Coconut Head not been consulted before the marriage? She had assumed that, just as Appa had sought her acceptance, he had also telegraphed Coconut Head to make sure he approved of the arrangement. The possibility that Coconut Head had been given no voice in the matter was most definitely awkward and worrisome. But not having a face to associate with the idea of a husband, Reva could muster neither the sympathy nor the understanding for her new life partner. Since she could think of nothing that could change the situation, she decided to focus on the people who were present around her at the moment. Like Mai.

It seemed that Reva had etched herself into Mai's bad books already. Reva did not blame her for it. Her own mother would have been just as upset if any major decision about her child had been taken without her opinion and approval.

"I still think your activism sometimes goes a little too far," Mai persisted. "How many girls are you going to save like that? Are you not doing enough by talking to the villagers and stopping them from getting their young children married off and giving money to the schools? And we don't even have a daughter."

"Uma!" Appa had heard enough. "We didn't have a daughter before. But now we do. The subject is closed. Let's wait for the child to rest and get comfortable with her new home. I know what I need to do next."

The sound of feet approaching the *divankholi* triggered Reva to instinctively dash back towards the stairway. In her haste, her foot caught in one of the many cascading folds of her *loogduh*. She stumbled and collided with a pile of books that exclaimed, "*Array-ray*! Are you blind?!"

A second later, a man rushed to apologize, "Forgive me, I thought you were one of the servants. They are forever rushing around cross-eyed."

As Reva regained her composure, the man eyed her with a frank gaze, unmindful that it was not appropriate for a man to be looking at an unknown woman with such shameless curiosity. Reva lowered her eyes and stared at the books strewn on the floor—English titles. On one of the covers, there was that stern-faced Tilak, the fiery Indian freedom fighter. She frowned. She was not on good terms with Tilak; he wanted the British out of India and was known to provoke the locals into rebelling against the colonists, like Miss Tytler. How could Tilak even doubt the intention of people as noble and full of grace as her teacher? Now here he was again glaring at her from the floor.

"Err ... I don't mean to be rude....but who are you?" the man with the books finally asked. His voice seemed friendly.

Tongue-tied, Reva was wondering the same thing, but she dared not look up. She started to gather the books on the floor, angry with herself for forgetting the nine yards of fabric that were the bane of her existence. Unfortunately, the commotion in the early hours of the morning had drawn the entire household to the *divankholi* as ants to sugar.

Appa hurried over to where Reva knelt on the floor. "When did you wake up, *pori*? It's early, and you had a long day yesterday."

"There was a scary sound outside my window..." Reva stammered, her voice barely audible.

"To be sure just a *dhole* straying away from the jungle. You can see those wild dogs often in these mountains. But they rarely come out in the village. So don't be afraid." Appa smiled. "*Aso*, let it be, since you are awake now, come and meet everyone."

Reva stood up uncertainly, patting down her *loogduh* as she disengaged her foot from yet another fold, conscious of her disheveled appearance being scrutinized. She locked her gaze on the tile beneath her feet as though it was a lifeline.

"I think it would be better if she cleaned herself up first," Mai's voice rang out distinctly. "We will meet in the dining room for breakfast at nine o'clock. Gopi, take Revati back to her room and show her all the things she needs." Mai had taken control of the situation.

The authority in the voice confirmed Reva's suspicion that she was indeed in the presence of her mother-in-law. She took a step forward, bending to touch Mai's feet and receive her blessing, but her mother-in-law stepped away.

"First things first. We never greet each other without taking a bath. That is a form of respect you give to the family. Then, you must go to pray in the *devghar* and only after, come to the dining room," Mai continued. Her tone was a pointed reminder of the unconquerable difference between the lowly plains and the lofty hills.

"Maadhu, Revati's trunk is still on the porch. Take it upstairs and keep it outside her room. Gopi can unpack it from there." Mai's instructions to the servants were clear and concise and demanded immediate attention. From the corner of her eye, Reva noticed a girl, not much older than herself, spring into action, walking briskly from the entrance of what was possibly the kitchen to the foot of the stairs, waiting for Reva to follow her.

Reva didn't mind the instructions. She was glad to know exactly what was expected of her. But the coldness alarmed her. Mai seemed just as eager to push her away as Appa was trying to pull her closer into the family.

Reva followed Gopi up the stairs, still conscious of the amused gaze of the stranger with the English books. Realizing she never had a chance to find out who he was, she slowed down to peek over the bannister when she reached the landing. The man was as tall as Appa. He was wearing a long-sleeved white cotton shirt with a sleeveless tan jacket on a white *dhoti* like Appa. His black wavy hair was longer than the boys she had seen in her village and was parted on one side. He had the golden color of wheat, like Mai, and the sun-kissed warmth of Appa on his face.

"Appa, what have you done? She is just a child," the stranger said.

"That is why I did what I did. She will grow up as a daughter of this house. There will always be room for one more here."

"A child bride in the house of the Tambays! How can we tell the villagers to keep their daughters in school when we haven't practiced what we preach?" the stranger asked earnestly.

"Viraj, that is enough. I don't have to answer to anyone." Appa's tone reflected his annoyance, but also a mixture of fatigue and helplessness. "My conscience is clear. I have done the right thing."

"Appa, I understand the situation. I am not sure though if your decision and actions were not hasty."

Reva was starting to feel afraid for this stranger who was boldly challenging an elder of the family. In her Kaka's house, this conversation would have been nipped in the bud long before it even started.

"But what has happened has happened," the young man relented, continuing to follow Appa, who had taken a seat on the *divan*.

"So I have a new sister-in-law... I am happy to have some company in Avi *dada*'s absence. Let's just hope Avi *dada* is happy about it too. Wouldn't I love to see his face now?" The young man chuckled.

Dada. He had referred to Coconut Head as *Dada*. This man was Coconut Head's younger brother.

In the safety of her room, Reva recalled with a tinge of relief how Viraj had admitted that he was happy she was here. Maybe it was too early to call him an ally, but at least he didn't hate her. Unlike Mai.

After a long journey and an uncomfortable start to the day, Reva gave herself up to the joys of a hot bath. Unfortunately, Mai's image kept popping in her mind. Mai was a few inches shorter than Appa, but her upright posture made her look almost the same height. Her face was handsome—olive skin with dark brown eyes that seemed to possess three-hundred-and-sixty- degree vision. Her eyebrows were long and barely separated at the nose, suggesting the presence of a frown lurking beneath that might be revealed at a moment's notice. The red *kumkum* that adorned most of her forehead left no doubt of her status in society as a married woman and her pride in achieving it—its presence just as attention grabbing on Mai's forehead as its absence had been on Aai's. Even at that early hour, Mai had been immaculately groomed and in control. She looked every bit the queen that ran this palace. Her *loogduh* was of the finest cotton with tasteful delicate gold borders. But it was the style with which she wore it that captured Reva's attention. Shorter in length than Reva's, it was draped around the body in a way that flattered and flowed. Reva had seen a photograph of a woman who had draped it in a similar manner printed in the newspaper not too long ago. It was a style that was gaining popularity with the royalty and the rich. Reva was intrigued. She was tired of feeling and looking like a pumpkin.

As the warm water ran down her body, her thoughts wandered to Coconut Head. Reva could not help but wonder about the product of two grand personalities such as Appa and Mai. She had already seen one, Viraj, and had been impressed. Viraj was more handsome than any other men she had met in her young life. His clothes were *deshi*, local, but the confidence and superiority he exuded in them made Reva think of the *firang* world, the English world. He was respectful towards his parents, and yet spoke his mind fearlessly. His Marathi was flawless, but his books hinted at a fluency in the English language as well. Was the older brother just a more accomplished version of Viraj, or as different from him as Mai was from Appa? If only there was a way to find out.

Eight loud tolls of what could only be a giant clock somewhere in the house snapped Reva back into the moment. She hurried out of the bathroom and dressed in her new clothes. Just as she was wondering how to summon Gopi, the girl appeared at the door. Giggling at Reva's ballooned, *loogduh*-clad body, Gopi showed her the way to the dining room after a brief stop to pray, and for Reva to marvel at the rich altar in the *devghar*.

Feeling more like an awkward clown than a budding mistress of the house, Reva settled herself at the table in the dining room and waited for the rest of the family.

"They will be here in a few minutes," Gopi told her as she headed to the kitchen, still giggling.

Reva wondered if she had met all the family or if there were more surprises to come.

Chapter 6

October 1900

Reva could count up to a hundred in English, but her speed was no match to the swift movement of the seconds on the polished wooden clock in the dining room. Tick-tick-tick-tick. One-two-three-four. Her unwavering focus on counting the steady ticking of the clock kept the knot in her stomach from growing. Any moment now, Mai would walk into the dining room. Reva had no reason to believe that this meeting would be any more favorable than their early morning exchange.

"Twenty-three...twenty-four...twenty-five..." She struggled aloud with the English numbers, hoping the sound of her voice would subdue the thudding of her heart. Unfortunately, time would not slow down for her foggy mind to remember the next string of the foreign numbers. She switched to counting the minutes. It gave her time to breathe. Three minutes passed before she sensed that she was being observed.

Turning her gaze away from the clock, her eyes cautiously traveled the room. Like the mythological giant *Kumbhkaran*, cursed to sleep a hundred years, the massive dining table lay sprawled in the center of the space. A row of tall windows, similar to the ones in her room, lined one side of the wall. A heavy buffet sat alongside the other, topped with a table runner made of the most elegant handcrafted lace. The soft light from the windows illuminated a lifesize portrait hanging on the wall above the buffet. The man's head was held high as if gauging a distant mountain top, his eyes imagining its conquest. Bits of silk vest and tunic peeked beneath his strings of pearls, rubies, and gold necklaces. The face could have been Appa's when he was younger, but without his smile, Reva could not tell with certainty.

Moving past the portrait, Reva's eyes rested on a large armchair in the corner. Camouflaged by the upholstery sat a man wearing dark khaki pants and a white shirt, the kind worn by the English officers who had visited Uruli occasionally. His face was obscured behind the newspaper. Reva fidgeted slightly in her seat as she adjusted her *loogduh*. In response, the man suddenly lowered the newspaper as though aware of company for the first time. Reva flushed, hoping that her face wouldn't register her surprise as she realized it was Viraj, her brother-in-law. Gone was the Indian attire, the *dhoti-kurta*, he'd worn earlier. Now he looked like a perfect *saheb*, the white man. What little familiarity or comfort Reva had felt regarding Viraj suddenly evaporated into thin air. The knot in her stomach now extended to her tongue.

What could Reva say to Viraj? Would it be good manners to speak to him without being properly introduced by Appa? But then again, she couldn't possibly just sit here ignoring him. Reva reasoned that as long as she addressed him respectfully, it would be alright. She remembered Aai addressing her Kaka as *Bhauji*, or brother. She would begin there.

"*Bhauji*, I am sorry, I did not see you here. ...I would not have been so loud with my foolish counting," said Reva timidly as she wiggled out of her chair intending to leave the room.

"It was entertaining," admitted Viraj good naturedly, his face breaking into a mischievous grin.

Reva thought his poking fun at her went against the gentlemanly image his outfit projected. She took a step towards the door.

"You don't have to leave on my account," Viraj stopped her. "Appa will here any minute now, and Mai will approve if you are five minutes before time. I assume you have already met our *Ajoba*, grandfather." Viraj pointed to the portrait, and the likeness to Appa suddenly made perfect sense. By making the hills his home, Appa's father had indeed won over this land, and as Reva looked closely at the eyes again, she caught a glimpse of the same pride and love that Appa had expressed for the hills.

Viraj folded the newspaper and stepped towards the dining table. Reva panicked.

"Let...let me get Gopi," she mumbled, still unsure of the proper etiquette.

"If you are worried about talking to me alone in this room, please don't be," Viraj said. "Appa does not care for the old cumbersome ways of conversation between men and women, especially within the family. Tradition is important, but respect, practical thinking, and acting freely is paramount... You will not get into trouble for breathing the same air as me or exchanging greetings with me," he added with a small laugh.

Reva exhaled.

"...Mai, on the other hand, walks the fence," Viraj continued. "Although her sari might display the latest style, her thinking at times reflects the *purdah* tradition where women hide behind veils. She attempts to keep up with Appa's progressive thoughts, but sometimes her conservative sensibility prevails. You will just have to figure it out as you go." Viraj paused for this important nugget of information to sink into Reva's mind.

"And another thing," he said after a moment, "you do not have to call me *Bhauji*. I have a name. It is Viraj. I'd like you to use it, seeing that I am closest to you in age here." Viraj smiled broadly at Reva as he finished his introduction, and the warmth that flooded his face made Reva feel as though she was in Appa's presence.

Reva guessed that Viraj was perhaps not really as close to her age as he pretended. Was this his way of extending a hand of friendship? Reva welcomed the encouragement. She had much to learn, and he appeared to be a willing teacher. As her knot began to dissolve, Reva was tempted to ask Viraj the myriad questions buzzing in her mind. But just then, Appa entered the room, followed by Mai.

"You are ready, child?" Appa greeted Reva. "*Chhaan*. Very good. Tell Gopi to serve the food. It looks like Tai-Aaji is not feeling strong enough to come to breakfast today. Mai has already taken the food to her room."

Reva's ears perked. Tai-Aaji? Another member of the family that she had yet to meet.

As Reva pondered who Tai-Aaji might be, Appa settled at the head of the table with Mai and Viraj on either side of him. Seeing the empty chairs between Mai and Reva, Appa smiled good-naturedly at Viraj, who immediately moved one spot over. Appa motioned for Reva to sit next to him on the seat recently warmed by his son. Reva hesitated briefly to glance at Mai, but her face was as unreadable to Reva as the titles on Viraj's books. Fully expecting a sharp directive from her mother-in-law at any moment, she moved cautiously next to Appa. But Mai remained silent as Gopi appeared in the doorway with a large wooden tray.

The room was instantly flooded with the aroma of *kaande-pohe*, soft rice flakes and onions tempered with mustard seeds, turmeric, curry leaves and chillies, topped with a generous sprinkling of chopped coriander leaves. The sight of food lifted Reva's mood as surely as the steam rising from it. She was famished. She welcomed the warm familiarity of the breakfast—Aai used to make *kaande- pohe* for Reva after she came home from school. It took all of Reva's willpower to wait until the men had been served. And that was just as well, because Reva realized that digging into her food with her hands was not advisable. Appa and Viraj were eating with spoons just like Reva had seen Miss Tytler do in her office. Reva struggled to get the elusive flakes of rice onto the spoon and then keep them there as she precariously raised the spoon to her mouth. It seemed like too much effort for too little food.

"Reva, do you have everything you need in your room?" Appa inquired. "Otherwise tell Gopi to get whatever is missing. Uma, I am going to meet the new British Resident appointed to Tarapore. He is planning to change some of the land laws, and I would like to get a sense of what he is thinking. I will be back for a late lunch as usual. You have much to do today," Appa addressed Mai while smiling at Reva.

Reva was fascinated by Appa's agenda—his words revealed that he was going to a meeting with the white man, but the relaxed tone seemed to suggest a meeting of equals. Reva had heard about the protests flaring in big cities demanding that white people stop treating the natives as their inferiors, as incompetent and uncivilized. There were Indian leaders demanding a voice in government. They wanted self rule. Then there were others like Tilak who just wanted the English colonists out of the country. And yet here was Appa, cocooned high in the hills, engaged in a comfortable and unlikely friendship with the English people. Reva was beginning to feel like an authority on strange connections.

"Appa, I would like to go to our fields and inspect the new carrot plantings. I will ride part of the way with you," Viraj chimed in.

"Of course. And once Reva settles down, we can show her the land as well. Maybe even try to get some *serbeti*." Appa's eyes twinkled in a conspiratorial way.

Reva blushed. She still could not recall the correct name of the fruit, but knew for certain now that it was most definitely not the name she had conferred upon it. While Appa cleared the confusion, and Viraj joined in the amusement, Reva sneaked a glance at Mai. Unsmiling. Their eyes met, and Reva looked away hurriedly. Mai's stern look hurt Reva. Would she not offer even one kind word?

Mai's gaze openly demanded, "Why are you here?"

Surrounded by the grandness of her new home and the novelty of her husband's family, Reva had temporarily forgotten the reason that had pushed her into marrying Coconut Head. Mai's coldness reminded her of her mission.

"Appa..." Reva whispered nervously, twisting and untwisting the loose end of her *loogduh* around her fingers, "what about school?"

"What was that?" Mai asked sharply. "Speak up, Revati."

Hearing Mai call her by her full name brought back unpleasant memories of Kaku's endless scolding.

"Appa ... school..." Reva mumbled.

"First, you will learn the ways of this household, and then we shall see," said Mai. "You are fifteen years old. I am sure you can read enough to get by. Any more and it will get you into trouble."

Mai's words made no sense to Reva. How could learning to read and write harm her? Or anyone? What had she got herself into? That Mai was against her going to school was as clear has the lines of concern etched on Appa's face.

"She wants to study further, and there is no reason why she shouldn't," Appa finally said to Mai as he prepared to leave for the day. "Let me see what I can find out. I know someone who works in the village school. I will ask if you can start attending in the spring. That should give you enough time to settle in your new home and find your way around the hills, Reva."

Appa's voice was soft, contrary to the firm message it carried. Seeing Reva and Viraj following the conversation intently and Gopi being slower than usual in clearing away the table, Mai let the subject drop. But Reva knew that Appa would hear about it again in the privacy of his chambers. She implored God to give Appa the strength to keep his promise and for Mai to generate some sympathy for her new daughter-in-law.

Before leaving the room with Viraj, Appa turned back to Reva and, in a voice a little brighter than the gray flecks in his eyes, said, "If you feel strong enough for a bullock cart ride again today, you should go to the Krishnali temple. That way you will get to see some of this beautiful place and its people. It's a good way to start your new life, with the blessings of the Divine. Make sure you take Gopi with you. The paths in these hills can get very confusing, even dangerous for a newcomer."

The idea of getting out of the house to visit the temple appealed to Reva. Two hours into her day and she was already a mess of tangled feelings. Some fresh air and a dose of the Divine would help sort her out. Waiting for her mother-in-law to finish her conversation with Sita, the cook, Reva looked at herself in the reflection of the windows. A stranger returned her gaze. Reva felt cold. Exposed. She pulled the loose end of the *loogduh* tighter around her body.

"Revati, I want to speak to you before you go out. Sit down." Mai waited until the servants reluctantly resumed their chores, and the women were alone in the room.

Then Mai walked towards Reva and looking down at her said, "Appa has told me everything. I am sure you are just as unhappy about the situation as we are. First, to tragically lose your mother and then to be married off unexpectedly. Although, I do think the latter is inevitable for us women, and you are not as young as I was when I got married."

Sympathetic and callous in the same breath, Mai paused briefly, as if transported to her own past before continuing.

"I will be honest with you—in my opinion, your marriage into the other family would have worked out just as fine. From what I hear, the boy was decent, the family was well-to-do, and not far from your childhood home. What more can anyone want? This ridiculous arrangement happened because of your childish insistence to go to school and your good fortune that your wishes fell on Appa's kind ears and generous heart. But let me tell you, I did not go to any school, and yet I have learned my lessons well. Life is the best school, and there is plenty to learn from it, if one is so inclined."

The authority in Mai's voice was laced with a tinge of bitterness. Reva wondered if Mai's heart had ever been possessed by a struggle not unlike her own. Was Mai's stern objection to Reva's plans a result of her own crushed dreams? Reva desperately wanted to believe that Mai's firmness was out of her sincere concern that might someday grow into love for her as a daughter as well. But before she could utter a word, Mai spoke again, louder and harsher.

"To see my own son married off in the manner that it happened makes me angry. I am the groom's mother. I did not get a chance to choose my daughter-in-law, to plan a wedding, and to be given the respect due a boy's mother. In fact, this marriage has once again revealed the importance of my opinion. There is none."

Reva thought it best to remain silent. Some of the thoughts Mai was sharing did not make sense to her. She gathered that Mai was unhappy. And worse, that Mai held her responsible for her unhappiness.

Overwhelmed by the growing awareness that she was unwanted and unwelcome, Reva suddenly felt stifled in the room. But she could not leave until she was dismissed. And Mai was not finished with her yet.

"What is done is done." The displeasure in Mai's voice was palpable. "There is nothing I or anyone can do to change the situation. You are here, and now, in the eyes of God, you are a part of this family. But I will not pretend—it is going to take us both some time to get used to being together under the same roof. In the meantime, I do expect you to start learning your responsibilities as the future mistress in this house. We are an old, reputed family, respected by the village people and English visitors alike. We may be the bridge to the western world, but we are also guardians of traditions and our ancestral ways of life. We have to live up to very high expectations. That alone will keep you busy from morning to night. I imagine there will be no time for school. I am telling you upfront just so that you do not build any castles in the air."

With that blunt warning, Mai took a few steps back and turned towards the door.

"Now it's time for my morning walk. Take Gopi with you when you go to the temple."

Mai left before Reva had a chance to utter a word. She was too dumbfounded to move, let alone respond. What could she possibly have said?

"Hirkani, you were wrong," Reva whispered to herself. Marrying this Coconut Head was indeed like going over a cliff and, at that moment, Reva was convinced that being hurled down by Mai hurt more than if she had jumped off herself.

Chapter 7

October 1900

Two hours after lunch, Reva found herself in Maadhu Kaka's bullock cart on her way to the Krishnali temple with Gopi as her companion. Appa had not lied. Tarapore was unlike any place she had visited before. Gazing at the lofty peaks in the distance, the lush greenery all around, and the pristine landscape delicately tinged by a rising fog of red dust as the cart made its slow journey towards the temple, Reva could not help but feel the magic of the hills beginning to tingle in her bones. Appa had described it aptly—a piece of heaven on earth.

Gopi started to hum a tune unfamiliar to Reva but, from the rhythmic bob of Maadhu Kaka's turbaned head, it had to be a song known to the locals. Her song was interrupted only by brief comments to Maadhu Kaka and small shrieks of joy as she dangled her feet from the cart, encouraging Reva to let her guard down cautiously. Relief seeped into Reva's body as the cart moved farther and farther away from the house... from the one particular woman in the house.

Seeing Gopi's childlike delight, Reva sensed that Gopi did not get many opportunities to venture outside the house during her workday. While Gopi chatted with Maadhu Kaka about her last visit to the temple,

Reva observed her new companion closely for the first time. She was not much older than Reva. Gopi was shorter and stockier, but she sat with her shoulders back and chest thrust out as if she owned the world instead of serving it. Her long black hair, gleaming and fragrant with coconut oil and neatly parted in the center, was double braided in a way that combined fashion with functionality and drew attention to her face. A face that spoke volumes. Friendly. Eager. Accepting.

The Krishnali temple was a twenty-minute ride along crimson paths bordered by tall Arjuna trees and bushes enflamed with brilliant yellow flowers. Alongside the road, tucked in the hillside corners, and playing hide and seek among the boulders were the most delicate plants—each stem made up of the tiniest leaves, the color of parrots that stopped to rest in Reva's village during summertime. As her eyes scanned the passing shrubbery, Reva realized they were in the thousands.

"Gopi," she called out, her curiosity getting the better of her shyness.

Gopi quickly scrambled backward into the cart eager to be of service to this new mistress. Reva pointed to the fragile fronds that were now appearing in bunches, some as tall as the wheels of the bullock cart.

"What are these plants?" Reva asked. "I've never seen them before."

"Reva *tai*..." Gopi began, fidgeting on the seat cushion. Seeing her awkwardness as she settled into the soft companion seat inside the cart, Reva wondered for an instant if Gopi's place was always in front, beside Maadhu Kaka. Had Reva crossed some social boundary inadvertently? But Maadhu Kaka had not reprimanded Gopi or even cast a disapproving look as she had scooted inside the cart.

"These are *pheruns*, Reva *tai*," Gopi replied. "They grow wild on these hills, but you won't find any down in the plains of Waikan. The plains are too hot for these delicate things ... just like the *goray*, the white people." Gopi giggled at the spontaneous comparison.

"The *goray* go crazy over these *pheruns*...But, tell me Reva *tai*, where are the flowers? See—no flowers at all. Where is the beauty in that?" Gopi said dismissively.

Ferns. Reva remembered the drawings that Miss Tytler had shared with her class. Looking at the brilliant ocean of ferns dancing in waves around her, Reva felt a growing understanding of Miss Tytler's attraction to Tarapore. Unknowingly, Reva had landed in a place that was as English as she'd ever know.

The hills stretched out in the distance. The air smelled woody and crisp. The warmth of the sun was inviting. And the chaotic twitter of the birds made Reva wonder if they had sensed a stranger in their midst.

"Where are all the people, Gopi?" Reva asked, eying the deserted path.

"People? There aren't many people here at this time of the year. Most of the big houses are locked up for the winter, like ghost houses. It's too cold and wet for visitors. Which *bindok*, idiot, wants to be drenched in the monsoons or freeze here in the cold? Other than us locals, of course. You couldn't pay me enough to live anywhere else. This is where I was born, and this is where I will die," Gopi proclaimed dramatically with a flourish of her hands.

"There are some hut settlements built by farmers and others like me who work on Appa's land and the *firang* houses," Gopi explained. "Then there are patients who come from the plains to get better. You must have heard, this air in the hills is like magic. It heals the body and the mind. Come sick, leave strong and healthy. That's how it is here," she declared proudly.

Reva smiled. Just like Appa, Gopi was a part of this land, and it was a part of her.

"The hospital for the white people is close to the village. And there is one for the rest of us, not too far from our house. Appa is *dev-manoos*. He is the one who started the hospital for us locals." Gopi paused and folded her hands together as if praying in gratitude to Appa.

"Then there are some shops, a bazaar, in the village square. Further down the hill, there are more huts, but it's just like this in the monsoons and in the winter—quiet and boring. So I wait for the summer," Gopi ended with her voice slightly raised and quavering.

"Why? What happens in the summer?" Reva wondered aloud even though she had an inkling of what she would hear. She wanted Gopi to keep talking.

Gopi straightened up and hugged her knees tightly as if to contain her excitement.

"*All* the white people come to Tarapore as the summer begins in the plains. They cannot stand the heat, those *phuskay*, weaklings," Gopi mocked as she rolled her eyes and then smiled brightly. "They come to escape from the hot air in Bombay and Poona and make this village their home for a few months. All the ghost houses on the outskirts of the village come alive and their lights glimmer on the hills like fireflies. You know, Reva *tai*, when they are around, you can smell the *majja*, fun, in the air."

"*Majja*? What do you mean, Gopi?" Like a sponge, Reva was absorbing all that Gopi was offering.

"You can see the *firangi*, foreigners, in the market or in their carriages. Wearing their long-long gowns made of the fanciest cloth and the brightest colors. Some even ride horses. Who knows what they say to each other! But it sounds *lai goad*, very sweet. Some come to the house to visit Appa, and Appa speaks to them in that same tongue. Very knowledgeable, our Appa is. Then every evening they gather in that big red brick house, the *culub*. They play music and some even dance right there in the *verandah* in front of everybody. Men and women together!"

Gopi covered her mouth with her hands giggling at the picture of the foreigners dancing with abandon. Then, realizing that perhaps she had spoken more than she should have, she stopped abruptly, worry beginning to creep into her eyes as she looked expectantly at Reva. But Reva was just getting started. Gopi was promising to be an excellent informant, and she needed one desperately right now.

"Do Appa and the whole family also go to the club?" Reva persisted.

The continued probing was all the reassurance that Gopi needed.

"Oh no no! Only white people can go to the *culub*. No *deshi*, Indian, allowed. Isn't that funny? It is on our land, and yet we cannot go in. Not even Appa. It's just as well that Appa is not interested. So he doesn't mind. But Viraj *dada* does not like that. He gets *lai* angry. He says he will not go even if invited. Viraj *dada* does not care much for the white people."

Reva shivered with excitement. She had always fantasized about Miss Tytler's world and its ways. And now she was so close to it, she could almost taste it.

A spurt of rustling in the tree canopy made Gopi squeal softly in delight.

"Reva *tai*! There may not be many people here, but we have the monkeys—just like people. No? Look!" Gopi pointed to a group of macaques that had made themselves visible among the leafy branches. They remained unfazed by the rattling of the cart and the presence of people in their environment. Some even bared their teeth at the passing bullock cart. Was it a welcome, or was it a warning to this newcomer in the hills? Reva shooed the troublesome thought away and shared Gopi's joy as she watched the monkeys suddenly appear in clusters, swinging and jumping for one tree to the other. Her eyes fixed on a female with a little baby clinging to her underside. The mother sat upright for a few moments fondling her baby before leaping to another branch and disappearing with her offspring into the foliage. Reva tried to remember what it had been like in the comfort of her mother's shadow, not caring what she was doing or where she was going. A memory of her following Aai around the house drifted in her mind and a bittersweet lump started to form in her throat.

Staring intently at Reva's transformed face, Gopi nudged her gently.

"Reva *tai*, we have to walk from here. The cart cannot go on that tiny path," Gopi said, pointing to a narrow dirt track through the dense shrubbery. The bullock cart had come to a halt. The sun was still high in the sky, but on the trail ahead, it looked like the hour before sundown.

Reva disengaged her feet from the folds of her *loogduh* as she climbed out of the cart. She felt a sudden urge to run down the path. It was a feeling that had been on the edge of her mind and on the tip of feet since she had come across Viraj in the dining room that morning. The instinct to flee. Here, on this lonely dirt trail hidden by the trees, there was no one to see her or scold her for running. Gopi seemed like she could keep a secret. But Reva decided that she could not risk her *loogduh* unraveling. Monkeys have eyes too, and they were known to chatter. She would never forgive herself if she caused Appa any embarrassment.

Then, of course, there was the persistent voice that taunted her with cruel questions—from whom was she fleeing, and worse, where could she flee? Reminding herself that she was the daughter-in-law of a very prestigious family and the sooner she forgot her childhood ways the better, Reva planted one careful step in front of another, her gaze fixed on what lay at the end of the trail.

Reva and Gopi had walked about hundred yards in friendly silence masked only by the sound of their *chappal* on gravel and the incessant chirping of birds when suddenly, without any warning, the shrubbery parted and through the clearing Reva got her first view of the Krishnali temple. She stared in awe.

The trail had opened up behind the temple and Reva stood facing its back wall. Vibrant moss climbed all over the facade in changing shades of green, interrupted by some insolent patches of brown. Vines of flowering ivy covered the parts the moss had missed. As she stepped closer, Reva saw the massive black stones of the walls under the thriving green. Solid. Dependent. Full of life.

Reva's eyes traveled the length of the back wall and along the side all the way to the front. The temple was constructed as a small open courtyard surrounded on three sides by thick stone walls. A sheer drop into the valley formed the fourth—the front of the temple was at the edge of a cliff! Reva felt invisible roots under her own feet bury deeper in the earth as she realized just how high up she was in the hills.

Gopi's careless shuffling behind her as she reached for the wildflowers growing abundantly around the temple reassured Reva. She tried to calm her mind now conflicted between this newfound fear of heights and her curiosity to explore.

"There is a story that this temple was made by the Pandav princes when they were in exile a thousand years ago," Gopi explained. "You can see the whole valley if you go closer to the front of the temple, Reva *tai*."

Not wanting to admit her fear to Gopi, Reva inched towards the open courtyard of the temple at the edge of the precipice. In the distant valley below, she saw the river Krishna, blue and brimming, bank to bank, snaking through the red earth that changed to yellows and browns as the river headed away from the hills and into the plains. Seeing the river again planted a tiny seed of courage.

As Reva drew closer to the open courtyard, she was relieved to find that the edge of the cliff was at a safe distance of about fifty yards from the entrance. She could access the temple without needing to stare down into the vertical drop. She let out a shaky breath and turned her back to the valley to face the deserted temple.

"This Krishnali temple is the place where the Krishna river begins. It is the main source of water for the hills and the valley. So villagers come here to pray for their water. In Waikan, there is a big *utsav*, festival, for the Krishna river. Appa took us to see the *utsav* one time. I bought new bangles then," Gopi rambled.

The dark, moss-studded stone made Reva pull the loose end of her *loogduh* around her body like a shawl. She ran her gaze over the intricate carvings that made up the interior of the three walls, the ceiling supported by columns made of the same stone. Straight ahead, fifty feet away, she saw the door to the inner sanctum of the temple where lay the source of the river Krishna. The gentle sound of running water mesmerized Reva and created a sudden need for solitude.

"Gopi, wait outside, in case Maadhu Kaka comes to find us. I will take a quick *darshan*, view, inside the temple," said Reva, remembering how Mai had spoken to Gopi and yet not wanting to sound like her.

Gopi was only to happy to oblige. "I couldn't come in even if I wanted to Reva *tai*," she responded casually.

Reva cursed herself for her blunder. Of course, Gopi was not allowed into the inner sanctum for the same reason that Reva could not hug Hirkani the vegetable seller back home. They were both of a lower social caste. This invisible wall that separated people was as strong and as grounded into their lives as the massive stones of the temple. Even the majestic hills were not spared from its dark shadow.

Although this bitter truth bothered Reva, Gopi seemed unperturbed. She volunteered to find mulberries in the shrubbery and disappeared in the next instant. Reva smiled. For all the responsibilities Gopi had, she could not help but reveal her youthful exuberance at times. Reva was almost certain now that Gopi was close to her age even though Gopi's conversation with Maadhu Kaka had revealed that she had two little children waiting for her every night. Reva wondered if her own story was destined to be frighteningly similar.

Chhoom chhoom chhoom ....

In the quiet of the temple, Reva's thoughts were interrupted by the soft but unmistakable chime of tiny bells. Just like the ones that hung around Gau, her beloved cow that she had left behind in Uruli. She listened closely, imagining her faithful four legged friend to be close-by. The chimes sounded again, almost inaudible to a careless ear. With no grazing space for any cattle around the temple, Reva was mystified. She followed the sound further into the temple courtyard. Just before the entrance to the inner sanctum, she came across a small rectangular cistern. Steep, narrow steps from the four sides of the cistern led down to a pool of shallow water. A beautiful water spout channeled the waters from the sanctum into the outer courtyard and dispensed it into the cistern. The spout was a sculpture of a cow head, *gomukh*, with the water flowing through its delicately carved mouth. Suddenly, Reva missed Gau. She missed Aai. The picture of the baby macaque clinging to its mother flashed before her eyes as she remembered the countless times she had gone looking for her mother in the temple at Uruli and then finding her there. But now her mother was lost to her forever. Tears collected in her eyes and threatened to trickle unchecked like the river water flowing out of the spout. Her legs trembled and she flopped on the step next to the water spout.

Reva tried to console herself that in a situation where things could have been worse, she had ended up in a safe place. She knew she was lucky, but her heart felt burdened with feelings of anger and injustice. Like Mai, Reva wanted to hold someone accountable. For pulling a mother away from a fatherless child. For marrying her to a man she still had not seen and into a family that wanted to shun her but was obliged to keep her. For being in a strange land with unfamiliar people. And for the prospect of school growing dim with Mai's objections.

The tears started to flow in the stillness of the temple. Reva cried until the loose end of her *loogduh* was damp and wrinkled. She had no idea how long she had been sitting there. But by the time the shadows on the wall got longer, Reva's breath had calmed. She willed her bad mood to wash away with the last of her tears. She could see Gopi patiently waiting near the trail with Maadhu Kaka. The rays of the descending sun cast a soft light on the black stone. It did not look as forbidding as before. As if prompted by this magic of the changing light, Reva reconsidered her situation. What would Aai have done?

Reva tried to pinpoint the cause of her despair. Her marriage had been inevitable—if not now, a few years from now. Even her mother would not have been able to keep the marriage prospects and society pressures away indefinitely. Her new home was grand. Her new village was in heaven, at least the English people thought so, and they should know—they were heaven-born. She was going to eat a *serbeti* soon. Her new husband was expected to be handsome, English-educated and, for now, conveniently absent. And Appa had promised she would study further. He had given her no reason to distrust his word.

Suddenly, Reva imagined she heard Aai scolding her for lamenting what might even be her good luck, for being greedy for more. What was the more she wanted? What was mucking the waters of a seemingly favorable future? She played around the obvious. Soon she was compelled to name it. It was Mai. She wanted Mai to accept her. Like her, even.

Chapter 8

October 1900

"Our Mai is *dev-manoos*," Gopi said, pausing to feast on the succulent mulberries heaped in her lap, as they headed home from the temple.

Reva was momentarily alarmed that the mulberries were creating a toxic reaction in Gopi. How else would anyone agree with Gopi's description of Mai as godlike? But Reva held her tongue and listened as Gopi shared her own story.

Gopi's mother had worked with the family until the pain in her joints made the trip up the hills impossible. She had sent Gopi instead when she was only eight years old. Mai had paid for all the medicines and for household expenses as needed. Gopi, married at ten into a local family, had moved to her husband's home at twelve years of age. She continued her service in Mai's house. Four years later, the sixteen-year-old Gopi was mother to two little boys that her mother-in-law cared for while Gopi worked. Her husband had a small vegetable store in the village. Mai now paid Gopi extra money so the children could go to school and get prompt medical attention when needed. Gopi was forever in her debt.

Reva's heart warmed a little when Gopi uttered Mai's name with such reverence. Aai had admired Miss Tytler for the same reason. Despite her own discomforts, Miss Tytler had built her life in a little village to teach children. Mai helped in other ways, but the end result was the same. They made life better for people around them. Would Mai then not make Reva's life better too? Perhaps she had judged her mother-in-law in haste.

The next morning, Reva woke at the break of dawn. After her visit to the Krishnali temple, a plan of action had started forming in her head. The solution to her problem had been staring in her face. But it had been Gopi's vivid portrait of a benevolent Mai that had cast an illuminating light on it. The plan was simple: Reva had to prove to Mai that she could do both—attend school *and* take care of the house. Surely Mai's heart would melt when she saw Reva's determination to work hard and be part of the family. Aai had always remarked what a quick learner she was, and a smart helper too. Mai just needed to get a taste of Reva's efficiency around the house before she broached the subject of school again.

The sun was beginning to peek over the horizon when, freshly bathed, Reva went downstairs and headed to the *devghar*, prayer room. She would join Mai in prayer and then request to learn the ways of the kitchen. She would observe and learn as Mai met with the villagers and as Gopi and the other servants kept the household running smoothly under Mai's supervision.

It was early, but Reva's keen ear detected movement—a muffled cough, a creaking door, the faint sound of running water. Life was beginning to stir. The day was full of promise. Reva stepped into the kitchen. Sita had not started the stove yet. Reva rummaged through the shelves for a basket. She planned to gather fresh flowers as an offering to the gods. Reva had seen a blooming red hibiscus tree in the garden.

She knew that hibiscus was the flower of choice for Ganapati who sat majestically in the *devghar*. She could use a little help from this Almighty as she tried to win her mother-in-law's favor.

Reva found a laced metal basket washed and now drying on the window sill. That would do perfectly. She washed it carefully one more time not knowing whose hands had touched it last. Opening the front door quietly, Reva stepped out in the yard. In the tender morning light, she paused to enjoy the woody fragrance of the trees mingled with the lingering scent of the night jasmine. Then she deftly cut some hibiscus and marigolds, smiling to herself as a silly thought crossed her mind—not having a husband to woo, she would woo her mother-in-law instead.

In the prayer room, Reva set the flowers down by the altar and looked around for the lamps and the incense sticks. Morning prayers were a feast for the senses—the imposing statue of the deity, the flowers, the incense, the chiming bells, and the fruit offerings. How could one resist the magic of such a moment? How could one not feel a burst of tenderness, of love, in such an environment? For a few minutes, the vision of the Ganapati temple in Waikan on the banks of the river Krishna that she had passed a few days ago recaptured Reva's imagination. The prayer recited by the priest floated into her mind, and she started to chant it softly as she arranged the flowers prettily for Mai to use. She was about to light the altar lamp when a voice thundered the names of the Trinity from the doorway like a battle cry.

"*RAMA! SHIVA! GOVINDA!*"

The lit matchstick in Reva's hand fell into the flower basket, scorching the hibiscus.

Terrified, Reva turned around to see a woman, bent at the waist, blocking the entire doorway. The wrinkles on her body contrasted eerily with the vigor in her voice. She was hunched over a thick cane of gleaming dark wood. Her sari was a fiery red, spun of the finest cotton, and her head was covered unto her forehead, framing an enraged face.

"What are you doing girl?" her voice boomed again.

Reva sat transfixed. Who was this woman? Why was she screaming at her?

"I was just..."

"Now the whole room will have to be washed and cleaned again before prayer. *Bindok*, idiot! Did the birds eat your brains for breakfast, girl?" The woman's anger scared Reva.

Within minutes, Mai appeared in the doorway, followed by Appa, and even Viraj. In the background, Reva could see Sita and Gopi straining to catch a glimpse of the scene inside the prayer room. Reva fought the tears that materialized on the rim of her eyelid. There must be some misunderstanding. She was just trying to help.

"I was just..." Reva started again.

"Uma, do you see what your daughter-in-law has done? The basket touched by Gopi and Sita and god alone knows which other pair of filthy hands is in the prayer room. *My* prayer room. The whole room is now polluted. *You* will have to sweep and wash it again before my prayers."

Reva glanced at Mai to assure her that she had washed the basket herself before bringing it into the prayer room. She was shocked by Mai's transformation. Mai's eyes were downcast. Her face was drained of color. Her hands were so tightly clasped that they would probably leave fingerprint bruises on her skin for days.

"This is the chit of a girl who is supposed to be my Avinash's wife?" the old woman said scornfully. "She does not have the sense to live in a prestigious house, let alone run it. Appa, forget sending her to school. She needs to learn the ways of the house first if she is to be a decent daughter-in-law."

Reva could feel the flush on her cheeks deepen as she fought to restrain the hot tears. This old woman knew her dreams. Worse, she appeared to have the power to crush them.

"Tai-Aaji...," Appa started to mollify the woman.

"Enough, Appa." Tai-Aaji raised her stick in warning, as if it was an extension of her bony finger. "I tolerate your forward thinking, your western ways. I didn't say anything when you sent Avinash to the Christian land. I look the other way when those unclean meat-eating *firangi* visitors come into our home. I even ignored the disrespect you showed me and our traditions by bringing a daughter-in-law in the house without even informing me, let alone consulting with me, the elder in the family. But I will not keep quiet today! This prayer room is mine. You hear me, MINE! I will not stand for any change in the way it is to be run."

Appa tried again, "My dear Tai-Aaji. No one is—"

But Tai-Aaji had no patience for his mild words. She turned her attention on Reva once more.

"You, girl. Appa tells me you want to learn English and study and matriculate. You cannot form a simple sentence from that deformed mouth. What English are you going to speak? First take care of your home, then look into your neighbor's yard. Ignorant fool!"

Then Tai-Aaji hobbled towards Mai.

"Uma, you have failed as the mistress of this house today. Never has the purity of my *devghar* been compromised so carelessly. Do as I say now. I will come back for my prayers only after this room is spotlessly clean and purified again."

Tai-Aaji hobbled away, mumbling the names of the Trinity, "Rama, Shiva, Govinda," over and over again as if she were reprimanding rather than appealing to them.

For a few seconds, aside from the receding sound of Tai-Aaji's cane pounding on the floor, the room was deathly quiet. Tai-Aaji's tirade had left everyone frozen and numb. Reva sat stunned. Her finger throbbed from the burning flame of the matchstick, but it was nothing compared to sting of the harsh words that had spilled from Tai-Aaji's mouth. Even Mai had not been spared from Tai-Aaji's wrath.

"Mai," she uttered softly, trying to explain that she had taken enough precaution by washing the basket herself, that the room was not impure as Tai-Aaji had mistakenly assumed.

"I would like everyone to be out of the prayer room. Especially you, Reva. Get out of here, before you create any more trouble. I have work to do." Mai's voice rang out in the silence and sent a chill down Reva's spine urging her instantly into action. While Reva had acknowledged the injustice of Mai's humiliation, it was obvious that Mai had turned a blind eye to the injustice meted out to Reva.

With a reckless blurred vision, Reva dashed out of the *devghar*, past the dining room, through the main entrance, and out the door. The brightness of the daylight made her steps falter long enough to register someone calling out her name. The recollection of the viciousness with which her name had been uttered in the prayer room urged Reva to sprint. Not knowing any of the paths around the house, she ran in the general direction of the temple, wanting to put as much distance as possible between herself and the dreadful scene.

The sun was higher up now, and the heaven that seemed promised to her just an hour ago was burning up in Reva's eyes. In that moment, Reva resented Appa's decision to make her his daughter-in-law. No one was happy with this marriage. Appa was probably at peace in his heart because he was helping a girl achieve her dream, but did he really like her? Would he have chosen her for his son if she had been a marriage prospect that had arrived by post rather than by calamity? Her ears still rang with Tai-Aaji's insults. *Tai* was a reference to an older sister. Caring. *Aaji* meant grandmother. Loving. Tai-Aaji was neither. She had not lived up to her name.

Reva hurried on, oblivious to her surroundings, recycling the cast of characters in her new family through her mind, willing them to cast a kindly look, utter a soothing word and show that they cared. But even her imagination would not comply. Before long, she realized that the path no longer appeared familiar. The ferns should have been lining up at her feet by now, but there wasn't even a frond in sight. She must have taken a wrong turn. But where? Her feet started to sting. In her rush to get out of the house, Reva had forgotten to slip on her *chappal*. Her bare feet, caked in mud, matched her eyes—a bright red. Reva remembered the times at home when she had ground henna leaves on stone and caked the wet pulp on her hands and feet to get the same pretty red. Her mother had loved the color of henna and the fragrance of its leaves. But she had to be content watching Reva. Widowhood was colorless, dull, and as Reva had recently discovered ... frightening. Like Tai-Aaji. A shiver went down Reva's spine.

Even though her mind was unwilling, her body was starting to insist that she turn back. She was exhausted. She was alone. She had to go home to Appa. What else could she do? Whether they liked it or not, she was there to stay.

"I beg your pardon, can I help you?" a voice called out, bringing Reva back to her present predicament. It was the first kind voice that she had heard that day. The words were English. Reva did not understand completely. But she knew one of the words—help. It was exactly what she needed at the moment.

Reva looked up and saw a young woman with fair skin, rosy cheeks, gray eyes, and hair that was spun gold. Her dress was made of simple green cotton, but with lace trim and bows, she made Miss Tytler look ordinary. On her shoulders was a warm woolen shawl of a darker green. She carried a covered basket that had a cross painted on the side. Reva blushed as she realized that she was in the presence of her first white woman in the hills, and all she wanted at that moment was for the earth to open up and swallow her.

The woman eyed Reva cautiously. Tear-stained face, mud-caked feet, hair wild, and clothes disheveled, it would be hard for anyone to believe that she was from Appa's house. Would Appa be angry, or worse, disappointed, that she had let a stranger see a member of his family in this state?

"Do you need help?" the stranger asked again.

Reva shook her head. She needed to get back. But she managed a shaky smile as she turned around. Then with her head held high, mustering the rest of her shredded dignity, she walked resolutely in the direction from where she had come, praying that it would take her back to the house. She could feel the puzzled stare of the beautiful woman on her back all the way until she turned the corner on the trail.

Chapter 9

October 1900

Reva's feet were bare and bruised. She had been walking since the sun had just made its appearance on the horizon. It was almost overhead now. The cut on the side of her foot was bleeding, leaving a faint trail that disappeared promptly in the red dirt. Overcome by fatigue, she wished she could simply close her eyes and wake up on the other side of this nightmare.

She glanced over her shoulder, then scanned the trail ahead as a shadow of concern crept into her eyes. She should have arrived at the house by now, but once again Reva found herself on an unknown path, well-trodden but deserted. The birds had gone silent and the sound of the wind blowing through the trees sounded like a hushed murmur of voices ridiculing her, the witless newcomer to the majestic hills, the misfit in Appa's esteemed family.

The breeze had picked up slightly, fanning Reva as beads of perspiration started to form on her forehead. She sensed in her step that she was heading in the wrong direction. But before she could retrace in her mind the turns she had taken, a sudden movement in the thicket accompanied by a menacingly low grunt made her scream in terror and sprint down the narrow offshoot of the trail that led her away from the impending threat. The wild dogs that Appa had mentioned, the ferocious grins of the macaques, and Gopi's stories of cheetahs and hyenas that brazenly prowled the hills in the winter months loomed in her mind. The rustling followed on her heels as she ran, screaming for help.

Suddenly the thicket parted and Reva's feet skidded to an abrupt halt. Her screams carried on forward at full speed, only to be flung back at her in mocking echoes. Heart thudding wildly, Reva realized that she was at the edge of a cliff, the small rocks loosened by her feet rolling precariously down the path Reva would have found herself on had she kept going. She stood hypnotized by terror as her ears followed the sound of rocks free falling down the cliff towards the valley and disappearing into the dark crevices along the way.

As she stood on the edge, the wind lashed against Reva's body as if urging her to retreat. But as the seconds blended into minutes, her fear befriended a strange, dark fantasy that kept her feet rooted to the spot—there was, after all, a way out of this nightmare, and it was only a few steps away. There was a way to be with Aai again.

The shrill ring of a bicycle approaching from behind shook Reva out of her reverie and released her from the twisted fatalistic thoughts. Gasping, she backed away from the cliff and limped hurriedly back to the main trail towards the insistent ringing of the bell, vowing to stay away from the treacherous cliffs.

As the bicycle came into view, Reva was relieved to see a familiar face.

"Thank goodness I found you, Reva. Where were you? We have been looking all over for you. I heard you scream and all kinds of bad thoughts came to my mind. Thank goodness you are safe!"

It was Viraj. His voice was loud, almost frantic. Sweating from his ride, he was staring at Reva, brows drawn.

She nodded silently, her speech still lost in the jumble of terror and relief. After a few moments of silence, Viraj continued in a calmer voice, "Everyone is very worried. The hills can be dangerous especially for a newcomer. And the way you took off running... Let's go back home now."

Like cattle answering the call of a cowherd, Reva started limping on the path again.

"That's not the right direction. You are going further into the forest," Viraj said impatiently. Then noticing her limp, he exclaimed, "You are hurt! Your foot. It's bleeding. We must take care of it quickly."

Reva looked at her foot. It did look frightening, but her loneliness and heartache had made the pain of the wound inconsequential.

"Reva, sit on my bicycle carrier," Viraj ordered. "I will take you back."

Reva hesitated. She lacked the strength to face another scolding for riding on the backseat with her brother-in-law.

"Appa will understand, and I will make Mai understand," Viraj urged.

Reva had no choice but to comply. While Viraj held his bicycle steady, she carefully sat on the carrier trying to find a position on the little passenger seat that would necessitate minimum physical contact with the rider. Regardless of the assurances Viraj gave, Reva knew she was headed for trouble, double-seated on this ride with a man who was not her husband. As Viraj maneuvered the bicycle with ease, Reva had to admit that it felt good to take the weight off her feet. With her foot dangling above the ground, Reva could see the blood dripping from the wound as they pedaled away.

Before she knew it, they were on the same path where Reva had, just a short while earlier, attempted to salvage her dignity in front of the English woman. The bicycle clattered down the dirt track all the way to the end, passing underneath an arch displaying the words '*Janata Rugnalay*', Hospital of the People. An unexpected but welcome landscape unraveled before her eyes.

Overlooking the lush green hills and the Krishna valley stood a small building with a large cross painted on it. In Uruli, on a rare occasion when her mother's homemade remedy had not cured her stomachache, Reva remembered being taken to see the doctor who visited their village weekly, carrying a case with a similar sign. At first, her aunt had warned the family to stay away from that white man, that foreigner who wanted them all to follow a different god, to become Christians. But Miss Tytler had told the children that he was a doctor who could help them get better. And he had. Reva concluded that she was in a hospital.

Around the main building were blocks of rooms, each surrounded by an abundance of flowers, their colors as bright and dazzling as fresh paint. The air smelled crisp and clean. Reva's eyes, hungry for the sight of people, fixed on the few patients sprinkled in the landscape—some sitting on little cots placed in the sun, others taking walks along the pathways lined with ferns and *sadaphuli*, periwinkle. A tiger butterfly flew around the bicycle for a few seconds and then disappeared into the open sky. How different this little nook in the hills looked compared to the cliffs she had just left behind.

"We are going to take care of your foot before we go home," Viraj told Reva as he parked the bicycle outside the main building. "Stay here. I am going to get help."

Viraj hurried inside and returned with the same woman that Reva had seen an hour before. The woman exclaimed in recognition when she saw Reva. Reva fidgeted with embarrassment for a moment, staring at

Viraj as he spoke to the woman in English. He uttered the words as if he had been born with that tongue. Confident and commanding. How Reva wished she was not so ignorant. They were talking about her, and she could barely understand a handful of words.

A few moments later, Viraj addressed Reva.

"Reva, this is Miss Annie. She runs this hospital. I have asked her to clean and dress your wound. I will wait outside for you. Go with her."

Annie. Miss Annie. Reva liked the sound of her name. It was the kind of name that instantly made a friend out of a stranger. Gopi had talked about a sanatorium, a hospital, that Appa had started, and Reva considered the possibility that she was in it right now.

Miss Annie took Reva's hand so she could take her weight off her foot as they walked. Miss Annie's hands were milky white and soft. Reva smelled roses. As though she was handling a newborn, Miss Annie led Reva into a sitting room, minimally furnished but inviting. Smiling, she patted Reva's hand as she settled her patient in a wicker chair and rang the bell to summon help.

Reva basked in Miss Annie's care and kindness. She looked around the tiny room, imagining how delightful it would be to stay in this cozy corner instead of the cold mansion that she could not call a home. Her eyes focused on a lone picture hanging on the wall, and she saw Appa's robust frame and friendly smile beside the petite figure of Miss Annie in what seemed to be a ground-breaking ceremony for the sanatorium. Reva's initial suspicion was confirmed—this hospital was Appa's. Studying the picture a little more intently, Reva noticed a faint outline of two young men in the background. She wondered if they were Viraj and Coconut Head. For an instant, she was tempted to disregard Miss Annie's instructions to remain seated in order to get a glimpse of her still faceless husband. But the sound of voices approaching dismissed the thought.

A young village girl appeared in the doorway. If Reva had been impressed by Viraj speaking in English, she was now riveted as she watched Miss Annie instruct the girl in simple Marathi to wash and disinfect Reva's foot in a basin of water. Emerging from Miss Annie's mouth, the words sounded like a musical composition—familiar notes in a mesmerizing arrangement.

Reva felt the sting as the girl poured cool water on her foot. Miss Annie then used the gentlest of words to soothe Reva while she applied medicine and dressed the wound. Reva felt herself healing even before Miss Annie had finished wrapping the bandage on her foot. Finally, Miss Annie led the limping Reva back to the entrance where Viraj was waiting, reading the newspaper with a calmness that suggested a mundane morning. The two exchanged some words again. Every now and then, Reva felt Miss Annie glancing in her direction as she listened to Viraj. Her face was kind, inviting Reva to let her guard down.

Observing Miss Annie and Viraj from a distance, Reva could not help but notice how perfect they seemed together. She wondered if they felt it, too.

As Viraj got his bicycle ready for the ride back home, Miss Annie helped Reva seat herself on the carrier again. When Reva shyly mumbled a thank you in English, Viraj looked surprised for an instant, and then smiled. Reva smiled in response.

Once back on the road home, Viraj said, "You will like Miss Annie once you get to know her. She is a blessing to our village."

Reva bit her lip, afraid that the meddlesome question that had grazed her mind earlier might escape her lips. It was none of her business.

Instead she asked, "Why do you say that?"

"Miss Annie is a nurse who was working in the sanatorium for the white people in the village. She realized there was no medical help for the locals who had to travel all the way to Waikan to see a decent doctor. So she approached Appa with a plan. Appa gave her money and resources to build the hospital. She now manages the place. She has even convinced the doctor from the English hospital to visit two times a week. But when the English hospital gets busy, the doctor's visits dwindle. Miss Annie then does the best she can to take care of the sick."

"Why doesn't she just become a doctor then? I am sure in England anything is possible."

Viraj laughed. "We give the white people more credit than they deserve. There are times when their society feels only a tiny step ahead of ours. Even in England, women doctors are frowned upon. So Miss Annie chose the next best thing—to be a nurse, to spend her life doing what she wanted to do. Helping people get better. She has been here for five years now. I trust her judgment just as much or even more than the *gora*, the white doctor."

The admiration in his voice was unmasked, as was the respect in his words. Reva had never heard a man speak about a woman so reverently. She liked it. She wanted it for herself. Even if she was not a *gori*, a white woman.

The sun was descending in the sky as the mansion materialized in the distance. The ominous feeling returned.

"I can get down and walk back from here. My foot feels better already," Reva said, anxious to do the right thing.

"I know that you are afraid to go back with me. But I have told you already, taking care of family comes first, and that is what I am doing.

I will explain to Mai if I have to. I will only advise you to keep out of Tai-Aaji's way as much as possible. She has had a hard life, and while we don't always agree with a lot of things she says, we respect her, and all she has done for the family."

Reva wondered if having had a hard life gave one the right to make life hard for other people. Aai had never done so.

"One more thing, Tai-Aaji does not need to know that Miss Annie took care of your foot," Viraj continued after a moment. "The English are like untouchables for her—any association violates her religion. But she stays in her room most of the time these days. So you don't have to worry too much about it. When we reach home, I'll take care of the explanations. You can go to your room with Gopi's help and rest your foot. I will instruct Sita to take your lunch to your room."

Viraj's commands, just like Mai's, demanded obedience. It was just as well that Reva had no inclination to put into action the rest of her original plan of wooing Mai. After the disastrous events of the morning, it seemed like a naive thought in the first place.

Gopi was at the door waiting to sound the word as she saw Viraj and Reva approaching. She dashed inside the house to notify Appa and Mai. Then she reappeared, ran up the pathway, and then behind the bicycle all the way to the front door of the house. Double seated on the bicycle with Viraj, Reva could not bring herself to look at Mai fearing her disapproval. There was really nothing Reva could have done about the situation. Fortunately, Mai retreated into the house before Reva had even steadied herself on the ground.

"What happened Reva? Are you okay, my child? I was just about to get Maadhu and search for you myself," Appa exclaimed. Then seeing Reva limp, his brows further deepened, "Are you hurt, my dear?"

"I will explain everything, Appa," Viraj interrupted. "But first, Gopi, take Reva to her room. She has hurt her foot, so she cannot walk by herself."

For a few minutes, Reva enjoyed the concern that was showered on her as the household noticed her bandaged and swollen foot. Appa. Viraj. Gopi. Sita. As much as her wound hurt, Reva wished she could freeze this moment forever.

Chapter 10

October 1900

Reva struggled to open her eyes the next morning. Turning her head towards the windows to register the progress of the sun, she felt a moment's panic. Insolent clouds were peeking through the windows, then passing on, not having seen anything of interest. Had she dreamed her return to the house the day before? Or had she indeed been one of the rocks free falling down the cliff-face to her destiny? Was she in heaven? Would Aai glide into her room riding on one of these soft white tufts?

The haziness of the scene outside the window resembled the confusion inside her head. But as her senses adjusted to her environment, Reva recalled that this was the blanket of fog descending on the hills in winter mornings. The magic began to rub off on her. She sat up in her bed, bidding her fatigue to roll away with the fog.

Reva eyed her bandaged foot, propped on the pillow. Still swollen. She would have to stay upstairs the entire day. Reva was thankful for this forced solitary confinement. She pulled the thick woolen blanket closer around her. She could feel the stiff fabric of her *loogduh* collected in lumps around her body. A curse escaped her lips spontaneously just as a soft knock sounded on the door. Gopi entered the room, a mischievous smile forming on her lips.

"Reva *tai*, it's more auspicious to start the day taking God's name, and not the Devil's," she teased. The next instant Gopi's smile disappeared as she realized she had overstepped her boundaries. She had no business talking to Reva as if they were equals.

Ignorant in the etiquette of a true mistress of the house and desperate for a friend, Reva immediately retorted, "I tried flattering the Gods yesterday. Look where it got me! Perhaps I will have better luck with the Devil."

The girls giggled. Then Gopi glanced at the door quickly and approached Reva's bed.

In a hushed voice, Gopi said, "What a scene in the house yesterday, Reva *tai*! Viraj *dada* dashed after you, calling to you. But you ran like the house was on fire. Where did you go? Mai had to sweep and mop the whole prayer room by herself. Then she had to wash all the items on the altar. I am not allowed to go into that room, otherwise I would've done it, you know. Of course, you don't. That's why you messed up Tai-Aaji's *pooja*. Appa paced the house the whole time. I think he was angry with Tai-Aaji, but he does not go against her word, you know. Of course, you don't. How could you? Poor Mai has to do all that she says. Thank goodness that ever since Tai-Aaji has returned from her pilgrimage earlier this year, she has decided to stay mostly in her room taking God's name. But tell me Reva *tai*, what's the point of taking God's name in the room and speaking like the Devil outside? She should not have yelled at you like that, the little girl that you are and new to this house too. That was not very nice."

Gopi's acknowledgement of the injustice that Reva had suffered was like a soothing balm on Reva's wounds. She felt thankful that she had a sympathizer in the household.

"How is your foot feeling?" Gopi asked, trying to locate the wounded foot amidst the mound of fabric that had bunched up at Reva's feet.

Reva made a face. "I'll let you know as soon as I find it, Gopi. I hate this *loogduh*! Even if I was not hurt, how can I ever do anything with this balloon always in my way?" she complained. "At least you can wear yours high up so your legs are unbound and free to move. Maybe I should wear it that way too."

Gopi giggled again. "Mai would skin you alive. Women of this family never show their bare legs."

"Easy for Mai to say," Reva grumbled. "Her *loogduh* seems so much easier to manage and looks prettier too. So fashionable."

"That it is." Gopi nodded in agreement. "It is not as long as yours, for one thing."

"Where did she get it?" Reva asked.

"From Satara. And it is not a *loogduh*. It is called a *saadee*. Mai goes to the city once every two months for a meeting of important women. Appa wishes Mai to be part of that group and try to help the women in the hills, so Mai dutifully goes. A year ago, she came back with a *sadee*. It is only *paach-vaari*, five yards, in length and it is worn differently. It's the fashion of the rich. Mai would never do anything without the approval from Appa, which he readily gave. I haven't seen her wear a nine-yard *loogduh* since that day."

Reva was intrigued. "I wonder how it feels?" she said aloud.

"I can show you. I helped Mai learn to drape it when it was all new. Can you stand up? Let me show you," Gopi offered eagerly.

Reva's excitement overpowered the discomfort of her foot. She stood gingerly near the bed while Gopi worked the long *loogduh* around her slim frame, tucking, pleating, and tugging until at last she stepped back to observe her handiwork. Carefully, she led Reva to the full length mirror in the room. Both girls stared at the reflection for a minute, as their lips spread wider and wider into smiles that refused to be quelled. Soon they were laughing uncontrollably. Reva, wearing the nine yards of fabric in a five yard style, still looked like a balloon—a balloon that popped the moment the girls heard the sound of a throat delicately clearing. Both whirled around towards the door and saw Mai waiting patiently.

Panic-stricken, Gopi mumbled an excuse and a fervent apology and hurried out of the room. Mai's gaze followed her until she disappeared from sight. As Gopi descended the stairs and the sound of her footsteps receded into the kitchen, Mai stepped inside the room. Reva sat nervously on the edge of the bed in order to rest her foot, which had started to throb again.

"Is your foot a little better today?" Mai inquired, not unkindly.

Reva responded quickly, wanting to please Mai, "*Ho*, yes. I can come down if you need me there. I can..."

"No, that will not be necessary," Mai nipped her offer in the bud. "Your foot needs to heal completely first. I will send lunch to your room."

Mai prepared to make her exit. But in the doorway, she paused, as though debating a thought. Then, glancing over her shoulder at Reva, she said, "Gopi can chat the whole day away. But she has work to do and, soon, so will you. You must learn when and how much to encourage her and when to keep your distance. Remember, you will one day be the mistress in this house."

Mai left the room, and for a brief moment Reva wondered if she had only imagined a touch of kindness in her tone and a hint of a smile on her face. As she propped her foot back up on the bed and made herself comfortable, she wished she had summoned the courage to speak up and tell Mai that she had only been trying to help her in the prayer room the previous day. But then again, keeping her mouth shut had also not been a bad idea. It had kept her out of trouble.

On the third day of her confinement, Reva woke up listless and bored. She enjoyed being pampered by Gopi, but it also meant that she had very little to do. Her foot was healing and her mind refused to regurgitate the multiplication facts or her sanskrit prayers anymore. What was the point anyway?

When Gopi brought in the breakfast, Reva ambushed her with a question that had been playing on her mind.

"Tell me, Gopi," she said, "sometimes the house seems so quiet. Where does everyone go?"

"I have to hear Sita's chatter the whole day, so I don't know what quiet you are talking about," Gopi responded.

"I mean what does Appa do the whole day?" Reva asked, a trifle annoyed with the simple-minded servant.

"Appa is busy from morning to night. He spends most of the day in the fields. The farmers tend them but Appa helps them. He knows a lot about the soil and the plants that can grow here. Some days Appa also goes to the local villages to talk some sense to the people—to be clean, to send the children to school, to take care of their girls. Very nice man, Appa. He tried to tell my father too, to not get me married so fast. But my father was too worried about what people will say. So no use. Appa also talks to the English people if villagers are not happy with them. He tries, anyway. The English people are good on the outside but not on the inside. Some are like ripe golden mangoes with rotten pits."

Reva ignored the judgment. What would the village-bound uneducated Gopi know about the character of people, especially the white people?

"And Mai?" Reva pursued.

"Mai? Mai meets with the women in the villages and does what Appa tells her to. She spends most of the time managing the kitchen and house expenses and of course, catering to Tai-Aaji's every demand. Sometimes I feel bad for her. My mother says that Mai still works as she did when she was a brand new daughter-in-law in the house. Poor woman," Gopi murmured. After a moment's pause, she remarked, "I better get back, or Mai will take on Tai-Aaji's spirit. I will come back for the dirty dishes later."

After Gopi had left, Reva couldn't stop thinking about Mai and Tai-Aaji. When would Mai finally get her freedom?

It was obvious that Mai resented Reva's going to school. But as Reva pieced together the bits of information that Gopi had shared, the situation started making sense. If Reva were in school, Mai would remain the beast of burden in the house catering to Tai-Aaji's whims and the social responsibilities that come with being an important family in the village. Even if Appa was able to convince Mai, Tai-Aaji was bound to learn sooner or later about Reva's school, and Reva knew it would be Mai who would bear the brunt of Tai-Aaji's disapproval and subsequent anger. Mai was stuck in an unpleasant situation, and having a dutiful, house-bound daughter-in-law was probably her ticket out of it—even if Reva was not the daughter-in-law she would've chosen.

What could Reva do?

The next afternoon, Reva decided that she would put an end to her convalescence. The prospect of spending some time in the garden sounded appealing. Before leaving her room, she listened for the sound of Tai-Aaji's voice. Convinced that the coast was clear, Reva hobbled down the stairs and out the back door into the garden to breathe in the fresh air and feel the warm sun on her skin. The winter vegetables had started to flower. Reva spotted some snake gourd hanging on the vine, the stubborn remnant of warmer days. She would ask Mai's permission to cook the gourd for the family the next day. Mai would have to like that idea.

As Reva planned her next move, she heard a sniffle. Then the sound of feet shuffling. Who else was in the garden? Reva feared it might be a wild critter.

"Who is there?" she asked, getting ready to beat a hasty retreat into the house if needed. Silence. Then to her surprise, Mai came into view with a basket full of *gulmohar* and a nose as red as the flowers.

"It's me," Mai said turning her head away as she walked past Reva. At the door, she said, "Looks like your foot has healed. Now come inside quickly before you catch a cold and have to lie in bed again for days."

Before Reva could say a word, Mai had disappeared into the house. Mai sure was a complicated person. Impulsively, Reva decided she would try harder to make Mai happy. And if it required Reva to put away her dream of going to school that spring, then she would do so. But just for a little while. Once the family got to know how hard working and responsible she was, once they trusted her to be a good daughter-in-law, she would revive the idea of her going to school. Perhaps Coconut Head could help her then too. The sudden appearance of Coconut Head in her thoughts annoyed Reva, and she swatted away his vague image as she would a pesky fly.

Now that Reva had conjured a plan she could live with temporarily, she could not wait to tell Appa of her decision. How relieved he would be to put down the burden of the promise he had made to Reva. Just for a little while. Reva herself was surprised at the relief she felt at the thought of not being in conflict with Mai and even Tai-Aaji. The picture of a happy family fueled Reva's imagination as she went to look for Appa.

Reva found Appa reading in the front porch and catching the morning sun.

"Appa, I wanted to tell you something," she said, mustering all her determination. Without waiting for his response, lest she changed her mind, Reva continued, "If you are worried about my school and what Tai-Aaji or Mai will say, you don't have to anymore. I have realized that I don't have to go to school right away this spring. I can be happy helping Mai and learning how to run the household with her. Maybe then she and Tai-Aaji won't be upset with me."

The spoken words sounded less convincing than her thoughts.

Appa sighed as he shook his head.

"How life makes a grownup of a child before its time. My dear, come sit by me. I have been wishing to talk to you but wanted you to recover first. Tell me *pori*, is your foot better?"

Reva nodded. She barely remembered her father, but he must've been like Appa. They had been friends, after all.

"Even if you want to give up school, I will not let you. You must learn. Become someone. Not just Appa's daughter-in-law or Avinash's wife, but an identity that is meaningful to *you*. You will become whatever you want to be. And I will see to it that you do. Tai-Aaji, even Mai, needs some time to adjust," Appa said.

Appa's words made Reva feel like bursting into a song, but the shadow of Tai-Aaji's anger kept the notes in check.

"You see, Tai-Aaji has lived a very sad life ..." Appa folded his newspaper carefully as he spoke. "As a widow, she is shunned as bad luck everywhere except in this house and, of course, in the house of God. The little relief that she gets as a valued elder in this house pales compared to the miserable treatment she has received after her husband died. You may not know this, but she is my father's sister. She was married when she was eight years old. Her husband died of the plague when she was ten and still living at home with her own family."

Appa's voice trailed off as he got lost in the tangle of prickly memories.

Reva waited for a few minutes before fidgeting in her seat. Appa recovered and continued, "Her husband's family claimed that it was Tai-Aaji's cursed shadow that fell upon their son and caused his death. Their heartless accusation ruined a young girl's life. Tai-Aaji became a widow without ever knowing her husband or his home. A child widow. But she was the one who raised me after my own mother died when I was only four. She has been with me since. She is the reason I started questioning the ways of our world, the baseless superstitions and suffocating practices and yet ... and yet, she is the one who fights change the most."

Appa's face registered the pain and the suffering that he felt for Tai-Aaji, and Reva's heart softened.

Tai-Aaji's story was worse than her mother's. At least Aai had been a little older when she had been married off. She had enjoyed her husband's love and attention for a few years. It was true that the family had followed the unjust, even cruel, traditions of widowhood, but they had not disowned her Aai. And Aai had had Reva. They had taken care of each other. Tai-Aaji had been alone. She had every right to guard her small world fiercely.

"My child, all I am going to say for now is to give Tai-Aaji some time," Appa concluded. "She has nothing against you. She just needs to make peace with the changes in her home. As for your school, I have already talked to the headmaster of the village school. He is of the opinion that you will not get an adequate education there since the children are much younger than you. So I have spread the word in the community to see if I can find a private tutor who can come here and teach. It might take a little longer, but I want you to get the best teacher possible."

Reva's spirit soared. Her dream was safe in Appa's hands.

"I have not forgotten about the ... about the ... what did you call it ... *serbeti* ...either." Appa started to chuckle.

"But we have to wait a while for the right season. The fruit appears at the same time our English friends flock to these hills to escape the heat. It's our busiest time of the year in Tarapore ... that's when you will taste your *serbeti*. I will arrange it with my English friends."

After the few unnerving days of quiet, Appa's relaxed banter reassured Reva.

"...and Reva," Appa said kindly, " ... listen ... I got a letter from Avinash. He is well and learning a lot. He will come back as soon as he completes his training."

Reva did not know how to react. Other than a mild curiosity, she felt nothing. As a matter of fact, the prospect of getting to know the *serbeti* was more intriguing to her at the present time than Coconut Head. But one day she was going to need all the puzzle pieces to put the idea of her husband together. So she listened attentively. And she wondered. Hundreds of kilometers across the ocean, in the land of the beautiful white people, what was Coconut Head thinking?

Chapter 11

November 1900

Two weeks following her run-in with Tai-Aaji, Reva's foot had healed completely, and she put herself at Mai's disposal, quietly observing the day to day household functions and picking up the ways of the family. She noted that Appa liked his rice mushy with a generous dollop of ghee and never took more than a single serving. Viraj loved savory food and did not care for sweets. He always made it a point to compliment Sita, the cook, at the end of the meal. The best of Sita's cooking would only elicit a small nod of appreciation from Mai. But when Mai cooked on special occasions, the compliments from Appa and Viraj overflowed. Mai personally prepared Tai-Aaji's meager meals every day because Sita was of a lower caste. Unlike her childhood home, where the men ate first followed by the women, Appa's whole family ate the evening meal together precisely at half past seven. Reva wondered if Appa had borrowed this tradition from the foreigners in the hills.

The initial turmoil of arriving into a strange village, a new home, and an unknown family had given way to a mostly peaceful existence, and Reva began to feel more comfortable with her lot. *So what if I don't go to school right away? I am still learning new things.* Reva squashed her doubts each time they reared their troublesome head.

She took pleasure in observing that Mai was slowly warming up to her, even though Mai's brief business-like conversations with her were still in a voice that made Reva feel like a five-year-old child. That morning, Reva had entered her room to find a stack of brand new *saadee*, saris, on her bed. Gopi had readily spilled the beans. Sensing Reva's frustrations with the unwieldy *loogduh*, Mai had sent a request for the five yard saris from the store in Satara and instructed Gopi to train and assist Reva in draping the new style of sari. Staring at her transformed reflection in the mirror, Reva had felt like a butterfly emerging from its chrysalis, unfurling its wrinkled wings, tentative in the novelty of its beauty, yet trusting in the promise it carried.

The delight on Appa's face, the admiration on Viraj's, and the approval on Mai's as Reva entered the dining room clad in her new comfortable clothes that evening boosted Reva's confidence.

"Thank you, Mai, for these saris..." she began demurely before exclaiming, "I HATED the *loogduh*! I felt like a stuffed eggplant."

Viraj stifled a chuckle, and Mai looked up from the table sternly not favoring Reva with the smile she had expected.

"The clothes may be new, but our customs are unchanged. We do not talk so loudly no matter what. Keep that in mind."

Reva wished she could climb back into her chrysalis.

"Let it go," Appa said good-naturedly, "she is just a child, and children have every right to display their feelings."

Mai pointed out, "She is also the wife of an officer. Avi must have a good match in his wife. This new style suits you, Reva. Avi will definitely prefer this sari to the ones you were wearing. You can give those away to Gopi. You will not need them anymore."

Heedless of whether Mai's gift was motivated by her growing fondness for her daughter-in-law or her concern for her son's preferences, Reva sat down at the dinner table feeling more a part of the family than ever before.

While the housework kept Reva occupied in the mornings and evenings, it was the time in between that stretched out minute by minute. Mai had no use for her after lunch, and Appa and Viraj got busy with monitoring the harvests.

The search for a tutor was taking longer than Appa had expected. One afternoon, Reva found him pacing in the porch, agitated. In his hand, he clutched a well-traveled letter that Maadhu had just delivered.

"These men call themselves educated ... teachers of this new century ... and yet they have their pea-brains stuck in old suffocating ways! He has the nerve to tell me that he thinks his effort will be wasted here, teaching a girl, whose destiny is to manage her husband's home!" Appa waved the letter in frustration as he voiced his anger to Maadhu. Then, seeing Reva hovering in the doorway, he calmed down.

"*Aso*, let it be. We will continue our search. The winter weather right now does not tempt anyone to come to our hilltop village either. I am sure spring will bring us the solution we need," Appa said, smiling at Reva as she handed him a cup of tea. "Don't be discouraged, my child," he added.

Much to her own surprise, Reva was not discouraged. She was settling into her new home and her new family, gaining Mai's trust and chipping away at Tai-Aaji's distrust one day at a time. She did not want to sabotage her budding relations by broaching again the idea of pursuing her lessons. She could wait. For a little while.

Weeks turned into months. The days grew longer. The cool mornings got warmer as the fog retreated earlier to make way for the sun. The family began preparing to celebrate the spring festival of *Gudi Padwa*, the new year. Reva noticed new faces around the house as windows were scrubbed, floors were washed, and *punkhas* were unfurled and dusted. Fiery marigolds and glossy mango leaves were strung in intricate designs and hung on the doorways to welcome auspicious spirits into the house. Mai began to plan the lunch menu for *Gudi Padwa* while Appa and Viraj discussed the pay raises that they would give their workers as an appreciation for the hard work the previous year. The land had been more than generous, and Appa believed in sharing its bounty with the people toiling on it day and night.

The day before *Gudi Padwa*, Reva found herself heading to the Krishnali temple. It wouldn't hurt to start the new year with the blessings of the deity and, perhaps, the solid cool stones of the temple would calm the restlessness that had begun sprouting in her mind.

White periwinkle had blossomed in profusion all around the temple courtyard, leaving no doubt that it was springtime on the hills. Gopi waited in the cart with Maadhu Kaka while Reva went inside. Two pilgrims, illuminated by the rays of the overhead sun, were dipping in the holy waters of the cistern and softly chanting hymns in praise of Krishna. As Reva walked down the cistern steps, she thought of how much her mother would have loved this temple. Reva listened for the sound of the bells she had heard before. But the temple remained silent except for the soft gurgling of the water as it flowed through the spout.

Reva sat on the bottommost step and watched her reflection in the water forming and changing every few seconds. The events of the past two months flashed before her eyes. Aai would have been proud to know that she was adjusting to her life. That she was making sacrifices for the good of her new family. She was no longer the selfish little girl who had escaped from kitchen chores to watch the swell of the river or insisted on a storytelling at night knowing well that her mother was bone tired. She would obey Mai's wish that she stay in the house and manage the home fires, and she would do it so well that her new family would have to agree that Coconut Head would not have found a better wife even if the family had searched across the seven seas. Reva was happy. Or maybe, she was just not sad anymore.

"*Agga bai!* Oh my goodness! If it isn't my little Reva!" A loud voice shattered the quiet.

The voice was familiar. But it couldn't be.

"Hirkani?" Reva mumbled with confusion.

Why would Hirkani, the vegetable seller from Uruli, be here in Tarapore? Reva thought she was dreaming as indeed her friend and confidant materialized as if out of thin air right behind her. Hirkani had grown a little thinner, but there was no mistaking that it was her.

Reva shrieked and jumped up from her perch. "I cannot believe my eyes! What are you doing here, Hirkani?"

Annoyed, the two pilgrims looked angrily towards Reva for disturbing the serenity of the temple, but Reva had seen a trusted friend, and she was not going to hold back. Hirkani's smile stretched from ear to ear. However, anticipating a fierce hug from Reva, she stepped back, glancing at the pilgrims who eyed them disapprovingly. Reva's step slowed. They had both traveled a long way from home, but not far enough to ignore that Reva still belonged to a high caste and Hirkani to a lower caste. They must not hug. Reva would be reprimanded. But the consequences would be far harsher for poor Hirkani.

"Let's go to the back of the temple. No inquisitive eyes will spy on us there," Hirkani whispered, motioning for Reva to follow. They retreated to a little nook carved out in the thick green shrubs behind the temple.

"If I knew you were here, in this village, I would've come much earlier," Hirkani said. "Look at you Reva, you look different. All grown up in a few months. In fashionable clothes too! Where is that little girl of mine?"

"I am the same, Hirkani," Reva laughed. It felt good to laugh.

"Tell me quickly Hirkani, what are you doing here?" Reva could not bear the suspense any longer.

Hirkani's smile disappeared as creases surfaced on her forehead like ripples in still water.

"Where should I begin? A few weeks after you left, my life turned upside down. My family lost the little land we had in our village because of the new road that is being built. In a blink of an eye, our vegetable garden and our home were gone. Snatched from us. The road was necessary for the progress of the village, those beasts said. What kind of progress is this that breaks the backs and sucks the life out of poor people like us? But there was nothing we could do about it. For a while, we lived off the small sum of money the white man had given us for our land, but it was not enough to last a winter, let alone buy more land or a livelihood...it was a nightmare. I hope, *pori*, you never ever have to put your children to sleep with just air and water in their bellies. My ears still ring with their whimpering as they lulled themselves to sleep, hungry and hopeless."

Hirkani's eyes teared, and Reva bristled at the injustice her friend had suffered.

Hirkani continued, "Then someone in the village told the husband about the hills—that in the summer the white people people need a lot of help. My husband wanted to try his luck. So first we went to Marungaon.

But it was too crowded. My brother-in-law told us about Tarapore. I kept telling myself I had heard the name before. And now I know where—it was from you of course. *Me bindok!* Stupid me! I had forgotten. So we packed our things and headed to these hills. My husband now works the fields at the foothills, and I sell vegetables there. I heard of the beauty and the sanctity of this Krishnali temple and wanted to see for myself, so I came here. And good thing I did!"

Hirkani hastily wiped away the tears that had formed in her eyes.

"And good thing I did!" she repeated, her smile so contagious that Reva let go of the troubling story and rejoiced that fate had brought her friend back into her life. She was determined to use her own good fortune to make life a little easier for her friend.

"Don't you worry about a thing now, Hirkani. I will talk to Appa about you. We have fields too. I can see if you can work here. I can also talk to Appa about a house for you closeby. Then we can see each other everyday."

"Not if my life depended on it!" Hirkani exclaimed in shock. "I am from your mother's village. I cannot take any favors from your in-laws. What will our village people say if they find out? I may be poor, but I haven't lost my self-respect yet. Besides, we have enough to feed our children for now. What more can we want?"

Seeing Reva's smile evaporate, Hirkani hastily added, "But you can be sure that whenever I get my tired bones up this hill, I will try to see you. Hopefully, I won't bother you in your studies. I cannot wait to see my Reva all educated and smart. Unlike the ignorant me!"

The world turned uncomfortably quiet as Hirkani's words settled in Reva's mind.

"You are not ignorant, Hirkani. You talk to people. You go to different places and see things. You manage your household. You know the ways of the world. You are just as smart as anyone else. You don't have to go to school to be smart," Reva argued. Her voice rang sharp as it attempted to hide the tinge of uncertainty that lurked within.

Hirkani shook her head sadly. "Only the hunchback knows how he can lie comfortably," she muttered. "Dear girl... none of that knowledge was any use when the village head came home with papers and a white man to take our land. Said our land was theirs. Showed the thumbprint that my ignorant husband had put on it, thinking he was selling the produce from the land to the white people. And just like that, we lost everything. Now tell me Reva, if I could read, if I could understand the language of that white man, wouldn't I have done something to help my family, to save the little piece of land that was the support of my old age? *Nai, nai, tey kai nai!* No, no, don't even think about it! Your going to school is the best thing that can happen to you. And my blessings on Appa who is going to help you do it."

Reva toyed with the idea of hiding the truth from Hirkani. But she couldn't deceive her friend.

"Hirkani ... I am not going ... to school," Reva confided.

Hirkani froze.

"...For now," Reva added quickly.

"What's this nonsense now? Did you say you are not going to school? Were you tricked into marrying that Coconut Head then?" Hirkani demanded, as much shocked as puzzled.

"Hirkani, didn't you tell me, some time ago, that an arrow must be pull backward before it can go forward and find its mark?"

Reva explained her situation, and Hirkani listened without comment. Then, with an uncharacteristic grimness, she said, "Listen to me, Reva. It sounds to me like you are putting your arrow back in its quiver. What use is it then? An opportunity like this may not come again. Don't turn it away while trying to please the world. There is no pleasing the world. Appa, the *man* of the house, is supporting you in this dream. Take the offer while you can. Who knows what's in store for tomorrow?"

Hirkani's voice rose. "Continue your studies, learn the language of the white people, become something. You should not have to depend on anyone else for your happiness. You might not be able to hear the voices so high in the hills, but the whole country is calling for independence. Then why not us women?"

Hirkani's impassioned speech shook Reva. And Hirkani was not done yet.

"Don't get caught up with the household matters yet. There will be time for that later. God has favored the family that they lack nothing. So you don't have to feel guilty to follow your dream. You must go to school. You must!" Hirkani seemed agitated now.

Reva sympathized with Hirkani—having her land and livelihood taken away made her suspicious of everyone and everything. Reva did not wish to argue with her friend, especially when they had just reunited.

"*Bara bara, theek ahai!* Okay! Okay! There is still time to settle this question. And Appa *is* looking for a tutor. Now, come with me. I'll show you where I live. Then maybe next time you can come to our house with your vegetables."

"Some other time, *pori*. I must get going. It will take me an hour at least to get to my village, and though the sun is still high on the horizon, night arrives early on these trails."

Reva was disappointed, but she knew Hirkani was right. She did not want her to get lost in the darkness. Reva's terrifying daytime adventure when she had first arrived on the hills was still fresh in her mind.

"You will come again to see me, won't you Hirkani? You can ask anyone in the village where the Tambay house is, and they can direct you there," Reva insisted before they parted ways.

Hirkani raised her hand in blessing and whispered softly, "I will, my child. You can be sure of that."

As Reva watched Hirkani's figure disappear on the trail behind the temple, her doubts resurfaced. She thought of the misfortune that Hirkani blamed on her ignorance. Reva herself was no stranger to misfortune. Was she choosing to stay ignorant by tucking away her dream of going to school? As the bullock cart rattled home, Reva wished she could cast away the troublesome thoughts with every bump on the dirt road and restore her peace of mind that was proving to be as fragile as a butterfly's wing.

Back at the house, Reva descended from the cart, still lost in her thoughts, when Gopi tapped her arm to direct her attention to Viraj approaching.

"I wonder what world problems are being solved in that head that you wouldn't even acknowledge my calling out to you, Reva," he joked.

Reva blushed, embarrassed. She started to smile, grateful to be rescued from her unpleasant thoughts.

However, her smile tightened as Viraj continued, "Let me guess. You were consumed with decisions—whether to make sweet *puran poli* or *shrikhand* for lunch tomorrow? Or perhaps even, going to Satara to shop for some more saris ..."

Reva knew Viraj was trying to be friendly, but his comments annoyed her. Was that all he thought she was capable of? Would he say the same thing to Miss Annie?

Viraj finally came to the point. "Reva, I met Miss Annie in the village today. She was asking about you."

Coming closer, he said, "Miss Annie wants to meet you again. I think she likes you. I can take you tomorrow afternoon if you'd like. I usually go to the hospital on Thursdays."

Her curiosity getting the better of her delight over Miss Annie's interest, Reva asked, "Every Thursday? Why do you go? Are you sick?"

"No, no, I am hale and hearty," Viraj assured her, "but I help families of the patients talk to the English doctor who visits the hospital every Thursday. It eases Miss Annie's work a little."

"Where did you learn to speak so well?" asked Reva, genuinely interested.

"The same place your husband did," teased Viraj. "At Saint Peter's School in Panchgar—another village very close to here."

The mention of her husband triggered a new worry in Reva's mind. Her plan of postponing school might bring her closer to Mai, but would it jeopardize her future with her English-educated officer husband?

"I have to go help Appa in the fields now. We'll go after lunch tomorrow. Be ready," Viraj instructed as he mounted his bicycle and pedaled away, oblivious to the real concerns swirling in Reva's head.

The next day at the hospital, Miss Annie welcomed Reva warmly.

"I declare," said Miss Annie, "I haven't seen you at all since your foot has healed! You must be very busy in that beautiful house of yours. Do stay awhile, now that you are here."

Seeing Reva's mouth droop, as soon as Miss Annie was out of earshot, Viraj asked, "Why that sad face?"

"If counting flies the whole day is your idea of keeping busy, then yes one could say I have a busy life in the house," Reva replied dejectedly.

Viraj cast a probing look, but before he could pursue the conversation further, he was called to assist Miss Annie as she struggled to explain to a patient the importance of taking the medicine prescribed for him in addition to chanting his *mantras* for a quick recovery.

Reva observed the scene with much interest.

"Viraj," said Reva, when he returned to her side, "I was thinking ... can I help around the hospital like you do? There is not much for me to do at home in the afternoon—Sita does most of the cooking, Gopi does the other chores. There are more servants in the house than I have fingers on my hands. And who knows when Appa will find a teacher for me. I am going out of my mind with boredom. I feel like a ghost roaming the halls in the house, present but invisible. I want to do something."

Viraj considered her words carefully.

"I think that's a good idea," he said after a minute, "I can talk to Miss Annie about it. But you have to check with Appa first, and Mai, of course. I think they will be happy with your idea of helping the villagers at our hospital, but get their permission first."

Reva hesitated. She had one further request, but Viraj might see it as an imposition.

"Viraj, I want to learn to speak English, too. I always did. Now I want it even more. I want to help, and I am a quick learner."

"I understand ... but I can't do anything about that," Viraj said, unsure of what Reva wanted him to do.

"Can *you* teach me until I get a tutor?" The words popped out of Reva's mouth before she could stop herself. She wondered if she was overstepping boundaries. Would Mai frown upon this arrangement?

For a few minutes, Viraj was quiet.

"Let's start with your helping in the hospital," Viraj said. "If Appa agrees, I can walk with you and teach you along the way. No one needs to know about our conversations. Miss Annie can also help you with English while you are by her side. She can definitely use some more hands around here."

Satisfied with that answer, Reva's breathing relaxed, and she felt like she was not completely at odds with the strange path she found herself on and that appeared to lead her away from school. While Viraj spoke to Miss Annie, Reva planned how she would propose her plan to Appa.

"Reva, Miss Annie likes the idea very much," Viraj announced triumphantly when he rejoined Reva. "In fact, they are short of staff today. Would you stay for an hour or so to help get a room ready for a new patient? I have a meeting to attend here in the village. I can walk home with you when you are done. I think Mai and Appa would not object to you helping out in an emergency."

Looking at the radiant smile that flooded Reva's face, Viraj got the answer he needed.

Within minutes, Reva got busy helping the nurse set up the room for the patient who was expected to arrive shortly. She dilligently tucked in the edges and smoothed out every wrinkle on the fresh bedspread. She wiped down with ferocity the small table that would hold a pot of water and clean washcloths. She pondered over the precise placement of the rocking chair so that the sun would not invade the eye as it enjoyed the grand vistas framed by the window. Miss Annie could not help but smile each time she passed by the room. She even blew a kiss that confused Reva until the nurse giggled and explained its meaning. Reva was delighted.

Soon the room was ready. As the women adjusted the blankets on the bed one last time, the nurse sighed, "*Bichari*, unfortunate woman. Sick and alone. No family to look after her."

Reva gathered the nurse was talking about the future resident of the room. Although Reva no longer felt alone, she remembered the feeling vividly. She would not wish it on her worst enemy. She felt a pang of sympathy for this nameless, faceless person who would sleep under the very blanket that she had tucked in. She lingered a little longer and surveyed her work. The room was clean. It looked comfortable. It was ready for a patient to move in. And yet ...

Like a flash of lightening illuminating a dark night, Reva realized what was missing. She stepped outside and spotted some dahlias growing in the garden. She snipped three avoiding the keen eye of the gardener and arranged them prettily beside the bed. She may not be able to cure any sickness of the body like Miss Annie or the doctor, but she knew a thing or two about making the heart happier.

Seeing Viraj waiting for her, Reva waved a quick good bye to Miss Annie and hurried out. As Viraj and Reva walked out through the gate, they passed a bullock cart making its way towards the hospital. Reva could see a frail figure lying in the back with a blanket pulled all the way up to the head. Another woman sat at the patient's feet napping, unaware that they had reached their destination.

Reva prayed that the dahlias would serve their purpose. Reva prayed that she too would soon find her purpose.

Chapter 12

March 1901

"It is time," Appa said to Reva one morning a few days after *Gudi Padwa*.

"Now you will see the English flock to our village to escape the heat of the plains. They will swoop in when summer approaches and swarm out just before the rains begin. Here in the mountains, one has the sense of being in a storm even before the monsoons start." Appa smiled to himself.

As if waking from a deep restful sleep, Tarapore had indeed begun to stir and stretch, infusing tracks and trails with people and their possessions. One morning, Reva passed a caravan carrying four poster beds, wicker sofas, metal swings, and even a piano. Reva, now accustomed to exploring the hillside and the village with Gopi, noticed stores in the main bazaar stocking up on goods delivered from the bigger cities—furniture, rugs, pots, pans, mosquito nets, parasols, soaps and creams. Once Reva and Gopi had pondered the utility of a curious chair with a hole in the middle of the seat. Later, they had stared shamelessly as a servant from an English house carried it away but only after careful inspection and mock trial. Its use had dawned on them at the same moment, and they had laughed all the way home.

The houses on the outskirts of the village that had been shut in the winter were opened and aired out. Floors were scrubbed, gardens were tidied, and perfumed water was sprayed in the air to mask the musty signs of a closed house. To Reva, the flurry of activity resembled the chaos of the weeks before Diwali, the festival of lights that was still eight months away. Gopi had described this summer transformation to Reva, but it was exciting to witness that magic one day at a time.

"Maybe I'll learn more English words with so many English people around," Reva commented to Viraj at the breakfast table one morning, after Appa and Mai had left the dining room.

Viraj grimaced. "Only if they let you be around them long enough," he remarked with an uncharacteristic vehemence. "You will see what I mean. They will act as if they own this land. They will pretend that none of the local residents exist, and they will expect and take what is not theirs. They will make it obvious that they do not like Indians, and yet they will build their life here on the backs of the very same people." Viraj spat out the words with disgust.

"Appa doesn't see it that way," Reva countered lightly.

"How Appa can look the other way, I do not understand ... I saw the Resident's house being cleaned today. That's where they will gather in their beautiful clothes and scheming minds and while away the nights in merriment," Viraj muttered angrily.

Despite Viraj's pessimistic view, the picture in Reva's mind was tantalizing. What a treat it would be to see all the fair ladies in their beautiful gowns and the officers in their dashing uniforms! She was puzzled with Viraj's attitude towards the foreigners. Miss Tytler and Miss Annie were two of the nicest people she knew. Surely there would be more like them. Reva was not so naive as to assume that none would fit the image Viraj conjured, but a few bad grains of rice did not make the whole pot inedible.

"These are the people who bite the hand that feeds them," continued Viraj.

Refusing to let Viraj's dark mood dampen her spirit, Reva said, "The people I know are kind. So what you are saying makes no sense to me."

"Well, one day it will bother you, and it should," Viraj retorted impatiently. "Don't you know what's going on around the country? Our own people are being abused. Our riches are being stolen to fill the Queen's treasury. And we have no voice in the future of our own motherland. I say enough is enough. We must join forces with other Indians who are rising up in arms against these white people. They are uniting under Tilak's leadership to liberate our great land. It's time for the British to pack their things and go home. We don't need guests that abuse our hospitality and overstay their welcome."

Reva stared at Viraj, unable to understand the reason for his outburst. Wasn't it western education that had made Viraj the person he was today—knowledgeable, open-minded, and confident? What had these English people done to offend her peaceful brother-in-law's sensibilities other than spend an innocent holiday in the hills? Reva had known that Viraj was not a supporter of these foreigners, but she had not anticipated such intense dislike of them. Reva decided to keep her arguments to herself. On this issue, they were not on the same side of the fence. Maybe Coconut Head would share her appreciation. After all, he had chosen to live with the *goray*, the white people, for many years.

Reva soon forgot Viraj's misgivings as more and more visitors arrived in an endless line of horse carriages and with luggage bearers on roads that led from the big cities of Bombay and Poona. They reminded her of an army of ants marching towards a sweet destination. Reva had started to relish the sweetness of the hills herself.

The business in the bazaar was booming as servants were sent frequently to buy supplies for the summer. When the processions passed through the small village square, Reva caught glimpses of the children and their mothers—their fair faces flushed from the arduous journey up the hills, finding relief in the beauty and chill of the mountains. She watched ladies escorted by gentlemen stroll on the trails, calling out to their children to stay close to their sides. She observed how they curtsied and bowed and nodded and smiled at the other visitors. Reva smiled at the little girls and their mothers, but they obviously did not see her. Why else would their faces remain unmoved and cheerless?

The visitors settled in Tarapore in the picture perfect cottages now abloom with flowers and festivities. They came with a few servants and soon hired a band of locals to cater to their every wish and whim. The Resident, who as Gopi explained was the biggest *saheb* amongst the foreigners, had his own grand bungalow in the most picturesque part of the hilly landscape. His house came alive each night with magical lights and tinkling of glasses, with soft musical notes interlaced with delicate laughter of the ladies and the rowdy jaunts of the officers. All white. Watching the frolicking from afar, Reva had to acknowledge that Viraj had some right to be offended by these visitors who maintained such exclusivity.

One afternoon, as Reva idly sucked on a piece of jaggery, she watched Appa entertain two white gentlemen on the porch. These visitors were old friends. Every year, Appa made their stay comfortable by helping them procure special produce and competent help, familiarizing them with the points of interest in the hills. Reva knew they had a mutual understanding— the English men were not allowed to enter Appa's house, fearing Tai-Aaji's wrath at allowing the foreigners to pollute the sanctity of her home. Appa, on the other hand, though obviously respected, was not extended an invitation to visit at the Resident's house or partake in any of the festivities.

This strange relationship confused Reva.

"Appa, don't you ever feel like going to their parties?" Reva asked as soon has the visitors had left.

"*Pori*, I look at it this way. After spending a long day with the villagers and the traders, I like to come home to the privacy of my home and the comfort of my family. The same way, for a few months in the summer, these English folks want to spend time with their kind, their friends, their family. I don't think too much of that."

That explanation made sense. Appa made sense. And if the situation was acceptable to Appa, then Reva had no bone to pick with it either. She would do as much as she could to be hospitable to these visitors. After all, in a few short months, Reva had begun to feel like a host in the hills too.

"Talking about friends, Reva, look what I have here in my hands. I got these just for you. Just as I had promised." Appa's eyes twinkled as he held out his hand.

In a small basket made out of a dried banana leaf, Reva saw a tiny mound of fresh berries. She was finally going to taste the *serbeti*! The intense redness of the fruit produced a strange heat that started in the pit of her stomach and made her heart beat a little faster. Wispy green shoots crowning the fruit only enhanced the desire to reach out and consume one. Reva took the basket of berries from Appa. Looking closely, she saw the fruit was delicately tinged with dark spots, as though nature was warding off the evil eye. She closed her eyes and inhaled deeply, letting herself be intoxicated by a fragrance that was both familiar and foreign.

Hastily, she gulped the last bit of jaggery down her throat, and then reached for the biggest berry. As she bit into its juicy flesh, the symphony that the berry had built around itself hit a faulty note. Reva's eyes squeezed shut, and her mouth puckered. The fruit tasted more sour than sweet. Cautiously, she ate another, trying to coax the sweetness that Miss Tytler had relished. The tartness subsided a little. Reva's mouth relaxed. Perhaps it was the lingering sweetness of the jaggery in her mouth that had overpowered the sugar in the strawberry.

Appa was watching her reaction excitedly. Not wanting to disappoint Appa who had obviously gone through much trouble to procure the *serbeti*, Reva forced a smile.

"It's delicious, Appa! So red. So juicy," Reva said, extending the basket towards him.

Appa popped a couple in his mouth. "I can taste the richness and the fragrance of the mountain dirt in these fruits," he remarked with pride.

Reva tried again. She could smell the earth too, but the sweetness eluded her taste buds.

"Should I take some inside for the others?" she asked.

"No, no. Mai and Viraj don't care for them, and Tai-Aaji best not know anything about them," Appa said mischievously.

In a few minutes the berries had disappeared. Rubbing his hands around his belly contentedly, Appa turned and headed inside the house.

Left standing in the porch with the empty basket in her hand, Reva decided that she would not judge the strawberry so hastily until she had tasted the fruit again. After all, if it looked so delicious, and it smelled so heavenly, it simply had to taste like sweet paradise. The fault probably lay in her own jaggery-coated compromised tongue.

One afternoon, Gopi and Reva walked to the main bazaar to explore the new merchandise being stocked for the visitors. As they fingered the small bars of soap and inhaled the heady rose and lavender fragrances, their attention was diverted by the sound of hooves in the village square. A group of riders had come to an abrupt halt, and the horses were neighing and kicking up a dust storm. The three English horsemen, dressed in impeccable riding attire, were studying the dirt tracks that radiated around the square. Their pale skin was flushed, their backs erect as they controlled their steeds. Their voices oozed confidence and command as they talked among themselves.

Local shoppers stopped and stared at the trio and little children edged closer to the group trying to earn some favors—perhaps some small change, a foreign trinket, or maybe even a kindly glance. One of the officers pointed to a little boy and demanded something. His words, laced with frustration and a tinge of anger, prompted the little boy to burst out crying. He ran to his mother, who grabbed his hand and hurried away. The man repeated the question to another young man who grinned vacantly and nodded his head but made no attempt to respond in words or action. Reva caught the words *rasta*, road, and Resident. She realized that they were trying to find their way to the Resident's bungalow. They were lost. They needed help. On instinct, she started to step forward to approach the group. Gopi held her back.

"Reva *tai*, you cannot talk to these white men," she warned. "Mai will be furious. Let them be. Someone will help them eventually."

Reva paused. Gopi was right about Mai ... but Appa would've helped them.

"Why should anyone be angry with me for merely helping someone find their way around our hills? I am not going to sit on the horse and show them the way, am I?" Reva retorted cheekily.

Reva walked tentatively towards the men. One of the riders noticed her approaching and called to his friends. Reva knew that her appearance intrigued them. She had the same pale skin and light eyes as them, but she was dressed as Indian as could be. She smiled uncertainly at the closest rider from twenty feet away. He smiled back slightly and continued to stare at her. Reva felt her breath quicken.

Before she lost her courage and her wits, Reva said to him, "*Rasta? Resident bungalow?*"

The man grinned and nodded.

Reva pointed to one of the trails leading away from the main bazaar.

The three riders quickly conversed amongst themselves and turned their horses in the direction Reva had pointed.

The man talking to Reva inched his horse closer and tipped his hat.

"Thank you, Miss. My name is Richard. And you are?" His voice was deep and smooth and reminded Reva of the sticky sweetness of molasses that lingers luxuriously in the mouth. His eyes were blue enough to drown her thoughts had she met his stare. This encounter was turning out to be more than Reva had bargained for. She did not have the courage to face the music at home if she brazenly had such an exchange with a strange white man. She turned around immediately and hurried towards the waiting Gopi. Behind her, she could hear soft chuckling and then the sound of hooves moving away from the village square.

"Mai is going to be furious when she hears how you talked to those white people. And all by yourself in public," Gopi's words revealed her nervousness. After all, as the chaperone, Gopi should've stopped Reva from having that conversation in the first place.

Reva, her nerves temporarily calmed, mustered all the authority she could find. Looking Gopi in the eye, she said, "Mai is not going to hear about this incident from us. Is she, Gopi?" Reva had seen Mai use this tactic with the help. She knew it worked.

"Now let's walk home quickly. It will be time for tea soon," continued Reva. She walked a few steps ahead of Gopi all the way home. Gopi need not know that Reva was equally nervous about the consequences for the impulsive exchange with the gentlemen.

Reva's warning to Gopi had been in vain. The report had already fallen on Appa and Mai's ears before they reached home. Reva realized that the grapevine in Tarapore was just as well-oiled and unforgiving as in Uruli. She received an earful from Mai that was as hot and scalding as the tea Gopi served that afternoon.

"I knew you were not the right choice for this family," Mai complained. "Every little thing has to be spelled out to you. Did your mother not teach you that you should never indulge in a conversation with an unknown man? A young white man. And you initiated it. The whole village is talking. The name of our family is being discussed in every little hut tonight, and not in a way we can be proud of." Mai fumed while Reva cried silently. Appa watched the scene from an armchair with the newspaper folded on his lap, and as he saw Mai get ready to launch into another tirade, he intervened.

"Reva, what Mai is saying has some truth to it. We want you to be safe. We don't know who these men were and indulging in a conversation with them would only draw unwanted attention and get your reputation ruined. But I appreciate the fact that you were trying to help, and the color or gender of the person did not stop you from doing that. Uma, let her be now. I think she has learned her lesson. I am sure she will not do it again."

Reva was dismissed. She was still not convinced that the small interaction she had had with the men warranted such a nasty scene. But it had bothered Mai and Appa, so she would do her best to refrain from participating in such situations in the future. If only her best was good enough.

Chapter 13

April 1901

With some explanation from Viraj, a convincing display of dullness and lethargy from Reva, and frustration arising from the fruitless search for a tutor, Appa agreed to let Reva help Miss Annie in the hospital for a few hours every afternoon. Her unbecoming encounter with the white man in the village square compelled Mai to give Reva's idle mind something worthwhile to do. She could perhaps even salvage her reputation with this selfless and noble deed. Reva's plan to learn English, however, remained a secret. She would keep it so until the time was right.

Getting ready for her first day of work, Reva checked her reflection in the mirror. She had picked out a cotton sari, a pale yellow like the color of magnolias. Under the pretext of maintaining their family status, Mai had generously ordered new saris for Reva in an array of colors and textures to suit every demand of the day. However, on that particular day, Reva did not wish to stand out like a sore thumb among the nurses in their plain *loogduh*, so she chose the simplest of the lot.

Her hair was oiled and pulled back neatly into a braid that fell all the way to the middle of her back. In her ears glistened her mother's pearl *kudis*. The black and gold beads of the *mangalsutra* around her neck and the small *kunku* on her forehead would announce to all the strangers she would encounter that she was a married woman. They would also be a good reminder for Reva to behave in a mature, dignified manner. She stared unhappily at the stack of gold and green glass bangles on each arm that clashed with the slightest movement of the hands. How could she do her best work at a hospital in these noisy contraptions? She could not remove them—a bare arm on a married woman was frowned on. Impulsively, Reva decided to keep a single bangle in each wrist. Satisfied that she was appropriately dressed for a productive day at the hospital, her gaze returned to her face. She wondered if anyone would notice in her hazel eyes the glimmer of excitement that she felt in her heart.

Miss Annie was in her office when Viraj walked Reva to the hospital. Her face broke into a strained smile when she saw Reva hovering in the doorway. Reva had the sense that she had arrived late to an appointment she had not made. Miss Annie seemed a little agitated. The nurse soon explained why.

The new patient, that Reva had prepared the room for when she last visited, was causing some anxiety among the caregivers. The staff called her *Abolee*, voiceless, since no one knew her real name, and she had said not a word. She had been first admitted to a Bombay hospital by a well-meaning citizen who had found her shivering and delirious in his barn, her body as hot as freshly extinguished coal. The doctors had treated her for malaria but could not pronounce her well enough to be released. It seemed that it was not her physical sickness that was impeding her recovery, but her troubled state of mind. She did not want to live. With no contact from any family during her stay in Bombay, the staff at the hospital had declared her abandoned and contacted Miss

Annie for further action. The expectation was that the fresh air and the high mountain landscape would renew a sense of hope and well-being in the patient.

And so Abolee had been transferred from the Bombay hospital to the hills. After days of observing her relentless silence, Miss Annie was now fearful of the outcome of this case. The patient indeed had no wish to live. She stared vacantly at the walls or out the windows. Her food remained untouched. Medicines had to be coaxed down her throat. Her thoughts remained sealed and buried under a mountain of untold stories.

"I don't know what more I can do," Miss Annie squeezed her hands in distress. "The poor girl will die if she goes on like this. I wonder sometimes if that is her plan. Reva, you seem to be the same age as her. Perhaps she will warm up to you. Will you try talking to her? You are my last resort now."

Miss Annie's words echoed in Reva's mind as she stepped out of the office.

Through all the turmoil that Reva had experienced in her own short life, she had never felt the desire to exit the world. Only for a few seconds, that first time on the cliff, had she subconsciously flirted with the possibility, but she had very definitely chosen to live. Reva had no idea what she could do or say that would help this young girl. On the way to Abolee's room, the nurse described how the only attempt to take Abolee out for a stroll one sunny morning had ended with the girl becoming hysterical and holding tightly on to the bed rails until her palm had started bleeding. Seeing the lines of worry forming on Reva's face, the nurse hurriedly assured her that the violent behavior was quite uncharacteristic, and that the patient was mostly quiet and subdued.

Reva peeked into the room to take stock of the situation. Abolee was seated in a chair facing the window, her back to the doorway. A cool breeze intent on bringing fresh life to the room merely ruffled her unevenly shorn shoulder length hair and left with its work undone. Reva could smell resignation in the air. The quiet in the room amplified the questions that started to crowd Reva's mind. Who was Abolee? How did she end up in the barn? Where was her family? What happened to her hair? Why would she not tell her story to Miss Annie, who was only trying to help?

Reva stepped into the room.

Reva's footsteps did not produce any reaction from the patient. She continued to stare through the window. Reva wished she had not removed her stack of bangles. Then she wouldn't have to work so hard to fill the uncomfortable silence. She sat down tentatively on one edge of the companion bed behind Abolee's chair, contemplating how to begin a conversation. Although Abolee appeared like a lifeless doll propped on the chair, her bandaged grip on the armrest seemed alert and alive, as if prepared to fend off any attempt to remove her from her safe place. An angry scar at the nape of her neck was visible through her roughly trimmed hair.

Reva's gaze moved from Abolee back to her bed, neatly made, holding no clue to the story of the person who had lain in it just a few hours ago. Reva wondered if the girl had slept at all.

Reva slid closer to Abolee. Abolee's back straightened ever so slightly. Then she stilled. She reminded Reva of the jungle deer, freezing … in readiness to flee. Reva's attention was once again drawn to Abolee's hands, skin stretched taut across the knuckles as the fingers gripped the chair. And right then, Reva's eyes discerned a blue-gray bean-shaped mark that lay exposed on Abolee's arm. As the mark took shape in Reva's mind, the air began inching out of her body. To a stranger, it might look like a slow healing bruise. But Reva was no stranger. Not anymore. She knew it was a birthmark.

Reva's mind could not accept what her eyes saw.

It had been four years since Reva had last seen this beloved birthmark. A tear slipped down her cheek as she eyed the tense body wrapped in white hospital clothes. There were no bangles on her arms, no earrings dangled in her ears, and the long dark lustrous crown of hair that had once been an object of Reva's envy, had all but disappeared. A single word escaped Reva's lips before a tear ran down her face.

"Sumi!"

The body in the chair jerked upright, and the next instant, Reva found herself face to face with her cousin and childhood friend. Sumi's gaze locked with Reva's for what seemed an eternity.

Yet no sound emerged from her lips.

Sumi's dark eyes reflected a tiny spark of emotion that shone a little brighter as she noticed Reva's tears. With a slight shake of her head, Sumi implored Reva's tears to stop. She released her hold on the chair and held out her hand to Reva. Her clasp was strong. Reva knew that grip. She knew then that Sumi was not running away from life; she was holding on to it desperately. The two of them sat in a stunned silence for some time, looking out the window, until Sumi rested her head on Reva's shoulder and shut her eyes. Reva did not move even when the breeze caught a slight chill.

The shock of seeing a corpse-like Sumi and then the joy at being reunited with her knocked the wind out of Reva's sails. Sumi, on the other hand, appeared to have found some comfort in her own silence. Her eyes followed some of the conversations around her, and her hands rested loosely in her lap, exhausted from days of clutching and clenching. Miss Annie observed that the change was a major breakthrough in her treatment. Reva's arrival at the hospital had already worked miracles.

Looking at Sumi, finally resting peacefully on her bed, Reva was certain that her story had been far from happy. Without her *mangalsutra* and *kunku*, it appeared that she was a widow. There was only one way to confirm.

"I can write to Kaka and Kaku to find out what happened to Sumi," Reva said. "They must be so worried about her. I must tell them. Perhaps then, she will feel better."

Miss Annie cautioned, "Her mind is in a very fragile state. We don't know if her mother and father had anything to do with her present situation. But I agree. The more information we have the better we can care for her. Yes, write to them Reva to inquire after her, but don't disclose Sumi's whereabouts to them and don't say a word to Sumi yet."

Reva resolved to get on the task that very night.

"What a day!" Viraj muttered as they walked home later that afternoon.

Reva was silent for a moment.

"I feel like I have a purpose now," she said slowly. "To look after Sumi and make her better. I cannot bear to see her like this. If you had known her then Viraj, you would understand my shock at seeing this Sumi ... the girl I remember was a beauty. Her hair was long and thick and always neatly braided. Her face spoke before her words formed. And they were always kind words. She was loved by everybody, adults and children alike."

Reva smiled as the memories started surfacing in her mind. "Sumi's brother used to tease her that her eyebrows looked like a *soorvant*, a caterpillar, was resting on her forehead when they came together in a frown. So Sumi never frowned. She only smiled. She smiled when she was happy and even when she was not. I remember how she had smiled when she heard she was going to get married. I had screamed and brought the house down. Kaka had scolded me and told everyone in the house that I was not to be given any food for the whole day for such low class behavior. But Sumi smuggled food for me, and we ate together on the terrace and talked about how life would be after getting married. I had insisted we talk to Miss Tytler to get Sumi out of that dreadful situation. But Sumi thought that such conspiring would only get her into trouble. She said she would be alright. She smiled even though she was afraid of getting married and having a husband. And look at her now. Every trace of that smile has vanished. I must help her, Viraj. I must."

As Reva rambled, she could not stop herself from crying.

"Sumi is safe now, Reva," Viraj tried consoling her.

They had stopped in their tracks so Reva could take a moment to recover. Watching her wipe her nose to the loose end of her sari, Viraj offered her a handkerchief, attempting to lighten her mood.

"Women in our house do not wipe their noses to their sari. Here. Use this."

Reva froze momentarily. She had been so involved in Sumi's story that she had forgotten about the women in her house.

Cleaning herself up, Reva asked Viraj, "What would Mai and Tai-Aaji say if they knew I was helping Sumi?"

With neither parents nor a husband by her side to protect her, Sumi would be considered by the locals to be a woman of questionable repute. Both Reva and Viraj knew that the social consequences of associating with such characters would malign the family name. Appa may not succumb to such suspicions, but Mai and Tai-Aaji were unpredictable. Most likely, they would disapprove.

"Best not to say anything to them for now," Viraj said.

"Surely Tai-Aaji would understand. She lived her whole life as a widow, without the protection of a man. She must know what Sumi is going through."

"Hmm ... I am not so sure about that. I have never understood myself Reva how people who are victims of an evil are also sometimes perpetrators of the same evil."

"What do you mean?" Reva was confused. The thought seemed too convoluted for her overwhelmed mind.

"Just don't say anything to anyone yet," Viraj said dismissing the question. "They have agreed to let you help at the hospital. Don't rock the boat. At least not yet."

Although Viraj's words did not make complete sense, Reva had grown to trust his judgment. Better to feign ignorance and get her hand slapped than sneak behind the back of the family after being expressly forbidden to form a friendship with a shunned woman. But no one knew Sumi like Reva did. Come what may, she would not let go of Sumi in her time of need.

Reva was not new to the world of secrets. Or lies, as some might call it. Miss Tytler had opened this whole world a few years ago, when Ram, a student, had magnanimously invited the entire class to his home to celebrate Diwali, the festival of lights. A wave of excitement had rippled through the class as they visualized plates of mouth watering *ladoos* and *chivda* waiting for them following a round of fireworks in Ram's courtyard. Spending a Diwali evening in Ram's home was an event none wanted to miss. No one had realized that Miss Tytler had entered the room silently and overheard the generous invitation.

With a twinkle in her eyes, she had said, "That's very sweet of you, Ram. What time should we come?"

Pin drop silence. Only Ram's feet could be heard scraping the floor as he had shifted uncomfortably from one foot to another. Everyone had felt his pain. Ram loved Miss Tytler. However, she was not welcome in his home because of her Christian religion. The children never figured out why she was entrusted with their care and yet not respected as a person in the village. But they never dared to question the elders.

"It will be very late in the evening, Miss Tytler. It will be past your bedtime," Ram had stammered.

Then Miss Tytler had patted Ram and laughed, "Now that's the kindest white lie I've heard."

A white lie? If lies had a color, Reva imagined it to be red, an angry shameful red, like the fingerprints that stung on bare skin upon delivering a lie.

"What is a white lie?" Ram had asked.

"My dear, a white lie is a harmless untruth uttered to avoid hurting someone's feelings—a well-intentioned lie," Miss Tytler had explained as she had got the class ready for the lesson.

Lies that were white. How could anything white be bad?

Reva reached home just in time to see Appa on the porch finishing up a conversation with his visitors. Reva did not like the idea of deceiving Appa. Surely he would understand Sumi's plight and the urgent need for a safe friendship. But Viraj had a point. Why ask for trouble right now? Why burden Appa with her secrets, however white they may be?

"Reva. Good, you are home. Come sit with me for a while," Appa called out.

Reva promptly obeyed and settled down at his feet.

"I have been thinking ... Seeing as there is no competent tutor available to teach you in our village, I have written to the girls' boarding school in Panchgar to check if there is space for you. It would mean that you have to stay there for a year or two, until matriculation. You wouldn't feel scared to be away from home now, would you?" Appa asked his brows drawn together in concern.

Reva was dismayed. A few hours ago, she would have jumped at the opportunity. But being away from Tarapore now meant she would be away from Sumi, a prospect that bothered her even more than not going to school for the moment ... until Sumi was Sumi again. Perhaps, she should confide in Appa after all.

"Of course, don't say anything to Mai yet." Appa was still preoccupied with his own plan for Reva. "I will take that bull by the horns only after I have heard from the school and your admission is confirmed. Until that time, we'll let sleeping demons lie." Appa smiled conspiratorially.

As Reva nodded her agreement, she decided to hold on to her own secret a little longer too. Sumi would surely recover quickly now that they had found each other. Perhaps, by the time Appa finalized the boarding school arrangement, Sumi would be ready to accompany her there as well.

"So tell me Reva, how was your first day at the hospital? Was there anything for you to do?" Appa asked.

Reva described how she had talked to patients, how she had tidied the rooms, how hard the two nurses and janitor worked and how wonderful Miss Annie was with her kind words and her gentle ways. Appa laughed as Reva acted out the confusing conversations she had with Miss Annie using her hand gestures. Reva reveled in the comfortable banter with Appa. She would be quiet about Sumi for now, but she would take the first opportunity to share her secret with Appa after Sumi recovered some more at the hospital. Reva felt satisfied with her decision.

Appa was still laughing at the scenes of Reva and Miss Annie conversing.

"You may have to get good at that kind of talking, Reva! What will you do if you have to say something to your husband? You know, he may leave his Marathi back in England…" teased Appa.

Reva blushed. Coconut Head was so removed from her daily life that she had temporarily forgotten that there was more to her presence in Tarapore than just being Appa's daughter.

"Talking about Avinash," Appa continued, "I received a letter from him today. He will not be home this summer. He still has a few months more to complete his work … to tell you the truth *pori*, my eyes are anxious to see my first born again, but if his arrival is delayed, it is probably a good thing. Both of you will have more time to get used to the idea of being married." Appa sighed.

Reva waited for more news from Coconut Head. Had he inquired about her? Or even mentioned her? But Appa said nothing more, and Reva realized that she really didn't mind. She had bigger concerns demanding her attention, and this delay in his arrival fit her plan perfectly. Coconut Head could stay with the Queen as long as he'd like. The longer the better.

As soon as Appa had left the porch, Reva hurried to her room. She had a letter of her own that needed to be written.

Chapter 14

May 1901

The sanatorium was a small facility consisting of a main building surrounded by ten small units, each equipped to house one patient and a companion. Small pathways lined with fragrant *mogra* led to the main building. Benches, safely situated on a narrow tree-lined path along the cliff, provided a resting space for patients wishing to take in the healing mountain air and to catch the changing light of the day on the opposite mountain face.

Miss Annie worked at the hospital seven days a week. Although not trained to be a doctor herself, she was familiar with the common sicknesses encountered and treatments administered. Some patients were recovering from tuberculosis, some needed relief from asthma, and some from the debilitating weakness brought on by a bout of malaria. Only recently, the sanatorium had taken in two patients who were fighting a 'sickness of the mind'. One was Sumi.

An English doctor visited two days a week. Miss Annie shared with him each patient's condition, complaints, and questions. In his absence, Miss Annie was the closest person to a doctor that the patients had.

Although Miss Annie's knowledge of Marathi was limited, she prepared her case notes meticulously. With Reva now forming relationships with the patients, especially with the women, Miss Annie had access to information that had previously been hard to gather. Reva would talk to them as a confidant to get information that could help in treatment or to simply put their mind at ease, a task that Viraj, being a man, could not perform adequately. Viraj would then translate Reva's reports for Miss Annie, a task Reva could not wait to take on.

Reva's English lessons had begun the first day she had set out with Viraj to volunteer at the hospital. From her work with Miss Tytler, she knew the words to greet people in English, but Viraj taught her how to speak with grace and confidence. She learned to receive and pay compliments. She learned to articulate her likes and dislikes, her agreements and refusals. She was familiar with the English alphabet, but he helped her play with the letters and form them into words. Cat—*maanzur*, sun—*surya*, pig—*dukkar*, pot—*bhaanda*. He labeled items that they came across on their walk—tree, flower, bird, boy, girl, man, woman. He quizzed her on their walk back. Viraj was a skillful and patient teacher, and Reva's grasp on the language doubled with each lesson.

She had a keen observation and a sharp ear. She listened intently to the conversations between Miss Annie and the doctor, Miss Annie and Viraj, and sometimes to the songs on the gramophone in Miss Annie's room at the hospital. She matched the body language of the speaker with the words that flowed from their mouths and learned new phrases using the context, surprising her teachers with her self-taught knowledge.

Viraj started helping out three days of the week at the hospital, a schedule that propelled Reva's English education further faster. The more she learned, the more she wanted to know. She wanted to talk like Viraj, without having to stop for words and hunt for meaning. She worked tirelessly to be eloquent and sweet sounding like Miss Annie. While her teachers were pleased with her progress, it required all of Reva's self-control to keep her learning adventures outside of the house, lest a word, a phrase, or a question to Viraj gave her away in front of the family. Mai was letting her make small decisions in the house, and Reva did not want anything to jeopardize the growing trust between them.

In the meantime, Appa had heard from the boarding school. They were closed for the summer and would reopen as soon as the monsoons ended. The possibility of admission would be revisited then. Appa was disappointed, even apologetic as he had shared the news with Reva. Reva had heaved a sigh of relief. Getting an education was still her dream, but going to boarding school would now be a nightmare. It would mean going away from Sumi.

Reva had received a troubling letter from Kaku in response to her inquiries about Sumi. Kaku had informed her that Sumi was indeed a widow; her husband had died last winter. Then, to Reva's horror, Kaku had written that Sumi herself was now dead to her parents because of the dishonor she had brought on the family name following her husband's death. Sumi had run away from her home, therby choosing a path of shame and sin, instead of a quiet pious life of widowhood. Kaka and Kaku did not want anything more to do with her.

She is dead to us ... Kaku's cruel words rang with such conviction and finality that Reva was tempted to think the same of her aunt and uncle. Her resolve to help Sumi strengthened further.

At the hospital, Reva settled into a comfortable routine. She arrived in the afternoon just after lunch when the patients were getting ready for their afternoon nap. She peeked in on Sumi, who was looking a little better each passing day. Then she went to help Miss Annie in the office, and on slow days, worked with her on English lessons. On the days Viraj visited the sanatorium, the three shared notes and updated the case files for the visiting doctors and discussed patient care.

At tea time, when the nurses went around to wake up the patients, Reva rushed to Sumi's room. Sumi was responding to the treatment but was still *abolee*, voiceless. Every afternoon, Reva settled herself next to her cousin and shared stories of her new life in Appa's home and reminisced of their childhood hoping to draw a word, a reaction from Sumi. Some days were more successful than others, when Reva's recollections elicited a small smile from Sumi.

Every day, Reva painstakingly oiled and combed Sumi's hair, arranging it to look as flattering as possible. She waited impatiently for it to grow out, as though the restored length of the hair would automatically restore the person she knew so many years ago. Some days Viraj sat with them on the cliffside benches, and Reva continued her English lesson in Sumi's company, hoping her curiosity and intellect might tempt her to say something. Anything. Viraj named the things in Sumi's room and challenged Reva to make sentences in English about them. They laughed at Reva's attempts and confusion. Reva hoped their easy camaraderie would reestablish some normalcy in Sumi's life which, she was now certain, had been traumatized.

One evening, Reva remarked to Viraj, "Sumi seemed happier today. I wish she would speak to me soon."

Viraj agreed, "Yes, she was looking ... rather beautiful. Did you see how she was following our lesson, her head moving ever so slightly as her eyes followed the words? That's very promising. If her mind is engaged, it might help her forget any unpleasant memories."

Reva was glad that she had Viraj on her side. The task of taking care of Sumi, in stealth, was too complex for her to manage alone.

"Has anyone come to visit her or asked about her?" Viraj inquired.

"No. Not a single person. No one knows she is here in Tarapore. Until we find out why she ran away from her home, I do not want to do anything that would jeopardize her recovery as Miss Annie warned."

Viraj agreed.

Under the care of the nurses, Reva, Miss Annie, and Viraj, Sumi had started resembling the person Reva had known five years ago. The dark circles under her eyes, just like the dark times in her past life, would take some time to fade, but Reva detected a brightness that was lacking a few weeks ago. She sat longer periods on the chair and looked almost happy when taken for a walk. Miss Annie was now of the opinion that the outcome of this case would be favorable after all.

One afternoon, Reva entered Miss Annie's office as usual, only to find it empty. But Miss Annie's desk, surprisingly, was a mess, littered with pictures of beautiful English women in clothes that were beyond Reva's wildest imagination. Her eyes were accosted with pastels and primes, silks and brocades, sheers, laces, trims and ruffles, fabric rising all the way to the chin or cascading scandalously low on the body. Some of the models were seated, holding dainty teacups; some were standing with parasols in exquisite gardens, each figure elegant and enticing. Reva was so mesmerized with the finery that she didn't hear Miss Annie enter the room and look over her shoulder.

"See something you like?" Miss Annie whispered in her ear.

Reva jumped, embarrassed to be caught with her nose fully grounded in Miss Annie's business.

"I was just ..." she stammered, but Miss Annie shooed away her discomfort.

"Pfff! No need to apologize. As a matter of fact, I would like to get your opinion. I need to buy a gown for the Summer Ball. I am trying to decide which one would best work for me," Miss Annie explained.

"A summer ball?" Reva questioned, wondering how a summer ball would be different from a winter ball. And wouldn't a bat be a better choice for a ball than a gown?

"Yes, a ball. A dance. We have such a gathering at the Club every year as the season ends, and this hilltop summer charade begins to wind down. I find them tiresome and dull. To begin with, it is only for us, the English folks. If that is not a recipe for boredom, I don't know what is." Miss Annie made a face as she sat down behind her desk gathering up the paper gowns in a stack.

"It sounds very exciting," Reva countered. "but if you don't like to go, why do you have to?" Reva had a hundred questions bouncing in her head.

"Because they will think I am a deserter, a traitor. And I am not. I just do not like those stuffy affairs. Unfortunately, I need to be friends with the people who attend the Ball. They help me out in managing this hospital that they would have stayed away from otherwise. Like our doctor friend who comes weekly to check on us," Miss Annie said matter of factly. Miss Annie did not paint a very rosy picture of her community, and Reva wondered if she had spent too much time working with Viraj.

"So will you help me pick out something to wear for the Ball? I need it in two weeks, so I must make haste and send my choice to the store today," Miss Annie said, laying the stack in front of Reva.

Eager to be of help, Reva looked closely at each one of them, contemplating with great seriousness the color that would best suit Miss Annie's fair complexion, the fabric that would best enhance her comfort, and the style that would best flatter her figure. Miss Annie delighted Reva with vivid descriptions of the past balls and and snippets of humorous conversations amongst the distinguished guests. Together they decided on a silk gown, the color of shelled pistachios, with two ruffles and a lace sash. It was simple and elegant, a style that complemented Miss Annie's personality. As Miss Annie placed the picture in an envelope, sealed it, and addressed it to a store in Bombay, Reva wondered how thrilling the actual event would be when merely the planning had made her jaw drop.

As the day of the Ball drew nearer, Gopi provided a running commentary of the preparations at the Club—how the local *dhobi*, washerman, was overburdened with the washing of the party linens, how two of her village friends were hired to polish the silverware and clean the lanterns, how a live band of musicians was practicing tunes the likes of which they had never heard before. On a few occasions, on way to the sanatorium, Reva and Viraj had to make way for carts laden with fresh fruits, vegetables, and flowers being delivered to the Club. A cartful of squawking chickens had momentarily transformed Reva's awe into distaste for the whole affair, but it evaporated as soon as she saw Miss Annie's dress that had arrived from the dressmaker just in the nick of time. It bore the promise to turn Miss Annie into a celestial *apsara*.

The night of the June full moon, Reva helped Miss Annie get ready for the Ball with a tinge of restlessness—not unlike an approaching sneeze that hovers awhile, then subsides without release. Without relief. The summer visitors would soon depart. The season would be a thing of the past. Would Reva ever witness, for herself, the grandeur that Miss Annie had described? Or, despite being so close to it, would she be destined to see it only through Miss Annie's eyes?

Chapter 15

June 1901

The Summer Ball was danced and done.

The foreigners were packed and gone.

The season was most definitely over.

And Sumi was still unreachable.

Reva's mood perfectly matched the dark clouds gathering outside her window that morning.

The rains had not made their appearance in the hills yet, but the sun had disappeared in anticipation. The afternoon breezes had turned cool, and a keen nose detected the sweet promise of fresh damp earth. It was time for the monsoons to make their arrival.

If the signs in nature were not proof enough, the flurry of housekeeping activities in Appa's home was a sure indication of the upcoming change in the season. The roof was inspected for leaks. The window bolts were tightened. Stone pavers, for a makeshift pathway through the dirt track leading to the porch, were laid. The garden furniture was packed in jute cloth and moved to the storeroom. Grains, dried fruits and vegetables were purchased in bulk and stored, as the monsoons would wash away the roads and stop the flow of supplies to the mountains.

Lately, every conversation Reva heard paid homage to the rain—'before the rains', 'after the rains', 'when it rains', 'because of the rains'.

"The rains are something else in Tarapore, you will see," Appa told her one evening as they sat on the porch eying the changing weather.

Appa made it sound as if the sky would rip open and unleash a deluge on the unsuspecting villagers. The haste with which the English visitors had packed up after the Ball, closed their cottages, dismissed their servants, and made a beeline back to the plains made Reva wonder how these white people who hunted the dreaded man-eaters of the jungles could be so nervous about the rains. Growing up in Uruli, Reva had lived through many monsoons too, and while they added to the inconvenience and hardship of daily life, they did not overwhelm it like they seemed to do in the hills.

As if reading her scornful thoughts and taking objection, early one morning, thunder rumbled through the clouds. It was a deep, hair-raising sound that rolled around menacingly in the sky, scrutinizing its earthly opponent before launching an attack. Reva scrambled out of bed and rushed downstairs as thunder swallowed the entire house.

Gopi and Sita had stepped out on the back porch. Their heads were turned towards the sky, watching the dense grey clouds with building excitement. Suddenly, Reva heard shrieks of laughter as Gopi and Sita were pelted with raindrops as big as marbles. Within seconds, the porch was soaking wet. A few minutes later, small streams of water ran down the steps into the garden. And before Reva could turn away, puddles had begun to form in the backyard. Soon, Reva could not see a leaf in the garden beyond five feet. She stood mesmerized by the downpour until Gopi tugged at her sari to urge her back into the house. With a start, Reva realized that she was completely wet. Another loud clap of thunder erupted. Her heart thudding in her ears, Reva wondered how she would ever get dressed all by herself in her room if every roar of thunder made her legs go weak.

"Gopi, it's very dark in my room. I am going to need a candle lit for my bath. You can also help me pick what to wear today when you come up to my room with the candle," she instructed, hoping to prolong Gopi's company while still guarding her newfound, almost childish, fear of the storm.

"I'll go get the matchsticks right now, Reva *tai*," Gopi said.

Reva dragged her feet up the stairs until she could hear Gopi following her. Then she quickened her step, feeling safe in the knowledge that she would not be alone in her room during the storm. Appa was right. This rain was something else.

She had almost made her peace with the thunder when a flash of lightning illuminated her entire room and sent her running towards Gopi, who was laying out her clothes from the closet.

"Reva *tai*! Are you afraid of this harmless rain?" Gopi teased.

Reva pretended not to hear her as another clap of thunder rumbled in the sky.

As Reva descended for breakfast, she noticed that the rain had not relented in the last hour. She heard it crashing on the roof, banging against her windows and trickling in the hidden corners of the house.

"Looks like you cannot go to the hospital today, Reva," Appa announced. "It is raining too hard. Maadhu was saying that the road into the village is already flooded in parts. Even the bullock cart will not have easy passage."

"Is Viraj staying home too?" Reva asked, biting her tongue instantly, thankful that Mai was not seated at the table yet.

"No, he must go. We cannot abandon our work in the village each time it rains. But I would rather worry about one of you than two."

Appa turned his attention back to the newspaper, and Reva realized that the subject was closed for further discussion.

No hospital.

No lessons.

No Sumi.

It was going to be a long day.

Later, Reva would wonder if it was the first flash of lightning that reminded her of the first day of the monsoons in Tarapore or Appa's electrifying words as the family gathered for afternoon tea.

Restlessly pacing in her room, Reva had come to the conclusion that she could not possibly pass two long months of monsoons the way she had passed the morning, She would go out of her mind. Perhaps it was time to reveal to Appa her secret about Sumi and about her English lessons with Viraj so that she could continue the learning at home. She would first explore her options with Viraj before saying a word to Appa. Viraj had not returned from the village yet.

Entering the *divankholi*, she noticed immediately that Appa's face was lit up as he paced up and down the length of the parlor. Having done the same for the last two hours, but more out of boredom than excitement, Reva was curious to know what was on his mind.

"Reva! Good. Good. You are here. I have some wonderful news," Appa announced as soon as he saw her. In his hand, he held a paper that seemed to be the origin of his joy. Could it be that he had heard from the boarding school in Panchgar?

Just then, Mai walked into the room followed by Gopi, who carried steaming cups of tea. Reva noticed that Mai's face mirrored Appa's joy. Then the news could not be what Reva had fantasized a minute ago. Mai wouldn't be happy if the school plan had surfaced again.

"Good news travels through all kinds of weather. Even through our Tarapore rains," Appa said waving the letter again. "Look Reva. This telegraph says that Avi, my Avi, is coming home in two weeks. He has successfully completed his work and is returning to Tarapore as an officer in the service of the Queen of England! They need him here. Just imagine Uma, our Avi is now an officer!"

If Reva was not already intimidated by the idea of a husband, this news overwhelmed her. Coconut Head, Avinash, was coming home in two weeks. The thunder and lightening that Reva had locked out of her room the entire day was here in front of her, sealed and delivered in an envelope.

Appa, reading her mind, said, "Avi is a good son. He will only follow my wishes. I can say with confidence that he will approve my choice as though it were his own. How can he not? I have chosen an angel for him."

Reva blushed. She glanced at Mai. Reva prayed that Avi's arrival would only enhance the fragile bond that she had started to build so painstakingly with her mother-in-law.

"Earthly angels need to be around to do any good," Mai stated cryptically to Appa. "And not on some remote hilltop studying numbers and words that are meaningless in daily life. No husband is happy with a distant wife."

Reva's eyes widened. So Mai had heard about Appa's plan to send Reva to a boarding school. Mai was not happy, and sadly Reva realized neither was she. Sumi's quiet image loomed in her head.

"Uma, we have already been through that discussion. When the monsoons are over, Reva will to go to boarding school in Panchgar. I have given you enough time to adjust to the idea, to see its wisdom. Reva will go to school and that is that."

Appa's voice was firm. It made Reva a little nervous about what she knew she needed to do. For Sumi.

"Appa, maybe going to boarding school right now is not a good idea. What Mai is saying is right. Maybe I should be around a little while longer now that ... now that ..." Reva did not know how to proceed.

"... Now that her husband is coming home," Viraj completed as he walked into the room.

Reva blushed.

"What are you trying to say, Reva?" Appa asked, puzzled. "Do you not want to learn? To go to school?"

"No, no, Appa," she replied hurriedly. "All I am saying is that if I have waited for this long, maybe waiting for a few more months won't make a difference in my future. But it would make a big difference at home right now."

"What's this? Your husband is not even here yet, and already, you don't want to leave him?" Viraj teased. "Here is a devoted wife if I ever saw one."

"Viraj, leave her alone," Mai's voice rang out. "You men will never understand us women. No matter how far we venture from home, there is always an invisible thread that ties us to our families, our husband and children. Naturally, Reva wants to spend time in the company of her husband. They must get to know each other. These first months are important for the foundation upon which they will build their married life. I agree with Reva. If she wants to drop the idea of going to school, I don't think anyone should force her. Appa, you were right. She is a good fit in this family after all. Her heart lies in the right place."

Mai smiled at Reva with a tenderness that she had not seen or felt before. It only heightened her despair. She did not agree with a word that Mai had said. The only real reason she needed to stay in Tarapore was to nurse Sumi back to health.

"Reva," Appa interrupted her furiously racing mind. "What do *you* want to do?" His own bewilderment at Reva's hesitation was obvious on his face. She came very close to disclosing the real reason, but a small voice cautioned her to steady her boat that was caught in this fast-moving monsoon current rather than rocking it further.

"Appa, I want to stay in Tarapore for some more time until ... until ... "

" ... until her husband ignores her and avoids her or worse makes her a slave to his every demand, and she realizes that school is where she wants to be," Viraj proclaimed dramatically. As his voice trailed off, Reva could see the realization dawn on his face.

"That's enough, Viraj," Mai scolded her younger son. "Leave her alone."

Viraj did not need any more admonishment.

"If that is what you want," Appa said to Reva, sounding defeated. "I will drop my talks with the school for a few more months ... but go to school you will," he ended resolutely, looking at Mai as if in warning.

Reva let out a shaky breath as her presence in Tarapore was assured for a little longer. But Viraj's jesting had unleashed another wave of worrisome thoughts. What if Avi was still angry about being married to her? What if she fell miserably short of the image he had for a wife? She was fair and light-eyed like the ladies he had probably met in England. But the resemblance ended there. What if Avi rejected her? Reva had no romantic motivation for her need to be approved by Avi. It was just that she had worked hard to become a part of the family—loved by some and tolerated by others, but part of the family nevertheless. That status was dangerously dependent on Avi's acceptance of her as his wife. She knew that as the eldest son in the family and the apple of Tai-Aaji's eye, Avi would be able to move mountains for her. Or at the very least support her need to go to school in the future. What if Appa's conviction that Avi would honor and trust his judgment crumbled? Reva shook her head as if willing the apprehension out of her mind.

Since her arrival, Reva had pieced together parts of a puzzle that was Coconut Head. The puzzle was far from complete, and her time had run out. She prayed that Avi would be as warm and agreeable as Viraj. It may take them some time to think of each other as husband and wife, but there was no reason they couldn't be friends. Reva talked herself into forced happy scenarios day after day as the rains continued to imprison her with her thoughts at home, and Avi's arrival loomed closer and closer.

One afternoon, Gopi came into Reva's room with something mysterious hidden in the folds of her *loogduh*. It was a photograph of Avi, taken when the family had visited Satara five years ago. Gopi had smuggled it out of Mai's room so Reva could take a quick look.

"Mai, must have taken it out of her cupboard today," Gopi said. "I had been looking for it the whole time. To show you of course. And there it was, lying on Mai's bed. Take it. I have to mop up the front porch before Mai and Appa come back from the village. You can feast your eyes on the picture until I finish. I must put it back before they return," Gopi said with a naughty smile as she left the room.

With bated breath, Reva turned her eyes to the face that was meant to be imprinted on her heart forever. She was relieved to find that the idea was not as horrifying as she had first imagined. Avi was a distinguished looking young man. A longish face crowned by jet black hair slicked back neatly. A wide forehead resting on proud eyebrows and intense eyes. His nose was slightly thick, giving him the rugged look of an explorer rather than the delicateness of a family man. Although the expression on his face suggested smiling would be blasphemous, Reva wished that he had. She could never understand why an unsmiling face was considered fashionable in photographs. If these pieces of paper were meant to capture the essence of a person, how could one leave out the most important part? A smile was a peek into one's heart, inviting warm or distant cold. Of course, a smile could also reveal deformed teeth or worse, missing teeth. That was the only convincing argument Reva could think of that would make someone keep those lips tightly sealed. But overall, Coconut Head was not bad looking. He was almost handsome. Five years ago.

Gopi passed by Reva's room with fresh sheets, pillows, and blankets, and a huge set of keys. Avi's room was being readied. Thankfully, Mai had situated Reva in the guest room when she had arrived in the house. Appa had insisted that Avi and Reva have their own rooms until they were ready to lead a life together.

Tai-Aaji had been furious. "What kind of a marriage is this? What will people say?"

"Tai-Aaji, Reva is still just a child, and Avi needs some time to adjust as well. If not Reva, think about Avi."

The mention of Avi's well-being mollified Tai-Aaji. But Reva was not sure how much time she had.

"You will finally meet your prince, your love, your life ...." Viraj teased Reva, his voice dripping sweetness and charm.

They were walking around the sanatorium grounds with Sumi. The rain clouds had let up that morning and the brave inhabitants of the village had seized the opportunity to indulge in life as they knew it before the rains. As soon as there was word that the road was dry and passable, Reva had convinced Appa to let her visit the sanatorium. Avi would be arriving in two days. It was Mai's expectation that once Avi arrived, Reva would spend as much time as possible at home in the company of her husband and in learning his ways. Avi would be her full time occupation. Therefore, with the weather turning favorable, Reva wanted to visit the hospital one last time to meet Miss Annie and assure her that she would resume her work with the patients as soon as her life attained a new normalcy.

It was imperative that she talk to Sumi herself about the changes taking place in Appa's house. Sumi may not be speaking, but Reva knew that she understood every word that fell on her ears. She needed to assure Sumi that she was in a safe place, and Reva was still close at hand. Sumi had made remarkable recovery, and Reva did not want any situation to hinder her progress.

"I saw Sumi checking her reflection in my office window today," Miss Annie had informed Viraj and Reva, her eyes twinkling with satisfaction. Reva had been pleased to hear it. It was a sign that Sumi had started caring about herself.

"Sumi, you must brace yourself, because the the next time you see your friend, she will annoy you with Avi this and Avi that," Viraj continued to jest.

Reva blushed.

"But let me tell you Reva," Viraj said, turning mock serious, "that older brother of mine is a *rakshas*—a demon. He used to bully me at every opportunity. You better be careful. I suggest that you keep a *lahtna* with you at all times. You know ... to defend yourself."

Reva couldn't help giggling nervously at Viraj's attempts to frighten her as she pictured herself chasing a faceless body with a rolling pin around Appa's house.

She turned to Sumi hoping to enlist her support to end Viraj's teasing. To her surprise, Sumi had stopped in her tracks. Her eyes were opened wide, unblinking. Reva saw that her terror had returned. Sumi started shaking her head as if in a trance repeating softly but viciously to herself, "*Naahi Naahi Naahi* No, No, No, No, No...."

Before Reva could recover from the shock of hearing Sumi's voice for the first time in years, Sumi turned around and ran back towards her room. Reva ran after her, shouting to Viraj to fetch Miss Annie. Sumi was now screaming out the words cupping her ears with her hands as if to block out her own voice.

Reva followed Sumi into her room and found her hunched in the corner, holding her legs together, tightly, as if willing her body to compress into a tinier mass with each rocking motion and eventually disappear. Tears flowed uncontrollably. Sumi was ranting. Words that had been sealed for months escaped and filled the room. Reva caught the word *rakshas*, demon, but nothing else made sense. Miss Annie rushed inside in a few moments. With soothing words, she led Sumi to her bed and gave her a sedative to calm her down. Reva held Sumi close until the medicine took effect, and Sumi drifted off into a restless sleep.

Viraj hovered outside the room anxiously. Reva watched as Miss Annie conferred with him, her agitation apparent on her face. What were they saying? What was happening to Sumi? She seemed to be well a few hours ago, and now she resembled the broken creature that had been first carted into the hospital. Reva could not hold back her tears. She let them escape as Sumi slipped deeper and deeper into a comforting darkness.

It was later than usual when Viraj and Reva started walking back to the house.

"What did Miss Annie say?" Reva asked as soon as she had the chance.

Viraj was silent.

"What is wrong with Sumi?" Reva asked, unable to control her rising voice.

"Miss Annie thinks her mental constitution is much weaker than we knew. Her mind is plagued with something dreadful that happened in her past. Her saying *rakshas* over and over again may point to someone that she is still afraid of or a particular memory that torments her."

Reva felt like she had been punched in the chest. She had been so focused on reliving her childhood with Sumi that she had disregarded that part of their lives when they had not been not together. She had assumed she knew Sumi's story just because she was a widow. But what if Sumi's story was not like her widowed mother's? What if Aai's life had been a bed of roses compared to Sumi's? What had really pushed Sumi to run away from home?

"What do we do now?" Reva thought aloud.

"Miss Annie said Sumi needs to be handled even more gently. Sickness of the mind is more complex than the body. The good thing is that whatever triggered her fear today has also brought back her speech. All we can hope is that soon she will be strong enough to talk about her bad experiences. Once the traumatic memories are released, her mind may recover through happier moments that we create for her at the hospital. But it will take time. Lots of time."

"With Coconut Head...er...your brother on his way, that's what I am short on," Reva replied.

Viraj concealed his smile as he pretended to ignore Reva's name for her husband.

"Viraj, Mai expects me to stay around the house now. With Sumi in this state, I will go crazy with worry. Can you make a trip to the hospital everyday to check on her and talk to Miss Annie about Sumi's progress and report back to me? I can write letters to Sumi that you can read to her."

Viraj nodded and smiled. "I would've done that even if you had not asked me to. Don't you worry."

Reva felt indebted to Viraj. She had never been more grateful for Viraj's friendship than that evening as they walked in silence the rest of the way home, each lost in thought. Reva could not help but gripe to herself—why did Coconut Head have to arrive precisely when Sumi needed her most? On the other hand, without his arrival as an excuse, how could she have avoided going away to boarding school?

Chapter 16

July 1901

Mai's frenzy of cooking and her obsession with arranging and re-arranging Avi's room kept Reva busy the next day. The aroma of fresh coconut roasted in ghee and flavored with sugar, raisins, and saffron wafted in the house as Mai made khobra vadi, coconut cakes, for Avi. Next Reva watched as a large pot of puffed rice flakes was tempered with curry leaves, mustard seeds, turmeric, and chili powder to make *bhadung*, a savory that packed too much heat for Reva's comfort. But these snacks were Avi's favorite and, according to Mai, would probably be the first of his demands on stepping into the house.

Reva followed Mai around observing, helping, and memorizing her husband's preferences for future use. It was only when Reva was called upon to simmer and stir the milk for thirty long minutes, until it gathered a creamy consistency to make *kheer*, that thoughts of Sumi sneaked into her mind. She wondered how well her cousin had recovered from the shock of the previous day. She had barely spoken to Viraj for a few minutes at lunch, and he had assured her Sumi was well. She was responding to instructions and answering questions in small spurts, but she still did not show any inclination to unravel her mysterious past. For now, Reva had to be content with the situation since there was nothing she could do about it.

The excitement in the house was contagious. While Tai-Aaji made no reference to Reva's existence, Mai had a matter of fact approach—Reva's husband was coming home, and she needed to know how to make him happy. Appa talked to Reva as though he was presenting her with a new best friend. Gopi, on the other hand, had lost all control on propriety, giggling in the crook of her arm each time she saw Reva. The innuendos made Reva blush. The innuendos made Reva toss and turn at night.

The morning dawned cloudless and clear as if wanting to do its part in making Coconut Head's journey home perfect. His ship was due to dock in the Bombay port late afternoon, and Appa was already on his way to meet him there. It would take another twenty-four hours for them to travel home. With every corner cleaned and every cushion plumped up, the household settled into a temporary quiet as each member eagerly awaited the homecoming.

That morning, Gopi tricked Reva into entering Coconut Head's room when Mai was busy with her prayers. At first, Reva pretended to resist the idea and feigned anger, but then her curiosity got the better of her. As soon as Gopi had left her alone, she wholeheartedly committed to exploring this space that had been locked for two years. The room was bigger than Reva's, with three windows overlooking the front yard. A closet stood in one corner with a full length mirror on one door. A sideboard ran alongside two of the windows, and Reva wondered what she would find in its drawers. A stack of books, held together with ivory bookends, were neatly arranged on the sideboard, the tallest to the shortest. Reva glanced at the titles and noticed that most of them were in English. She felt a slight shiver of anticipation. Finally, she could no longer avoid looking at the beautiful four poster bed that occupied the center of the room. With white cotton sheets and dark woolen blankets, it was inviting. She tried to picture the person inhabiting the space but all she could project was a fuzzy outline which changed form with her every breath. She tore her gaze away from the bed and found herself staring at her own flushed face in the closet mirror.

"In case you are thinking of peeking inside the closet, it's empty," Gopi announced, reentering the room. "Avi *dada* is going to bring all new clothes for himself from the foreign land. Sita's husband got all the old clothes. If my husband had been taller, maybe Mai would have given me some too. The clothes were fit for a king. And why not? Avi *dada* is no less than a king!"

Reva tried to imagine Coconut Head in *videshi*, foreign, clothes.

"I told you to peek in, and now you don't want to step out," teased Gopi, "Be patient my dear. It won't be long before this will be your room, too."

Reva fled. The idea was more shameful and scary than exciting. She cursed herself for letting Gopi get the better of her emotions.

That night, Reva dreamed of Avi's room, pitch dark with pops of color flashing like fireflies vaguely illuminating the back of a tall man engulfed in a light mist. His head reached the ceiling and his chest was as wide as the windows.

That night, Reva dreamed of scaling the mountains.

The next day was a waiting game. Coconut Head would arrive in the evening.

Reva paced the dining room trying to devise a way to meet Sumi. Viraj had delivered a message telling how much Sumi had missed her. Twiddling her thumbs at home when she could be at her cousin's side spurred Reva to pace like a caged cat.

"Your walking up and down without stopping is making *my* legs hurt. It's going to be a while before they arrive," Mai said, misreading Reva's agitation, as she arranged the flowers on the table.

Reva seized the opportunity.

"Mai, I am very restless today. Can I go to the Krishnali temple? I always feel calm after a visit there."

"Appa has taken Maadhu and the cart, and Viraj is also out inspecting the potato fields. How will you go? I cannot let you walk alone."

"But Mai, it has not rained for three days. The road to the temple will be dry, and I know it so well now. I will take Gopi with me and be back before lunch time."

Reva sighed with relief as Mai nodded and shooed her away.

As Reva hurried towards the Krishnali temple, she calculated how much time she would need to execute her impulsive plan. She would stop by the temple, so Gopi would not be part of her lying to Mai. While Gopi collected mulberries around the temple, as she usually did, Reva would exit from the back entrance and run to the sanatorium for a quick visit with Sumi. She would be back before Gopi had collected her fill of the berries.

Her plan worked, and soon Reva found herself out of breath in the main building of the sanatorium.

Miss Annie's office was empty. Reva hurried to Sumi's room. It was also empty.

"Sumi *tai* is in the garden," the nurse called from behind.

Reva smiled as she caught a glimpse of Miss Annie talking to another patient. Sumi must have ventured out alone. That was promising.

Reva followed the path to the bench where Sumi liked to sit. There was not a soul to be seen. The bench was empty, but Reva recognized the bicycle resting against the tree beside it. Reva was intrigued. That bicycle should've been by the potato fields.

Then Reva saw them—Sumi walking along a dirt path with Viraj a few feet away to her side. They were quiet, but their comfortable stroll and soft smiles spoke volumes. Sumi was twirling the end of her braid with her index finger. Reva knew the tick well. Reva could feel her heart starting to run wild. Sumi and Viraj. Before she had a chance to sort out the confusion in her head, she heard the nurse calling out to Sumi. Reva quickly hid behind the bushes as Sumi, startled, hurried towards her room, and a flustered Viraj collected his bicycle and headed in the opposite direction. If this furtive behavior was not evidence of a sweet budding guilt, then Reva had no plausible explanation for it.

Reva walked slowly towards Sumi's room. She needed time to think. For now, she pretended to have just arrived.

"There you are, dear. I was looking everywhere for you," Reva managed to say calmly.

"Reva! What are you doing here?" Sumi appeared a bit disoriented. Even a little scared.

Reva's heart melted when she heard Sumi's voice. It was just as sweet and comforting as Reva remembered it. She gave Sumi a long, fierce hug.

"I wanted to see for myself if you were feeling better. I couldn't come the last few days and most likely will be tied down for the next few weeks," Reva replied.

"Don't worry so much, Reva," Sumi laughed nervously. "I am alright now. Miss Annie takes good care of me."

Resisting the temptation to question, *Just Miss Annie?* Reva smiled and hugged Sumi again.

"Good. Then I will go. Otherwise, I'll be in trouble at home. I am happy to see you are more than alright," Reva's eyes twinkled as the significance of what she had witnessed grew bigger and clearer in her mind. She prayed to God she was right.

"Write to me when you can, won't you, Reva? I miss you when you are not around," Sumi said softly.

"I promise I will write, and I will make Viraj get a letter for you everyday. He may have more years on me, but I am the wife of his older brother. He has to listen and do as I say ... Would that make you happy?" Reva added mischievously.

If Sumi registered the teasing, she showed no indication. Nevertheless, now that Reva's suspicions were aroused, she silently vowed to not let anything, or anyone, get in the way of Sumi's happiness.

As Reva left the hospital premises, a heavy weight, that she had not even known was on her heart, lifted. Sumi's world could be rebuilt. And in that world, the two cousins might just share a home again, as they had done before. Suddenly, Reva no longer felt guilty about her own promising shot at happiness.

Coconut Head was just a few inches taller than Viraj, but his presence filled up the entire house and left Reva tongue-tied.

Mai met him at the door with a lighted lamp and flowers to shower blessings and to welcome him back. Reva watched as he touched the feet of all the elders. Then Appa summoned Reva.

"Avinash, this is your wife, Revati, but she prefers to be called Reva." Appa's introduction sounded unreal to Reva.

Avi glanced in her direction. It was not an unfriendly look. Reva had the feeling that Appa and Avi had exchanged more than pleasantries on their way home. Reva raised her eyes for a brief second and encountered Avi's cool gaze as he acknowledged her presence. She attempted an awkward smile as he abruptly turned towards Viraj and said, "And what has my good-for-nothing brother been up to while I was away?"

"Holding down the Indian front while you were strengthening the enemy lines," Viraj responded, tongue-in-cheek. Avi laughed good-naturedly. Reva got the sense that this brotherly banter was a continuation of a political conversation from earlier times.

"Wasting your time as always," Avi retorted.

Then he turned to Mai. "I smelled the *khobra vadi* the moment I walked into the house. Don't make me wait for it anymore."

A delighted Mai led the way into the dining room, where the snacks were laid out for the guest of honor.

As the group was about to step out of the *divankholi*, Appa reminded Avi to visit the temple with Reva first thing the next morning. Reva felt a tiny surge of hope when Avi complied readily.

"We will go at ten o'clock tomorrow," Avi said.

His voice was deep, and his speech was fluid and confident. Avi could possibly charm the cream off the cow's milk with his words.

For a few minutes, Reva stood in the *divankholi*, unsure what she was expected to do. She did not want to intrude on Mai's time with Avi, but at the same time, she couldn't disappear into her room nonchalantly as though she had just met a polite acquaintance. She wished Mai or Appa had given her precise instructions for her first day with Avi under the same roof. Attempting to read their minds instead, Reva headed towards the kitchen to make sure that dinner was under control. Mai had asked her to cook the stuffed brinjals, Reva's specialty, that had now become a family favorite. Even Mai had to admit that she had not eaten more flavorful, succulent brinjals than the ones Reva managed to produce. For Avi's homecoming dinner, the brinjals had been cooked to perfection that afternoon and were ready to enamor every person around the dinner table. But there was only one person that Reva wanted to impress that day.

As Reva tinkered with the dinner, she could not keep her mind off this man who was her husband and who had the whole house eating out of the palm of his hand, including Tai-Aaji. When Reva had cursed her fate at having to get married, had she been wrong? Was fate favoring her all along and she was just too young, too blind to see it? Avi was handsome, educated, respectful, and obviously loved by all. There was a strong possibility that he would want Reva to go to school. Would her own mother have found such an accomplished husband even if she had looked into all the corners of her tiny world? Somewhere in the warmth of the kitchen, on Avi's first day back home, unbeknownst to Reva, Coconut Head disappeared forever. Avi had appeared, and Avi was determined to stay.

The next morning, Reva woke up earlier than usual to get ready for her temple visit with Avi. For a few moments, her mind lingered over the disappointment at dinner the previous night. Avi had refused to touch the stuffed brinjals because some of the spices had in recent months started to make his stomach turn. Appa had casually lamented Avi's loss at being unable to savor Reva's delicious cooking. Avi had merely turned towards Reva and said, "I am sure they are delicious. I just cannot handle them anymore." Intense regret mingling with a strange understanding, Reva had searched desperately for words that would be appropriate, but the moment had passed and the conversation had changed. By the time dinner was over, Reva had convinced herself that Avi had not intentionally slighted her and that relationships were rarely built on a bowl of brinjals.

Reva selected a beautiful green sari that complemented her hazel eyes and light brown hair for her first outing with Avi. Lining her eyes with the dark *kajal*, she studied the person staring back at her. Her fair skin was glowing. The cold mountain air and her daily walks to the sanatorium had added a touch of pink to the cheeks. She could see traces of the Reva who had played with dolls and who had run around with abandon along the river's edge just a year ago, but those images were fading quickly. The replacements were far more more thrilling. She was now Avi's wife. Reva blushed as her mind turned in a direction that was not as repulsive anymore.

Shaking her head to dislodge the shameful thoughts, Reva quickly gathered her hair into a neat bun. She would stop in the garden to pluck a rose for her hair. She then pulled out the jewelry box from her closet. Her first instinct was to reach for the comfort of Aai's *kudis*. Instead, she chose a set of heirloom earrings, gifted by Mai, that dangled from each ear like a tiny intricately carved canopy. They complemented the nose ring, a simple gold wire studded with two carved gold beads that added an attractive softness to her face. The moon shaped *kunku* on her forehead drew attention to her eyes that revealed her heart in one glance. Reva wished she had some of the red color paste for her lips that she had seen Miss Annie use when she was headed to the Ball. If Avi had ambushed her mind since the moment he stepped foot inside the house, she was determined to make him suffer a similar fate.

"Reva," Appa called from below.

Reva ran out of the room and almost collided with Viraj.

"What's this?" he exclaimed. "Reva, is that you?"

His mouth slowly curled upwards, and Reva knew he was reading her mind. Embarrassed, she hurried downstairs. How stupid of her to make her intentions so obvious. She may look more grown up, but she felt like a child caught red-handed stealing sweets. It was too late to turn back now. The cart was waiting. And as she descended the stairs, she observed that Avi was waiting too.

Reva was suddenly glad she had taken extra care on her appearance. Avi was wearing a coat unlike the knee-length that Appa and Viraj wore. It ended mid thigh and enhanced his height. The dark gray color brought out the blue gray rims of his eyes. If it had not been for the darker color of his skin, he could've been mistaken for one of the English officers. Unlike Appa and Viraj who wore *dhotis*, Avi wore black pants which from the looks of it were stitched overseas. As Reva's eyes traveled up to his face, she saw a hint of humor in the set of his mouth and eyes. She realized with a shock that she had been staring at Avi. From the staircase, she could see Viraj taking in the show. From behind the dining room curtain, she could sense Gopi noting every detail to recount to her family over dinner that night, and from across the room, she saw Avi now eyeing her from head to toe. She cast her eyes down, thankful that Appa was preoccupied in getting ready to leave, and Mai and Tai-Aaji were in the prayer room.

"I asked Avi to drop me off in the village on the way to the temple. Let's get going," Appa said, sounding and looking twenty years younger.

Having Appa ride with them part of the way eased Reva's stress. She could listen quietly and get used to the sound of Avi's voice before being required to interact. It gave her time to collect her thoughts, scattered once again, before she spoke to her husband.

"So what have you decided now that you are back?" Appa asked Avi as soon as they were en route to the temple.

"I have been asked to work with the Resident here since Tarapore is becoming very popular with the English. They may need a local officer to assist in the development of the area."

"*Wah wah!* Good! That is music to my ears. I was thinking that you may be assigned to a distant office. But my prayers are answered—you will stay here at home. God is great!"

"Having grown up in this paradise also helped ... my white friends love these hills, and I know this land inside out," Avi responded with a laugh.

"The English have a good eye, no doubt. In people and in places. First, the development of the sanatorium, then the boarding schools and the summer residences. Not to mention that our weather is also suitable for their strawberry. Have you heard anything more about the Resident's plan to add more strawberry plantations?"

"Yes, Appa. I have heard some talk about it, and I think it's a good idea. It's the most delicious fruit I have tasted."

Reva disagreed. The sugarcane from Uruli was more deserving of that high praise, but she kept her opinion to herself.

"The English are trying to increase the production in Tarapore. They had some success on a small scale on the plot of land near the Officer's Club," Avi continued.

"Yes, I am aware of that project. We are lucky to receive such attention from the government."

"Indeed we are, Appa," Avi agreed. "If the strawberry takes to this land, we'll see even more agricultural and housing development. Tarapore will flourish."

Reva thought about Hirkani's family who had come to the hills in search of a livelihood. They would benefit if there was work, and food, and money for everyone. And Avi was going to make it happen. Her husband was going to make it happen.

"I will find out more today when I go to the Club," Avi said. Reva detected a hint of pride in that statement. Reva had learned from Miss Annie that as an officer in the Queen's service, Avi would be invited to the Club as a member, despite being an Indian. Reva's chest filled with admiration at the achievements of her husband. She decided to intensify her efforts to learn English so that she could be ready for the time when she would be invited to attend a gathering at the Club as Avi's wife.

Appa got off the cart in the village, and Avi and Reva continued for a while in silence enjoying the fresh air, the soothing sounds of the wheels turning on the soft dirt, interrupted only by the rising notes of the *kokila* bird.

Suddenly, Avi asked Maadhu Kaka to stop the cart. They were almost nearing the dirt track that led to the temple.

"Maadhu Kaka, you can wait here with the cart. We are going to walk the rest of the way."

Reva's heart raced as she realized that Avi wanted to talk to her without the presence of any inquisitive ears.

Avi helped Reva alight from the cart. On that cool morning, his hand was warm and his grasp strong. In the next instant, her hand was released just as abruptly as it was held.

The red dust on the dirt path rose in welcome and then settled on their feet, layer upon layer with each step.

"I wanted to talk to you alone, Reva," Avi began as soon as they were some distance away from the cart. His tone was one that Reva's uncle would use when he wanted no arguments. Just obedience. Reva bristled. And yet, Avi's voice compelled her to listen, to want to listen.

"Appa had written to me the circumstances of your family and the necessity of the decision he was forced to make. The fact that he took an instant liking to you made the decision easier for him, but your age and your ... my ... our...er...unreadiness... demands that the marriage remain only in name. Both Appa and I are in agreement about that. I will not expect you to be a wife. You do not have to look after me, or cook for me, or ... be my wife in any other way."

Avi paused, as if unsure whether the implication of his words was clear to this young girl.

"We will play the part of husband and wife when Tai-Aaji is around, and when Mai needs us to. When we have company. Rest assured that I consider you a part of the family now. My concern towards you will be of the same nature as Appa or Viraj or Mai."

Reva listened intently, growing more perplexed with each passing word. She had not wanted a husband so early in life. But it didn't mean that she did not want one for the rest of her life. If he never ever acknowledged this relationship, where would that leave Reva? A single married woman—able to enjoy neither the freedom of being single nor the family pleasures of a marriage.

Avi continued, "We will not talk about the bindings of our marriage until the time is right."

Reva heaved a small sigh of relief. Until the time is right. That is how Appa had explained this marriage to her. This was a fake marriage but only until Reva was older.

Avi's words were logical and true, but they were also cold and heart-less in stark contrast to Reva's changed frame of mind. And body. Two days ago, she would've been soaring like a kite on hearing these liber-ating words from Avi's mouth. Today, she was hurtling towards the ground with each passing second. All that time spent on taking Avi's breath away had backfired. It had only intensified the disappoint-ment and hurt she felt on hearing his words. How could she have even imagined herself to rise overnight up to Avi's notice, when he looked like the Prince of England himself, and she looked like the village bumpkin? Almost a decade younger, she could not speak coherent-ly in her own mother tongue in front of him, let alone converse in the Queen's language. Overdressed and undereducated. A far cry from the poised and graceful white women he had met in England. Reva stood as tall as his shoulders, and yet, in that moment, she felt as insignificant as the bricks that lined their path.

"Do you have anything to say?" Avi asked authoritatively. There was that annoying tone again. All she could do was shake her head. Avi was right. She was still very young. The fact that she had let his good looks and his achievements cloud her judgment, change her priorities, was evidence of how much growing up she had to do. How foolishly she had entertained ideas of a contented family life with Avi when she should've been pursuing her dream to go to school, to be independent. Then again she remembered Viraj and Sumi and the moment they had shared. It hurt.

From the direction of the temple, Reva heard the chimes. Faint but ringing insistently. Avi was offering her the privileges of having a well-placed husband without the responsibility of being a wife. Why then, did that good fortune make her heart ache?

Chapter 17

July 1901

Avi's arrival rocked Reva's boat. But as the days turned to weeks, Reva realized that Avi was as good as still being in England. She saw him briefly at breakfast after his morning walk, as he fortified himself on a boiled egg and toast, especially requested for him from the store that stocked European supplies. Amidst the aroma of fresh *thalipeeth*, spiced pancakes, and mango chutney that the rest of the family ate, the sight of the bald, bland egg made Reva's insides turn. He ate fruit with his fork, only after cutting it precisely in tiny uniform pieces with his knife. Reva admired his patience but pitied his need to destroy the joy of eating fruit. Avi wiped his hands and mouth on a napkin while the rest of the family washed their hands in the sink outside.

Reva had been, at first, awed by Avi's unusual routines and rituals, then disheartened at her glaring differences with him, and finally a little miffed at his flaunting his Englishness in front of them. Appa and Mai did not seem bothered by these customs. Viraj had tried to bait him by ridiculing his changed preferences, but his words were like water rolling off a duck's back. And even though Viraj's words reflected Reva's thoughts, she felt a tinge of irritation at Viraj's lack of sensitivity. After all, Avi had spent two years in a different land. How could one not be affected? It had only been eight months since her own arrival to Tarapore, and here she was, a simple girl from the plains, already dressed in fashionable clothes and feeling perfectly at home on the hills. Why should Avi have to pretend to be someone he was not anymore? In his own home?

She did not dare to venture further down that path of thinking. Appa had confidence that Avi would respect his father's wishes and do right by Reva. Reva stopped short of wondering how much of *that* Avi had changed. Fortunately, the torrential monsoon downpours washed away any doubts that threatened to sprout in her young mind. The hills were fresh and green just like Reva's future on them.

Avi spent most of the daytime at his office, much to the consternation of Tai-Aaji, who insisted on sending a home cooked meal lest her grandson be polluted by the meat-eating English people. Returning from the office in the afternoon for a nap and a change of clothes, a suited Avi headed to the Club for a leisurely dinner with the gentlemen. The Club was an imposing red brick building, alive every night with twinkling lights and foreign music that traveled over the silent hills, through the village streets, down the red dirt path, through the open windows, and into Reva's ear. Sometimes, Reva also imagined hearing Avi's deep laughter resonating in the warmth of an imaginary fireplace at the Club as he sat surrounded by his English friends. Avi's life overwhelmed Reva. And when she was wallowing in the notion that she had no hope of reaching the heights that Avi had scaled, she reminded herself that in a few short months she had already made a home in the mountains, fifteen hundred feet higher than her childhood home in the plains.

Two weeks after Avi's return, the family had resumed some sense of normalcy. Reva's days resembled her first weeks in Tarapore. Long, eventless, and filled with endless waiting—for whom or for what, she was unable to decipher. Avi barely acknowledged her. His indifference only fueled her need to be something. To do something. Anything. Her English lessons were in disarray, although in the confines of her room, she had role played and reviewed numerous times to assure herself that her learning was not lost. Sumi appeared more and more frequently in her thoughts. Reva needed to find the right time to broach the topic of her resuming work at the sanatorium. She wondered if Viraj would be as willing to help her again. In Reva's absence, Viraj had had many excuses and opportunities to meet with Sumi privately. Would he be happy to have her show up and be at Sumi's side at the sanatorium again? Reva convinced herself he would once he realized she would be a good accomplice in their crime.

One day on an afternoon that was unseasonably dry and warm, Reva decided to walk to the Krishnali temple. The monsoons had transformed the entire landscape in variant moods of green—tender and raging, vibrant and mellow, hopeful and optimistic. Reva's last visit with Avi had left her unsettled. She was determined to replace that memory and reclaim the temple as her peaceful haven. Gopi walked with Reva to the temple, and then without waiting to be told, disappeared down the little dirt path to look for mulberries. Reva headed towards the cistern to rest beside the water spout that had now become her favorite spot. It was quiet and the sound of the water was like a lullaby to Reva's over stimulated mind. She took in a few deep breaths.

A muffled sound coming from the inner sanctum made her aware that she was not alone. She also realized that she had never stepped inside that tiny space in the past visits. The day seemed as good as any to explore.

As Reva bent down to enter the inner sanctum through the small entrance, she reveled in the sound of flowing water that echoed against the black stone walls. In a few moments, her eyes adjusted to the darkness. She noticed five streams of water channeled into one small canal that led into the spout outside. Remembering that Aai had always referred to the river as a mother, Reva felt the urge to touch the water, to let it run through her fingers. She stepped towards the water channel and stumbled on a step that appeared out of nowhere. She groped wildly to restore her balance, but landed in a heap on the cool dark stone, the clashing of her bangles creating a ruckus inside the tiny space.

"*Hare Krishna!* Where does one have to go to get some sleep? Even God's house is crowded? *Hare Krishna* help me!"

Reva recognized the voice. "Hirkani?"

"Who's asking?" Hirkani demanded.

"It's me! Reva. Have you forgotten me? You never came up the mountain again. I thought you had gone to another village," Reva exclaimed.

"Bless my good stars! Finally I see the face of a friend!" Hirkani's tall frame rose in the darkness with her basket of fruits and vegetables beside her.

"Hirkani, why are you sleeping here? If the priest sees you he'll forbid you to come forever. And get you in serious trouble."

"He won't know unless a careless girl brings his attention to me," Hirkani said with a mock glare. "Let's go to the back garden before he returns and hears us. I was so tired from the walk up the mountains. I just needed a place to lay down for a few minutes without people, rains, and beasts bothering me. Except you, of course. I have been thinking about you."

Hirkani and Reva quickly exited the temple from the back entrance, and stepped outside into the inviting warmth of the sun.

Hirkani looked around the courtyard. "Now where is that husband of yours?" she asked Reva.

"How do you know my husband is back?" Reva asked. It had been four months since she had last seen Hirkani.

"Like the river, news trickles from the hilltop to the foot of the mountain, doesn't it? The whole village has been talking about it— Appa's son is back from the foreign land."

"So he is. Yes, Avi is back home," Reva confirmed taking in a deep breath as Avi's face flooded her mind.

"Avi?! What happened to Coconut Head?" Hirkani teased as Reva blushed at her own transparency. "I know ... I know ... he is very handsome." Hirkani's eyes twinkled with an intimate understanding. "Looks like he has pleased you as a husband too."

Reva smiled uncertainly. Gopi had on occasion teased her about being as good a wife to Avi in private as she was in public. When Reva had begged Gopi to explain how a wife is good in private, Gopi had turned as red as a mountain radish, and blurted, "That's not my job to tell. I am sure Avi *dada* will explain to you at the right time," she had giggled out the words, "...and in the best way." Gopi had run off leaving Reva speechless, nervous, and yet, as alive as she had never felt before.

"Have I lost you to your handsome prince? And in broad daylight too!" Hirkani's voice sliced through and cleared Reva's foggy mind.

"How do *you* know that Avi is handsome?" Reva asked, ignoring Hirkani's mischief.

"Because I saw him. As clearly as I am seeing you now. He came to our village with those nasty white people. He introduced himself to us as Appa's son. He told us he is now an officer in the English government and promised to work for the betterment of our land and our people. I am telling you Reva, we could not take our eyes off that husband of yours. So tall! And with such a commanding face! What confidence! No one wanted to miss a word that escaped his mouth. And such a well mannered boy. He touched the feet of the village elders, too."

Despite the distance between them, Reva felt a tinge of pride in the man who was her husband. By law and in God's eyes, at the very least.

Reva knew that Avi was an assistant to the Agriculture and Land Development officer, Mr. Jones. His office was responsible for the development of Tarapore and the surrounding area. Given the growing interest of the English in the region as a summer hill station, the demand for land was very high. Like Appa, most landlords leased the land to farmers who produced potatoes, radishes, and carrots for sustaining a meager but independent life in the hills. The relationship between the landlords and tenants was peaceful and mutually respectful. The farmers were hardworking, the produce was sufficient, and community life was simple and satisfying. Now Avi and his office would make this land flourish even more.

Hirkani continued, "All the people clapped and cheered for him. Then he and the white people talked *khoosoor-poosoor* among themselves for a little while and left. I don't trust those *goray*. But when I knew that Appa's son was working with them, my heart calmed down a bit."

Reva laughed at Hirkani's description of the sound of the English language and her fear of the English people. Poor Hirkani. She had the misfortune to meet the few bad grains, and now her opinion of the whole English race was forever soiled.

"Is he good to you?" Hirkani asked.

Reva paused before saying something that was untrue.

"He is not bad. That makes him good. Right?"

"Maybe. Does he talk to you?" Hirkani prodded.

"Not much. He leaves me alone. That's good isn't it?"

"Maybe. Are you happy?"

"I am."

"That's good. Is school keeping you busy?" Hirkani asked.

"Not yet. Avi's arrival has kept us all busy," Reva confessed, "But I have been helping at the sanatorium," Reva added the last part hurriedly to divert Hirkani's attention from the pesky subject of school. But the mention of the sanatorium also reminded Reva about the surprise she had for Hirkani.

"Hirkani, you will never believe who is in the sanatorium. Sumi! Remember Sumi?"

"How can I possibly forget little Sumi. The two of you were joined to the hip. But what is she doing here?"

Reva frowned at the troublesome memories.

"Sumi was sick. Very sick. So they got her here to recover. She is a widow now, Hirkani. Beyond that, we don't know anything, and she won't tell. She is all alone."

"Poor, poor girl. God be with her. Well, at least she is in a good place now. With you."

"Do you want to see her, Hirkani? I know she will be overjoyed to see you again."

"I will come one day, my dear. I will. To tell you the truth, just getting to this temple takes my breath away, then I have the whole journey home still waiting. But one day I will come," Hirkani assured her. "But tell me Reva, the monsoons are almost on their way out. So Appa will be sending you to school soon?"

Hirkani was persistent. Reva realized she couldn't avoid answering the question any longer.

"Appa wants me to go to a neighboring village ... a boarding school ..." Reva informed her.

"Bless his heart! When do you start?" Hirkani asked.

Reva wondered why her heart faltered each time she talked about her choice to stay in Tarapore.

"Not yet. I said no ... I am thinking that for a little while longer ... until Sumi is healthy ... I will just learn how to take care of the patients at the sanatorium ... from Miss Annie instead. That's an important job too ... just like a doctor," Reva said softly.

"But how can you become such a doctor without going to school?" Hirkani was puzzled.

Reva was not enjoying the direction of this conversation. It reignited dying flames.

"Listen, Hirkani. Miss Annie is no doctor either. But, if you ask me, I would rather have Miss Annie take care of me than any doctor," Reva blurted.

"You don't say! So she can cure the sick people by herself without ever studying. Then she must be a saint. I must bring these tired bones to the sanatorium for a *darshan*, viewing," Hirkani's voice was full of wonder.

"No, no, Hirkani. Not completely by herself. There is a doctor who comes once a week to look at the patients. Miss Annie and he talk about the patients, and he tells her what to do," Reva explained. As the words flowed out of her mouth Reva remembered the childhood frustration that Miss Annie had shared at being encouraged to be a nurse instead of a doctor because she was a woman. She would've been an excellent one too.

"My child," Hirkani interrupted Reva's uncomfortable thoughts and brought her back to the present. "I don't know this Miss Annie. But I know this. The world is bigger than this village and Appa and Miss Annie and your husband. And you should be ready for it. For what lies ahead."

"What lies ahead is very comfortable, Hirkani. Appa and the rest of the family take good care of me ..."

"Wasn't that the way things were when your mother was alive? But look what happened. I thought that way too. And look what happened to me. What is today is gone tomorrow. The world is changing. Make yourself ready for whatever comes your way. Go to school."

"But Hirkani," Reva grabbed at straws. "I can't abandon Sumi when she needs me most."

Even as Reva said the words, the image of Sumi in the garden with Viraj flashed before her eyes, and she knew that things were different now.

"Abandon? I thought you said this Miss Annie was an angel. It sounds to me like Sumi is in good hands already. Listen to me, Reva ... if not me, listen to Appa ... go to school."

"You are talking like Miss Tytler now!" Reva exclaimed surprised.

"Life does that to you. One day we had our land, the next day it was gone. And I couldn't tell you why or how. It's my ignorance. But what could I do? I was helpless. You are not. Appa will help you to be whoever you want to be. Don't pull your arrow back so much that it breaks the bow."

Reva listened quietly. In her heart, she knew Hirkani was right.

Chapter 18

August 1901

"Appa, Ganapati *utsav* is right around the corner. I think this year we should have a big celebration and invite all the villagers to join us in the festivities," Viraj suggested one morning at breakfast.

Ganapati, the beloved elephant-headed God, was worshiped each year at the end of the monsoons. For ten days, this indulgent God, in his idol form, was invited into beautifully decorated altars, prayed to morning and night, bribed with sweet coconut-stuffed *modaks*, and entertained by offerings of flowers and gratitude. Ganapati was also the Remover of Obstacles, and so, He had a special place in Reva's heart. There had always been some obstacle to remove in each year of Reva's life. This year was no different.

Reva's ears perked at Viraj's suggestion.

"We don't need to waste our time on any such nonsense, Appa," Avi responded calmly without lifting his eyes off the last three slices of bananas lying helplessly on his plate. "Our Ganapati worship is our private affair and should not be made into a show for the locals."

Avi's views reflected what Reva had been taught as a child—that one's relationship with God was personal and unique and need not be flaunted in front of others. Avi was right too.

"It wouldn't be a show. They pray in their houses; we do in ours. The idea is to come together and worship. It would bring our community closer," Viraj argued trying to match the logic in Avi's manner.

"And why do we need to do such a thing now?" Avi demanded.

Appa had stopped eating and was following the conversation intently. Mai, with a single glance, dismissed Gopi from the room before Gopi's mouth found the words to spread this exciting possibility in the community.

Viraj took in a deep breath. "Appa, the villagers are getting a little nervous. They are aware that the English people have taken a liking to the hills. They are seeing these people encroach a little more each day on the very land that has been used for generations to farm, to graze their cattle, or to build their homes. They are nervous because the English people are making rounds into their villages observing and marking the land. This communal celebration may help ease their anxiety that we are still a community. We are still together. And this is our home. We will look out for one another," Viraj concluded and, ignoring Avi's sigh of frustration, looked expectantly at Appa.

"Appa, I don't agree," Avi argued. "The villagers have nothing to fear. The English people are not monsters. Yes, they love the hills—it reminds them of their home in England. I should know. What is wrong with having a place to retreat after you have broken your back educating the ignorant locals and organizing the messy affairs of this land? Yes, they are looking to build houses and farms. Contrary to what the villagers think, such interest by the English government will only make them more prosperous. It will make their life better. Instead of spending time and money on empty celebrations, Viraj, talk to the people and explain to them what I just told you. God alone knows, my voice is hoarse from doing just that everyday, trying to knock some sense into their heads. And yet, now I see, it is of no use. They still choose to behave like ignorant simpletons."

Avi had finished eating, and the firm conviction in his voice would have made a tiger accept that it had spots not stripes.

Appa cleared his throat before Viraj could retort.

"Avi, your views are progressive, and your intentions are noble. But, under no circumstance will I allow you or anyone to belittle the people who have supported us for generations and who have been an important part of our success and happiness here in these mountains. Yes, they are simple-minded and ignorant. But that should only increase our responsibility towards them, not our frustration."

Avi listened. His face was expressionless.

"But I can understand your position too. There is more than enough land for all of us to live peacefully on the hills. The English people do not need to build their houses on top of ours. They are our friends. I know that by experience. The locals just need to be assured of that reality. So, you continue your good work. Talk to the villagers. They are our people. They will see their bright future eventually." Appa's voice had softened. It compelled Avi to force a smile.

"Appa, have you read the newspapers lately? Or talked to your friends in Satara?" Viraj persisted. "We may be thousands of meters high in the clouds but we need to keep our legs firmly planted on the plains. There is enough evidence all around that these *goray* are wolves in sheep's clothing. I am not saying that *Dada's* colleagues are the same. All I am saying is that we should be vigilant. And one way to stay vigilant and ready is to have a strong community. Lokmanya Tilak has been advocating Indians to come together for months. Ganapati *utsav* is just an excuse, but it brings people together. And unity makes people feel safe."

Lokmanya, the people's favorite. It had been a long time since Reva had heard the name of the national leader Tilak.

"Ah! I knew it. *Lokmanya* Tilak, the annoying pest of the plains." Avi slapped his napkin on the table. "That's what this is all about. You are choosing to support a man who wants to hold on to outdated traditions and unfair practices. A man who resists the English government's attempts to reform our backward ways, to end child marriages, to allow widows to marry ... That is the leader you want?"

"Perhaps you only get to read half the story in your English newspapers. Tilak is demanding that foreigners stop interfering in our affairs. Stop telling us what to do. That our own people should have a say, some representation, in the making and enforcing of the laws in our country We, Indians, should be responsible for our own reforms. Frankly, I agree," Viraj retorted.

"I don't believe this," Avi said, furious. "My own family inciting people against the British! Do you see how terrible it would be for me in the office? My own brother conspiring to block English interests in the hills? Where does that put me?"

"You are beginning to sound just like the people you serve," Viraj taunted Avi. "You are thinking only about yourself."

Avi stared at Viraj for a few moments. Then he looked at Appa, and his face softened.

"And you, Viraj, are sounding like the uneducated villagers you surround yourself with every day. There is nothing to fear. No reason to put on such a distasteful show of unity. Be sensible. Don't act purely on emotion," Avi responded, suddenly behaving like an indulgent older brother. He pushed back his chair. "One of these days, you should come with me on my land tour. Then you will see and hear for yourself the loftiness of the English plans for the hills and its residents."

Viraj accepted the olive branch that his older brother had offered, allowing Reva to breathe freely again. Appa had not only raised a fine son, but also a caring person. He did the right things. Reva could not help but hope.

"Appa, may I leave now? I am getting late for work," Avi asked.

Appa was lost in thought.

"Appa?" Avi repeated.

"Yes, yes," Appa said, "but before you go, I must say that I like Viraj's idea of including all the villagers in our Ganapati celebration this year. But not necessarily for the reason he put forth. I was thinking..." Appa looked at Mai. "We have been so fortunate this year...the harvest has been plenty, Avi has returned safe, sound, and successful from England, Viraj has taken up so much of my work and is doing it better than what I would do myself." Mai smiled in acknowledgement. "... And most importantly, this year I have been blessed with a daughter who makes me very happy. I want to share this happiness with all my friends in the village."

Reva's eyes teared up at this unexpected admission. She smiled gratefully at Appa. No one, not even Aai, had ever publicly acknowledged her importance in the family. Here was Appa hugging her with his words, knowing fully well the different, even contradictory, opinions that surrounded him. Now Appa had forever anchored her to the hills, to this house, to the people, even those who may not share his sentiments. If he loved each person in the family, then so would Reva.

Reva sneaked a glance at Avi, but saw only his squared back exiting the dining room. She wondered what part of Appa's announcement had further stiffened Avi's shoulders—his decision to hold a communal Ganapati celebration, or his joy in Reva's arrival.

The elephant-headed Ganapati was welcomed in Appa's home and wooed with great pomp and splendor. Villagers poured in and out of the house for ten days paying their respects to the deity and then to Appa and Mai, who represented the earthly forms of these dieties for the villagers. Tai-Aaji hovered around each morning balancing precariously on her stick and, on two separate occasions, accepting Reva's offered hand for support. With Viraj directing the crowd, the locals settled down in groups around the house talking and feasting on *modaks* and Reva's stuffed brinjals cooked fresh in huge brass pots each morning. Reva had declined all help and insisted on single handedly making enormous quantities of the vegetable, much to the delight of villagers and family alike. Blessings were showered on Reva morning, noon, and night. She collected them eagerly in an attempt to negotiate and convince Ganapati to crumble the obstacles in her life.

Hirkani had reignited Reva's dream of going to school. Viraj's interest in Sumi and Avi's indifference to Reva had fueled it. And when Mai patted Reva on her back after a particularly long day of worship and entertaining, Reva felt a sense of hope that her dream may be within reach now.

When the last day of the festival arrived, the family prepared to bid farewell to Ganapati. Amidst loud chanting and drumbeating, the idol of Ganapati was to be led in a village procession from the family altar to the lake and then immersed in the waters along with prayers and good wishes of the worshippers.

The fragrance of marigolds and incense hung thick inside the house and followed Reva as she looked for Appa in his usual spot on the front porch. He smiled as Reva stepped outdoors.

Appa was not alone.

"Come come, Reva. I want you meet my very good friend, Damoo Kaka. In fact, you can consider him my brother. He runs a thriving cloth business in Satara. Viraj and Avi have whiled away many summers with Daamoo Kaka's children in the city."

Damoo Kaka smiled at Reva as she bent to touch his feet in respect.

"*Sukhi raaha*, be happy," Damoo Kaka blessed her.

"*Pori*, you must be very tired. I have watched you work so hard the last two days. You have done more than a girl of your young age should do," Damoo Kaka said. "I was telling Appa that he is really fortunate to have borne such worthy sons, to have found such a gem of a daughter-in-law. And to have a home in this hilltop heaven."

Appa closed his eyes, breathing in the fragrance of the soil that had been released after an unexpected drizzle that morning. The last of the monsoon rains.

"Yes, I have been blessed to say the least. But Damoo, you know there is always room for you in this heaven. I am exhausted telling you to hand your business to your own worthy sons and move here. Let's spend our golden years together."

Damoo Kaka laughed good-naturedly, "We will see ... we will see ... I must go now. It's time for me to be on my way home. I must reach Satara before night fall."

After Damoo Kaka had left, Appa observed, "You have been working very hard Reva. You should rest a bit too."

"It was nothing Appa. I was actually happy to be busy. Ever since ..." Her voice trailed off.

"Ever since Avi arrived, you have been home. I know, my child. That was Mai's wish, and yours too, if I remember correctly. So I did not want to interfere. But I think you have spent enough time around the house. Avi's work is demanding, and he is not at home most of the time. I will talk to Mai. You can resume going to the sanatorium soon," Appa said.

Not getting the instant smile that Reva was so want to do, Appa prodded, "What's this? Is there something else you need?"

"Appa, I know I said I can give up school for a while until Mai agrees, but I really miss my lessons... perhaps now that things are settled around the house, Mai may agree to let me go .... Appa, I want to go to that boarding school," Reva ended breathlessly.

"I know you do. But there is nothing I can do for now," Appa responded.

"Appa!" Reva let out an involuntary cry. Had Appa changed his mind about sending her to school?

"You misunderstand, my child," Appa said gently. "Now that the monsoons are behind us, I have already started corresponding with the boarding school about the possibility of your attending there. I am waiting to hear back from them."

Reva could not believe her ears. While she had been struggling to make the right choice, Appa had already figured it out and was acting on it. He had truly meant it when he had promised he would let no one get in the way of Reva's dreams. Including Reva herself.

Reva sat at Appa's feet and started crying. He patted her head and continued, "Everything is up in the air at the moment. But rest assured, if not this school, I will look for another. And another. But go to school you will. Until then, continue your work at the sanatorium. It will keep your mind occupied and your heart engaged. I will talk to Mai when the time is right. No one deserves this chance at happiness more than you my child."

If it hadn't been for the villagers trickling in for the Ganapati immersion, Reva could've spent the entire day at Appa's feet listening to him speak. But they both had things to do and people to meet. As the village procession led by Viraj and Appa snaked through the hilly tracks towards the lake, Reva looked at the benevolent face of the elephant headed God, and could not help but see Appa's smiling face reflected in it. Her Appa was indeed the Remover of Obstacles.

A week after the Ganapati celebration, when every extra pot had been cleaned and stored in the attic, every silk sari inspected for stains and wrapped in tissue, and every piece of jewelry returned to its cheese-cloth home and handed to Appa for safekeeping, Reva had found herself once again walking with Viraj to the sanatorium. Despite Mai's reluctance, Appa had not only allowed Reva to resume her work, he had even encouraged it. Secretly, Reva was pleased at Mai's initial disapproval. She had a suspicion that Mai's objections were more because Mai had got used to having Reva around the house and less as a way to flaunt her authority. Viraj had seemed genuinely pleased with the idea of her getting back with Sumi, and Reva chastised herself for even doubting his feelings towards his sister-in-law.

Reva had languished as an ever-present wife of an absentee husband for too long. She could not wait to be with Sumi and the other patients again and to resume her English lessons. Viraj was pleased that she had not lost her learning during her long absence.

Sumi was waiting for Reva in her room at the sanatorium. Reva figured that Viraj would have shared the news of her return as soon as he got word. Miss Annie had warned them to handle Sumi with kid gloves, to avoid springing any kind of surprises on her, pleasant or otherwise. However, Sumi herself had none of those concerns, and astounded Reva with her improving health. She was conversing for longer periods of time, voicing her opinion frequently, and smiling with a genuineness that warmed Reva's heart. Sumi's hair had recovered its length and shine, as had the animation in her eyes and voice, especially when Viraj was around. Viraj's presence, his attention, seemed to have worked miracles on Sumi, leaving Reva with an added debt of gratitude and love towards her brother-in-law. The idea of going to boarding school now started sounding more and more favorable.

A few weeks later, as Reva walked along the garden path with her cousin, she pondered how Sumi's story was still unknown and therefore a stigma to her character. Why had she run away from home? Why couldn't she talk about it to anyone? Reva knew neither question bore well on a single woman's reputation in her community. Her skin bristled. Observing her sweet and gentle cousin delightedly recounting her humorous encounter with a macaque in the sanatorium garden, Reva determined that if Sumi wanted to forget the past and look forward to a fresh start with Viraj, then Reva had no problem with it. Mai's disapproving face and Tai-Aaji's harsh tongue hovered in Reva's mind for a brief second. The future may not be as simple as Reva was making it out to be, but she would fight for Sumi and Viraj. But what was it exactly that she was fighting for? Neither party had explicitly voiced their feelings for each other to her, although that truth was as glaring as the sunrise each morning.

Feeling a little mischievous, Reva made up her mind to prod into this budding romance.

"Sumi, you know ... I think everyone has a right to live a happy life. You and me included. And I think I know what makes you happy. In fact, I think I know *who* makes you happy."

Reva nudged her cousin knowingly and waited for the words to sink in. Sumi was looking at the floor, a strange mixture of emotions passing on her face. Reva waited, getting more anxious by the second. She had been careful not be mention the word 'widow' or 'husband'.

She had only talked about the present. Sumi's silence was worrisome. What was she thinking?

It was the sound of approaching bullock carts and a distant wailing that broke the seemingly endless pause in their conversation.

"What is happening? What's all that noise?" Sumi exclaimed, as if snapping out of a trance. "We must go and check."

Relieved that she had not pushed Sumi over the edge with her innocent comments, Reva grabbed her cousin's hand and the two ran to see what the commotion was all about.

Amidst a small crowd of distraught villagers, two bullock carts lined the outside of the main hospital building. A third was making its way through the entrance. Men were shouting for help as they unloaded injured people from the carts, some bleeding, some barely conscious. Within minutes, the two nurses and the janitor had their hands full, addressing the needs of the wounded the best they could. Miss Annie stood in the center giving orders, administering first aid, and trying to make sense of the stories that were emerging. Reva ran to help just as Miss Annie disappeared inside the building with the patients, casting a grateful glance at Reva who felt unequipped and even a little scared to deal with the impatient crowd. Viraj would not be at the hospital until later. She was on her own.

Sumi was standing in the shadows watching from afar. She seemed distant but calm. Reva had no choice but to turn her attention to the current situation. It was then that she saw the familiar faces and voices under the makeshift bandages and the pitiful groans—Gopi's brother-in-law who came to help with odds and ends in the house, Gopi's husband who farmed one of Appa's lands, the woman who had brought the first potato harvest to Appa for his blessing, and Sita's eldest son. These were farmers and tenants from the village. They had all been involved in a violent skirmish.

As the story came to light in bits and pieces, a panic-stricken Reva stumbled away from the crowd. She had to get home. To Appa. The horror at the sanatorium was just the tip of the iceberg. A parallel disaster was unfolding at home. Reva cast a desperate glance in Sumi's direction, but Sumi had followed Miss Annie into the building. Reva had no time to explain. Neither did she have the courage to put in words the fear growing in her mind like wildfire.

Without waiting for Viraj, she broke into a run. Her feet flew over the red, dusty road as her distress reconjured unpleasant memories of another day when she had found herself alone. Reva cried bitter tears as she stopped midway to catch her breath and collect her thoughts—this nightmare could not be happening. Surely she could not be orphaned twice?

Chapter 19

September 1901

The locals were angry, and like an injured man-eater, they had lashed out at the perceived threat with speed and ferocity. Unsuspecting, Appa had been caught in the deadly attack.

Reva reached home to find villagers gathering on the front porch. Recognizing a few of the anguished faces, she rushed past and headed to Appa's room only to find the door closed. On seeing Reva, a tearful Gopi unraveled the events of the day as coherently as she could.

That morning, Avi's office had made a startling announcement that had shaken up both the native landlords and their tenants. The English government had declared that a fifty kilometers radius of land around the village was reserved for the English government, and as such closed to farming, grazing, trading, or building by the locals. The land would be used to cultivate the exotic strawberry and build new houses to meet the demand of the increasing English population in the hills. The locals, who had built on and cultivated the land for years, would be forced to leave.

Reva recalled the enthusiasm with which Avi had described, to the family, the plans for expanding strawberry cultivation in the hills. Appa had expressed delight over the possiblity of experiencing a little bit of

England in their very own backyard. Now, with an injured Appa in the house, Reva did not like this English experience precisely because it was in her backyard.

"Appa, I think we are in the middle of a big change that is going to take us places, bigger and better places," Avi had boasted. Reva had heard ambition and excitement in Avi's voice, but even at that time she could not imagine leaving Tarapore and going anywhere else. She felt that the villagers angst of losing their land was justified. They were being treated unfairly, even cruelly.

To add fuel to the fire, in a seemingly magnanimous gesture, the English officers had informed the villagers that they would be given wage-earning jobs as servants and porters in the English households. Each English family that made its home in the hills during the summer season would need between ten to forty helping hands in order to sustain their elevated lifestyle.

"Reva *tai*, many of us never cared for a life of wage dependent servitude in the *firangi* houses, and we most certainly do not want it now. And have they thought about what we will eat the rest of the year?" Gopi protested, wiping away her tears.

"But Gopi," Reva persisted, "how can the white people take away Appa's land or drive away his tenants?"

"Reva *tai*, Appa does not own all the land in Tarapore. Just a portion—the house and some fields. The rest of Tarapore was given to the white people by the king of Satara many years ago in exchange for the village of Waikan that the king coveted and that was under *firangi* control. All these years, Appa had an arrangement with his white friends to allow the locals to continue living and farming their land for a small fee. The white people had never butted their nose in that understanding until now. Appa was just as shocked this morning."

Sniffling, Gopi had proceeded to recount the details of the violent encounter.

A small crowd of villagers had approached Mr. Jones and Avi outside their office and begged them to reconsider the law and pick other sites that were uninhabited and uncultivated. There was no dearth of useable land in the mountains. But Mr. Jones had turned a deaf ear and dismissed them. Avi had tried to appease the people by assuring them that they would not starve, that they would be given work, just a different kind of work. He had even commented how it was their ignorance that was making them suspicious of the white man and the progressive changes that he promised. When the villagers continued to protest, to the mounting impatience and frustration of Mr. Jones, Avi had instructed them to gather at Appa's house the following evening for a discussion. The two officers had soon after climbed into their carriage and headed out of the village, leaving the small restless crowd simmering in the dust.

Appa had heard of the dispute, as he was bound to, later that afternoon. He had immediately set out to meet his tenants and assure them that he would get to the bottom of this English policy and fight their case. On his way, he came across an angry mob marching towards the Club shouting angry slogans against the English colonists. Maadhu Kaku had implored Appa to remain inside the cart and let them pass. But Appa did not heed his words. These were his people and their troubles were his own. But they needed to stay calm and come together as a community to resolve this situation. As soon as he got out of the cart and stood in their way, arms upheld to stop their progress and to quiet them down, some hot-headed youngsters started cursing Avi by name.

"This is a misunderstanding. You are judging Avi too hastily. He is on our side," Appa had shouted back.

His words only inflamed the youngsters, who had pushed past him as they continued their march towards the Club. Appa had lost his balance and had fallen to the ground as the energized crowd jostled around him. A scuffle had ensued between the marching youngsters and the older farmers who rushed to help Appa.

Appa had been hurt in the trample. Maadhu Kaka had rushed him home, while others, injured, were taken to the sanatorium. Viraj had been summoned immediately.

"Reva *tai*, I have never seen Viraj *dada* so angry," Gopi confessed. "He kept saying how he knew something like this was going to happen. He even cursed Avi *dada* once. Tai-Aaji had to call him to the prayer room to calm him down before entering Appa's room. I don't know what's going to happen, Reva *tai*. In a blink of an eye, the roof has come crashing down on Appa's family." Gopi wiped another tear and ran to the kitchen.

Stunned, Reva squatted down outside Appa's room in the hope of snatching a glimpse or a word that would reassure her that her Appa was alright. She reminded herself that Appa had spent his whole life in the mountains that were known to work miracles on the body and the mind. He was strong enough to withstand this senseless attack. He had to be. She fumed silently at the brash young men who were responsible for Appa's fall. And as the minutes ticked by, she wondered who was ultimately to blame for this calamity.

Reva could hear the tinkling of the bell in the prayer room. Tai-Aaji had spent the whole evening at the altar. Mai was in the room with Appa, Viraj, and a village healer. Food lay untouched and cold in the dining room, as Sita had rushed to her home after hearing how her son had been involved in the incident. On receiving news that her husband was only scraped and bruised in the fight, Gopi had chosen to stay with family. Reva could hear her answering questions and taking care of the villagers waiting anxiously in the porch. The villagers were quietly lamenting the turn of events and praying for the safe keep of an innocent old man who was paying a heavy price for a crime he did not commit. The youngsters who had incited the violence were in the custody of the police. But in a brief moment of consciousness, Appa had managed to instruct Viraj that they must be released, for they had acted out of fear, out of their need to survive, and out of their God given right to be their own masters in life. Appa did not wish to bring any charges against them.

Refusing to let her mind entertain any sinister thoughts, Reva recalled the happier moments with Appa—the first day she had met him, their shared humor around the *serbeti*, the time Appa had referred to her as his own daughter, and how he was determined to send her to school. She did not know when the tears began to slide down her cheeks.

Avi's absence hung heavy on the house, and Reva wondered if the news of the violence had reached him. He traveled with Mr. Jones across the region and would probably not hear about this unfortunate incident until they returned at night fall the following day. How would he react? How could he continue to do a job that had risked his father's life?

A hurried shuffling of feet from within the room brought Reva back to the present. The village healer's urgent words drifted into her alert ears. Reva sprang to her feet and peeked through a small crack in the door, unable to resist the temptation anymore. She could not see Appa's face. His bed was surrounded—Mai was standing at the head, the color drained from her face. Viraj was calling out softly, insistently, to his father. Reva pressed her ear to the crack and listened, not daring to breathe. Appa did not respond. As Viraj's voice got louder, Appa's silence was deafening. Then the air in the house went still. Reva sank to the floor, her body limp, her mind numb. She knew Appa was now beyond reach.

Chapter 20

Avi made his appearance late evening the day after Appa died. A servant at the Club had informed him of the tragedy as soon as he returned from his tour. A ghostlike Avi had rushed home. To Reva's horror, Mai refused to meet with him. Tai-Aaji had already retired to her room with strict instructions that no one was to disturb her prayer and penance. Not even Avi.

Physically exhausted and emotionally drained, Viraj filled in the painful details as Reva, from the upstairs landing, watched Avi going through the same waves of grief, anger, and frustration that the rest of the family had confronted. Viraj broke the news to Avi that he had performed the last cremation rites for Appa, which was the highest duty of the eldest born. Reva felt an inexplicable urge to rush to Avi, hold him close and comfort him, when she saw the involuntary shuddering of his body and the torment in his face. The next instant she watched, stupefied, as Avi's grief transformed into an ugly fury that spilled out of his mouth in an eerily calm tone.

"Those ignorant, wretched fools. They had the nerve to lay their filthy hands on Appa. I had assured them I would meet with them as soon as

I returned from my tour. And this is what they do in my absence! They attack the most decent person that had ever crossed their foul path. Do you still wonder why the English want to maintain their distance from the natives? These are the brainless fools who spit on the very hands that are offered to them in aid. They will pay for this. Each and every one of them." Avi's voice rose. Viraj's face hardened. Reva stood flabbergasted—Avi was placing the entire blame on the villagers, the people who had regarded Appa as nothing short of God himself, the people who had prayed for the long life and the happiness of the whole family.

"Keep your voice down," Viraj addressed Avi in a manner that lacked his usual deference. "Mai is barely able to shut her eyes. Your senseless talk will steal whatever little peace she has left ... And the villagers did not attack Appa. He got caught in their angry demonstration. You should know that Appa has forgiven them. *All* of them. He understood that their actions were motivated by self defense. It was not the right thing to do, but it was not because they are evil-hearted as you make them out to be. You are in a state of shock right now and unable to see what is glaring in front of you. The white people and their cruel policies are the reason Appa is no longer with us. The earlier you realize it the better you will serve your own people, now that you inhabit the inner circles of the British Raj. I implore you to recognize this disaster as a call to awaken. Our hills, our home as we know it, are under attack, and if you think the locals are going to just watch and let that happen, then you, despite your western degree, are more ignorant than any of us."

Reva could taste the bitterness crackling in the air between the brothers.

"I can see that I have arrived late on the scene in many ways," Avi responded. "I understand you have a soft spot for the villagers, but if Appa's unfair death does not make your blood boil, then there is nothing more for us to discuss at present. I hope you have not filled Mai's ears with that anti-white nonsense."

Avi turned on his heels to head to his room. He had barely taken two steps past Viraj when his body slumped and another wave of grief engulfed him. He turned back, stretched out his hand and placed it gently on his brother's shoulder. Viraj did not acknowledge the conciliatory gesture, instead heading towards Mai's room. Reva could hear his knocking on her door that remained closed.

Avi's footsteps approaching on the stairs snapped Reva out of the trance-like state. She stood frozen on the landing. Avi paused near Reva. With one hand on the bannister, he ran the other over his strained face as if wishing for the horrific situation to change in that tiny sweeping movement.

Rather helplessly, he addressed Reva, "Can you tell Mai that I want to talk to her before breakfast tomorrow morning?"

Avi then retreated into his room without another glance at Reva. The tears that had only been curbed by Avi's arrival flooded down Reva's cheeks again as she dragged herself back into her room, her safe haven. Today it offered her no solace.

On the thirteenth day after Appa's passing, the priest conducted the rites that would enable Appa's soul to cut all earthly ties and proceed to its final destination. The sweet offerings in the lunch that followed were meant to enhance the joy of the soul's journey to its heavenly abode. Back on earth, it did little to ease the mind. When the last of the family well-wishers had left the house, and the sun hung low on the horizon, Viraj and Reva stood alone in the *divankholi*.

Reva heard Avi calling out to Gopi for a cup of tea. He was getting ready to head to the Club that had suddenly become his second home, away from the unvoiced accusations in Mai's silence and Viraj's curt responses.

Reva and Viraj stood in the quiet and stared, with grief laden hearts, at a photograph of Appa now hanging on the wall. Appa's smile was still contagious and his eyes full of love. Reva wished there had been some way of capturing the sound of Appa's laughter in the picture. The family needed it right now. Mai needed it most urgently.

Reva had heard of her own mother's overnight transformation from a married woman to a widow. Looking at Mai, Reva understood its pain. Mai had taken to dressing in dull whites and creams. She had chosen to keep her hair, and not shave it off as was the custom among widows. Appa would have vehemently objected to it. But her head was now covered with the loose end of the sari so precisely that not a strand of hair escaped its prison. The red *kunku* between her eyes was gone forever, leaving behind a round crater of bare skin paler than the rest of the forehead, a permanent reminder of what Mai had treasured and lost. The black beaded *mangalsutra* no longer adorned her neck, and her hands were bare, the green glass bangles reduced to a bunch of shards. But the worst to witness were Mai's eyes, constantly seeking Appa's empty chair on the porch or his seat at the dining table, her ears perking at the sound of footsteps, and in the next instant her forehead creasing in pain. The hardest to bear was how weak her voice sounded and how easily her back slumped. She had spent a greater part of the last two weeks at the altar with Tai-Aaji. Reva had heard their muffled conversations and words of comfort to each other and wished she could be part of it too. But she dared not intrude. With Appa gone, she felt uncertain of her place in the family once again.

When Aai had passed away, two years ago, Reva had focused her attention on school in order to guard her sanity. Without the comfort of lessons and Mai temporarily incapacitated, Reva plunged herself in the running of the household. She needed to keep her mind occupied. The thought of going to school receded further and further from Reva's mind. Her bow was broken, her arrow now aimless.

"In a twisted kind of way, I am glad Appa is not around to see the turmoil in his beloved Tarapore," Viraj commented quietly. "People are being driven out of their ancestral land just to humor the white people who will come here to vacation."

In the past few hours, Reva had heard whispered conversations among the mourners that validated Viraj's words.

"Till his last breath, Appa kept repeating 'they were doing it for their children, forgive them'. How could anyone not listen to such a kind soul? Why did the people just not talk to Appa or me instead of doing what they did? What a huge mistake and what a terrible price to pay! We are fighting amongst ourselves now." Viraj's voice mirrored his sorrow and frustration.

Reva thought about Sita and Gopi and their scattered families. The land reservation would take effect in six months. But some villagers had already started packing their meager belongings and heading out of the village in search of other lands to farm. Some left fearing a retaliation. After all, Avi was one of the white people now.

With the outbound men, went their wives, sons, and daughters, many of whom were employed in running Appa's house. Consequently, Reva found herself with lesser and lesser help with each passing day. Sita, the cook, had left two days after the incident to nurse her injured husband, and then, to appease his anger, she had quit working for the family. Gopi had not found the heart to leave the family in their time of need. She had sent her children with her mother-in-law to a relative's house in Poona while her husband traveled to other villages looking for work. Gopi would join her family in six months. Reva was grateful that she had Gopi as new help was hired and trained.

"Lives devastated. For what? For a season of fun and senseless merrymaking," Viraj continued. "Is that the party you are trying so hard to join, Reva?"

The question hung dangerously in the air for a moment before crashing on her with full force. The silence and loneliness in the house the past week, the tears withheld in a false show of bravery, and a sense of unfathomable loss erupted on Reva's face as she broke down and sobbed, her body slowly crumbling to the floor.

"No, no. Forgive me, that is not what I meant to say. You are not to blame, Reva. Forgive me. I spoke without thinking." Viraj was effusive in his apologies as he stood helplessly beside Reva's prone form. He called for Mai and Gopi to help. But no one came. Mai had retired to her room. Gopi had left for the day. Reva tried to regain some control on her emotions, but the harder she tried, the more the storm inside her raged. Hot tears ran down her cheeks. Finally, his concern for Reva overpowering what people might say, Viraj sat down beside her, and put his arms around her shoulders in comfort until Reva's tears slowed down to a stop.

"Don't worry, Reva. We'll be alright. I am still here."

The words were music to Reva's ears and for a few moments she let her head rest on his shoulder. Her brother. Her friend. Her protector. Just like Appa.

Hearing a sound on the upstairs landing Reva jerked back. She pulled herself together, smiled weakly at Viraj, and said, "Viraj, I was thinking .... I will start going to the sanatorium again. The sooner I start working the better. And you know Sumi will be waiting too."

In that instant, Reva realized that she would need a strong purpose in her life in order to survive Appa's death. Only the thought of settling Sumi's future held the promise of pulling her out of the life-leeching present.

Viraj fumbled with his words and then simply nodded. Reva noted his flustered response at the mention of Sumi's name but had no desire to pursue it further at that moment. She headed to her room and passed Avi on her way upstairs. His eyes were cold and his manner aloof. Reva hoped he had not witnessed her grief getting the better of her just a few moments ago. She wanted to be strong for the family. Appa would want her to be strong.

Avi's presence at home in recent days had started to generate a dangerously tense environment of unasked questions and insinuations. However, it still shocked Reva when one evening soon after, Avi packed his English life in his monogrammed trunk and moved out of the house and into the Club. Perhaps Viraj would have stopped him if he had been at home. Mai let him go.

The same night, Reva dreamed of the Club—its glittery lights like little flames of the funeral pyre and landscaped gardens alive with fanged demons that flitted through a thick fog. Their slimy extended arms grabbed and plundered all that crossed their paths. They fed on bloody red fruit that grew on spindly trees in the red dirt where lay buried the ashes of her innocent, peace-loving Appa. The pathway leading to the Club house was strewn with broken memories—a briefcase, a pencil, smithereens of green glass, a newspaper, a miniscule blue-tinged Krishna, and strands of long dark hair that traced its origins to the braid of a celestial *apsara* guarding the entrance. When Reva looked closely, she noticed that the *apsara* had Avi's gray blue eyes that were as tumultuous and menacing as an ocean on a stormy day. She woke up gasping.

Time crawled as the family struggled to resume life after Appa's untimely demise. On a brilliantly lit melancholy night of the October full moon, Reva quietly marked the passage of another birthday. She turned sixteen. She felt a hundred. If Goddess Laxmi had come knocking at the door that night to ask, "Who is awake?", she would have found Reva replaying in her mind the events of the fateful day and the weeks that had followed. Reva wondered if the Goddess would reward her for her vigilance on that particular night if the Goddess knew that Reva had been awake every night since Appa's death, falling into a troubled sleep only at dawn. Often, Reva would notice the candlelight seeping from under Mai's door when the night was the blackest.

Chapter 21

March 1902

The wrongful attack on Appa and his subsequent death sucked the air out of the villagers' amateur struggle to resist the changes on their land. Stories of proud, previously self-employed farmers leaving the village, routinely fell on Reva's ears and fanned Viraj's nationalist fire. The families that turned to wage employment out of necessity hung around the main bazaar in hopes of being able to feed their families in the summer and worrying about the future later. Having lost their homes to the reservation, they trekked daily for hours over the hills for work. Viraj and Reva suspected their own isolation from their community growing with each passing day.

If Avi had noticed it, on the few days he had visited with the family, he did not acknowledge it. Their conversation during the visits had been strained. After checking on the health of each member of the family and Maadhu Kaka, he had commented on the changing season. The days were long and the air warmer. Before the group settled into any semblance of a meaningful discussion about the implication of that change, the arrival of summer, Avi had taken his leave. He had sensed and recoiled from the questions swirling in everyone's minds. Would the land reservation continue as planned? What would happen to their village? What were the English thinking? How long before their own family would be forced to leave on some other senseless pretext? What would Avi do then?

One evening, Damoo Kaka came to pay his respects to the family. Reva saw the tremor in his fingers as she offered him tea, and heard it again in his voice as he grappled with his friend's absence.

"Appa and I had talked of spending our old age together in these beautiful hills. Of enjoying the chatter of our grandchildren together. Who could have forseen this calamity?" he said to Mai.

"Appa had urged me to hand over the business to my son and move up here as quickly as possible. He had threatened he would never speak to me if I postponed it again." Appa's friend's wiped his eyes.

"Daamoo Kaka, I can help you find a comfortable house closeby. The air here is definitely beneficial for good health," Viraj said.

"Bless you, my child. But it is not in our hands now. That freedom does not exist for me anymore."

"What do you mean?" Reva, who had been listening only half heartedly, chimed in.

"I had wanted to surprise Appa by acting on his words and buying a house nearby. The house belonging to the Pethe family, do you know which one I am talking about?" Daamoo Kaka asked, turing to Mai and then Viraj.

"Yes, yes, I know. It is less than a kilometer from here," Viraj answered.

"Well, I had met Pethe in Satara, and we had agreed to enter into a sale transaction since they wanted to live with their son in Poona. It seemed like the Tarapore house practically fell in my lap. I couldn't resist the temptation any longer to live out the rest of my life in the company of my old friend." Damoo Kaka paused.

"So then you are going to be our neighbor?" Viraj asked.

"I don't know. It looks like I am a victim to the changes planned for this village too. I have been told that for fifty kilometers around the hills, all land or house transactions had to get the approval of the English government. They have rejected my request once already saying the land is under the planning committee right now, and they are not allowing any purchase and sale transactions."

Now Reva was intrigued. Damoo Kaka was ready to buy an existing house in Tarapore close to their own. Why was he being refused a life in the hills? His house would not encroach upon any cultivated land. And if it did, so would theirs. It was only a matter of time.

"I have already been in touch with Avi about this matter, and he said he would look into it. I just hope this old bag of bones can last long enough to crumple in this red dirt," Kaka sighed. After a moment he looked around and remarked, "Talking about Avi, where is he? I don't see him here today."

Daamoo Kaka's visit raised questions in Reva's mind that refused to subside. What were the English planning? What was Avi planning? How long was Avi going to isolate himself? Mai may appear distant with him, but Reva had seen her sit in Avi's room frequently. Mai needed her sons; her daughter-in-law understood her pain.

Reva was getting restless watching the life that Appa had so lovingly created for his family and his community unravel like a faulty seam. But what could she do? There was one person who could help her make sense of the changes that were rocking their lives, and she barely got to speak to him. So Reva made up her mind to talk to Avi and prayed that she would have the courage to do so when the opportunity came.

One morning, feeling particularly optimistic, Reva sat down to write a note to Avi, imploring Appa's pencil to help her articulate the delicate nature of her message. She skipped the salutation, not knowing how to address a husband who pretended not to be one. She got straight to the point.

> *You had said that, as part of the family, you would treat me just as you would Appa or Mai or Viraj. I am request-ing you today to come home and talk to me, to all of us. It is very urgent. I have questions that only you can answer. The well-being of ~~our~~ the family depends on it.*
>
> *~~Yours~~ Respectfully,*
>
> *Reva*

Carefully, she folded the letter and inserted it in a blank envelope instructing a reluctant Maadhu Kaka to hand it over to Avi at the Club.

Maadhu Kaka returned a few hours later from his mission delivering the letter, but without an audience with Avi.

"Reva *tai*, please do not ask me to ever go to that place again. For this family I am ready to violate my religion, but the white man treated me as if I was an untouchable. It is too much to bear," he said.

"Maadhu Kaka, please forgive me for making you do it, but I don't know what else to do. I am desperate to get our family together again," Reva replied humbly.

Then she waited.

Walking to the sanatorium with Viraj days later, she wondered aloud, "Have you heard anything from your brother?"

"About the land reservation, I mean," she added hurriedly when Viraj cast a curious look.

"No, but I don't expect to either. He may have kept our name, but he has chosen his new family," Viraj responded grimly.

Reva panicked. Was Avi's silence an indication of his immense grief, or his lingering anger, or worse, his growing indifference? She would wait a few more days.

Reva had never been to the Club before. But on her way to the sanatorium, she had passed the turn in the road that led to the red brick building. She had even paused there a few times, pretending to give directions in English to an imaginary carriage driver. The pretense then had helped her practice the language. Standing at the junction now, she prayed that it would build her confidence. Her skills were going to be tried and tested if she carried out the plan she had hatched on a sleepless night. She was going to meet Avi at the Club to get some answers.

Reva knew she would have to execute her plan alone. Viraj's blood would boil at the very thought of walking into enemy territory. And what she needed most was a calm mind. With fewer helping hands at home, Gopi was busy morning to night. It would be impossible to get her away from the house as an escort or accomplice without undergoing a thorough interrogation from Mai about the reason for her absence. Reva did not want to invite that attention on her outing. Mai and Tai-Aaji would be furious with her for visiting the Club. A woman, from a reputed family, pursuing an audience with her husband in public was beyond shameful. And doing so without a proper escort was equivalent to signing a social and moral death wish. The risk was even higher now that Appa was not around to cast his protective net. But her life and Appa's dreams for his family and his land were at stake, and Reva could think of no other way to improve the situation. All she wanted to do was to talk and to get some answers. Only then could they work together to find a solution that would work for all.

Reva headed to the Club as soon as Viraj had dropped her off at the entrance to the sanatorium and was out of sight heading towards the village. The turn she had taken in her imagination time and again had become a reality, but she felt none of the excitement now. The road stretched endlessly in front of her. Keeping Appa's smiling face as her anchor, Reva proceeded towards the building that housed the Club. She had walked barely half a kilometer when the scenery changed. Gone were the wild brush and tangled trees. The road was lined with full blooming *gulmohar*, the bright red fronds a sign of the approaching summer. She could see the gardeners sitting in the shade at a distance eating their lunch and settling for a nap. They stared at Reva as she passed—a finely dressed young girl, unescorted, heading towards the Club, the gentlemen's Club. Reva covered her head with the loose end of her sari, and tilted her head such that they could not see her face and continued walking. Soon the red brick building came into view, but it was the sight along the path leading to the entrance that slowed down her step.

On both sides, arranged in neat rows that formed large rectangles, were small plants, the likes of which she had never seen before. The plants had long runners that touched the ground. On each stem hung tiny berries, their luscious red skin spotted with tiny black seeds. Reva recognized the fruit. *Serbeti!* Her heart welled as she remembered Appa's delight at offering her her first *serbeti*; she remembered Appa's hopes for the village that he had cultivated along with the rosy future of the strawberry. Here it was again, creating chaos in the hills. Was this tiny plant the real villain?

"Hello there," a voice called out.

Reva's heart started beating wildly as she glanced in the direction of the main building. An Englishman was approaching her. He stopped ten feet away. Reva recognized him. He was the horseman she had directed in the bazaar last summer. From the half-smile on his face, Reva suspected that he had recognized her too. She cast her eyes down quickly, uncomfortable as he studied her from head to toe.

"Hello. Miss ... ?"

Reva summoned her courage. "I am Revati, the wife of officer Avinash," she answered in English.

In the absence of Miss Annie and Viraj, the foreign words felt heavy rolling off Reva's tongue. Avi's name sounded cold. She had never said it aloud. She could already sense Avi's fury when he heard of her introduction. His anger would not be directed at uttering his name but more on the public acknowledgement of the relationship. But Reva needed to add that sliver of respectability to her outrageous plan. She was just looking for her husband.

"You don't say!" the man exclaimed. "Have a seat in the porch, and I'll get the old chap. Fancy that. Old Nash has a wife ... a very young wife." The man laughed, his gaze lingering for a few seconds longer on Reva before disappearing into the building.

Reva waited nervously. She was not sure anymore that the man had heard the name correctly. No one would call Avi 'old'. This visit was already promising to be a huge mistake. Within hours, the whole village would know of her transgression. The women in the family would house-jail her at the very least, if not disown her. Reva would be a joke in the eyes of the very people she had wanted to impress. And she could already see the quiet disdain in Avi's eyes as this story circulated in the gentlemen's circle. Maybe house-jail would not be such a bad idea.

The man returned.

"I am sorry, Miss. Nash, er...I mean, your husband is getting ready for an important meeting. He cannot be disturbed." The man walked away with a smile that showed there was more to the story than he had let on. Then he swung around and eyed Reva again, prompting her to turn on her heels and hurry away from the building.

Reva felt humiliated. What had she done that she did not deserve even a few minutes of Avi's attention? She might have walked into forbidden territory, but shouldn't Avi realize then that the matter was urgent? Was she no longer a part of his family? Avi's manner was puzzling. He may be bristling about Mai's and Tai-Aaji's rejection or Viraj's aloofness, but Reva had never shown that she held Avi responsible for any of the tragedy that had befallen the family. She genuinely did not know what to think or what to believe.

It was the month of May. The warm air was fragrant with a juicy sweetness—a sharp reminder of what was all around Reva but what she couldn't have. It was also an indicator of how close she had come. The brilliant red of the strawberries contrasting sharply with its lush green foliage creeping unchecked in the gardens was daring her to voice the obvious. Avi keeping his distance from the family when they needed his presence most was digging up the questions that Reva had tried to subdue all along. Was Avi guilty of conspiring against his land and his people? Was there darkness lurking beneath the dazzle of white?

Chapter 22

May 1902

Sumi planted the seed. Miss Annie nourished it. And Reva's imagination carried the idea to full bloom: If Avi refused to come to the house to meet with Reva, then Reva would sneak into the Club to force a meeting with him. Reva would attend the Summer Ball that year as Miss Annie's guest.

Yet some things were as certain as the morning fog in Tarapore.

Tai-Aaji would not allow Reva to even mention the Ball in her house, let alone attend it.

Mai would forbid her to go to the Ball even as Avi's guest, let alone Miss Annie's.

And Viraj would painstakingly highlight the insanity of a plan that involved Reva, an Indian woman, going to an English affair, unescorted by family, to confront an estranged husband.

Reva made up her mind to keep the family in the dark. She had done it before, and she could do it again. Her cause was urgent, her intentions noble. However, giving due consideration to all the presumed objections and knowing that as a native she would not be allowed entry into the Ball, Reva agreed to follow Miss Annie's suggestion—she would dress up as Miss Annie's English friend, temporarily visiting from the Northwest Province of India. Reva's fair complexion, hazel eyes, and brown hair created a solid foundation for the disguise already. Her name would be Miss Rose.

There was no doubt that not only was Reva's reputation on the line, but also the good standing of the entire family. In a village where Appa had worked tirelessly to uplift the residents, especially women, through education and practice, Reva's stunt, if exposed, would be used as an example of a family's downfall that is guaranteed when women are allowed any freedom. Appa's lifework in the hills would be undone. On the other hand, Appa had also held the family together, and cherished the togetherness in the community that was now being dangerously tested. Reva felt her actions were justified.

In Appa's absence, Reva had unconsciously assumed his obsession of safeguarding the family, her family, as best as she could. She was determined to get the answers that were keeping her awake at night— what was the future planned for their village? What was in store for their family? What was in store for her? She had less than four weeks to ensure the success of her plan.

The first and most exciting order of the day was to plan Reva's disguise. The women needed to pick an evening gown for Reva. Miss Annie had a handful from which Reva could choose. Sumi examined each one carefully to find one that would best suit Reva. Reva watched Sumi's animated face and followed with interest her exclamations and her deliberations. Sumi looked happy. Reva was fully convinced by now that Viraj had a big hand in Sumi's transformation. She resolved to come right out and ask Viraj about his intentions towards her cousin after the Ball. That part of the family also needed her attention.

For a moment, Reva was transported back to her childhood in Uruli when she would orchestrate the weddings of her dolls, hand stitching their trousseaus from scraps of cloth found around the house. She then recalled her first summer in Tarapore when Miss Annie had been the focus of this same exercise. Here she was one year later preparing for the Ball herself. It was as surreal as it was risky, and Reva was glad she had Sumi and Miss Annie with her as she tried to patch her family back together again.

Sumi settled on a pale blue chiffon with delicate plant motifs in velvet and silver thread appliquéd, making it a perfect choice for a girl of the hills, as Reva imagined herself to be. The water's edge pattern at the hem brought to mind the gentle lapping of river waves, creating an impression of gliding across the floor. To Reva's relief, not only was the gown the most exotic she had ever seen, it was also the most modest of the lot. Its full length ran all the way to the ground, the sleeves covered the whole arm, and the back was high. It was the front of the dress that gave her pause. The chest was more exposed than what Reva could handle. Miss Annie downplayed the bareness as the minimum required in order to carry out the disguise flawlessly. Reva realized that choosing imaginary gowns in a catalog was easy. Donning the unfamiliar contraptions was just the opposite.

Miss Annie suggested a simple but fashionable way to style Reva's hair. She had instructed Reva to refrain from oiling her hair the morning of the trial so that it would bounce and flow. As she undid her bun for Miss Annie to begin, Reva was pleased to hear Miss Annie gasp with admiration. Reva's hair hung beautifully in light waves when left loose. It was thick, shiny, and the natural highlights added interest with every turn of the head. Under the expert guidance of Miss Annie's fingers and a combination of pins and curlers, Reva's nondescript bun was transformed into a work of art fit for a queen. Sumi gushed with excitement, and together they reminisced the time when they had braided their shaggy cloth dolls to get them ready for their imaginary prince. What they were doing now was no different.

In addition to being an accomplished nurse, Miss Annie was also a magician with the needle and thread. A few tucks at the waist, hems along the train, a sash borrowed from an older gown, and Reva had a gorgeous dress made just for her. As she looked at herself in Miss Annie's mirror, she marveled at her own reflection. Cocooned in the numerous layers of her sari, Reva had overlooked how perfectly she had grown into the body of a young lady. Her round hips flattered the tiny waist that was accented by the sash on her dress. Her shoulders, visible through a wide neckline, were beautifully shaped. Miss Tytler's constant reminders to sit up in school had rewarded her with a natural elegant posture. Years of coconut oil scrubs had polished her skin to a glowing sheen that only highlighted the gentle rise and fall of her young full bosom. Reva's eyes rested nervously on her chest, somewhat bare and exposed. The gown had a deeper neck than her sari blouses. There was no *pudur* or scarf to cover the hint of cleavage that was just enough to fuel a heated imagination. Reva instinctively thought of Avi and blushed. She looked as beautiful as any of the women that she had admired in the catalogs. Desirable even.

Reva could picture the disapproving set of her own mother's mouth, the shame in Mai's eyes, and the fury in every shake of Tai-Aaji's head. But Avi? What would he think? What would he do? Her body tingled with thoughts she knew she should not entertain. But she let herself. For the moment. She was not Reva. She was Miss Rose, a young English woman. And Avi loved the English. Shameful as they were, Reva enjoyed the feelings that were washing over her as she stood staring at herself in Miss Annie's mirror.

"Well, hello Miss Rose. You are as tantalizing as your name!" Miss Annie exclaimed as she finished the last of the adjustments.

Suddenly conscious she was not alone, Reva immediately covered her chest with her arms crossed. Miss Annie burst into laughter.

"You look like someone bracing for an attack. That modesty will be a sure giveaway," Miss Annie reproached. "I know, you are not used to showing that beautiful skin of yours, but, God help me, you look ravishing. If I were a young English man, I would marry this local any day. That husband of yours has a big surprise in store. Talking to him is going to be the least of your worries. He'll be eating the words from the palm of your beautiful hand."

"You haven't said anything, Sumi," Reva observed, as she blushed again on hearing Miss Annie's comments.

"I don't have to tell you that you look lovely, but I am worried about what will happen when people find out. I had not thought the idea through when I suggested you meet with Avi in stealth. But this might be taking your freedom a little too far. It may infuriate Viraj as well. I don't want you to get into any trouble Reva," Sumi said.

Reva's excitement deflated. Sumi had put into words the thoughts that she had tried to bury under the exotic layers of her English disguise. Perhaps she needed to rethink the plan.

"...and I can't get over that bosom-blossom as well," Sumi added cheekily, as Reva snapped her arms across her body again.

Miss Annie chuckled. "But no one will find out you are Reva, except your husband ... when you tell him," Miss Annie reminded her. "Even if he does not follow you like a lamb the moment he sets his eyes on you, which I believe he will, do you really think he will expose your identity and become a laughingstock of his peers? If they don't know you are an Indian woman, they will not hold you to that standard ... and that ridicule. I'll be with you every minute of the party except when you get your chance to talk to Avi. We will leave as soon as you are done. I am certain this will work. Think about why you are doing this." Miss Annie shooed away the lingering doubts that were weighing down on Reva.

Reva wanted answers. This seemed to be the only way to trick Avi into a meeting and a conversation.

It did not take long for Sumi to fall in with the plan again. The three friends decided that Sumi would disclose the plan to Viraj after it was underway. This timing would ensure that he would not have a chance to stop them, but they would have a dependable male accomplice on hand should they need his help. The assurance with which Sumi spoke of handling Viraj further enlightened Reva on how far their courtship had progressed. Her heart warmed. Sumi deserved to be happy. And so did Reva.

With five days left before the Summer Ball, Reva had yet to come up with an excuse to be out of the house after sundown. She was usually home from the sanatorium in time to get the dinner preparations started. Mai had released her responsibilities around the house to Reva in the days following Appa's death. Most days Mai joined Tai-Aaji in the prayer room or sat in silence in the porch until Maadhu Kaka extinguished the lamps in the front porch on his way home at night. Appa's death had seeped her interest in her house and her work with the villagers. Lately, Viraj had become involved in a group that was tracking and following the plans for expansion of Tarapore closely. He too was away from home for long hours. Avi had stopped coming to the house. Instead, every week he sent a message about his well-being to Mai and inquired after her health. On Mai's request, Reva wrote back the same three words in response: *Me buree aahay, I am well.*

"Mai," Reva called out softly from the doorway of Mai's room. From the moisture-laden eyes that gazed back, Reva figured that the paper in Mai's hand was most likely some correspondence exchanged with Appa in the past. Or Avi at present.

"I can come back later," Reva said hurriedly, feeling like an intruder.

"*Pori*, later is going to be no different," Mai said.

Reva stopped in her tracks. Mai had used the same endearment that Appa used to call her. A lump formed in her throat as she contemplated the lies she was about to weave at a time Mai was at her most vulnerable. She prayed to God that Mai would never find out about the plan.

"Mai, one of the nurses has not been coming to the sanatorium because her husband is sick. Miss Annie is short on help. She is working tirelessly night and day tending to the patients and managing the office." Reva started building her house of cards, one wobbly piece at a time.

"Why are you telling me this?" Mai asked directly.

"On Saturday, three more patients are arriving from Bombay late in the evening. Miss Annie was asking if I could help her check and settle them in. If Viraj and Maadhu Kaka can come with the cart, I can return home with them later in the night. Otherwise, I can stay the night with Miss Annie in the sanatorium."

Even as she said the words, Reva thought how incredulous the plan was. No woman from a respectable home would stay the night in a strange location. She was going to get into trouble for merely proposing such a ludicrous plan. And just when Mai was making an effort to befriend her.

"My child," Mai said again. The lump in Reva's throat threatened to spill out.

"A year ago, my answer would have been a definite no. But now I ask myself, what would Appa have done? He lived his whole life for these hills and for the people in it. What you are asking sounds like something he would've allowed, even encouraged. So, yes, you can go to help Miss Annie. I will send Viraj with the cart at ten o'clock. Don't stay later than that. Maadhu Kaka has to go home to his family at a reasonable time too. Now ... I wish to be alone."

As Reva left Mai's room, she ran over the time constraints in her mind. The Summer Ball would start at eight in the evening. Given that Reva had a very focused goal, Miss Annie and Reva could be out of the Club in half an hour, leaving Reva time to change into her sari before Viraj arrived to pick her up. It was a dangerous plan that required every piece to fall in its devised place at the precise time.

Reva felt Appa's presence in every corner of the house that night. At times encouraging—what she was about to do was for the well-being of the people she loved. But mostly disapproving. The vision of herself as an English beauty had sprouted a hope and reignited a longing that she was ashamed to admit, even to herself. Was she jeopardizing the name of the family for her selfish interests ... for the momentary thrill of partaking in the English life that she had always fantasized?

Stopping herself from going down a path that would destroy their well laid out plan even before it went into action, Reva decided instead to practice her English in the privacy of her room. Every minute counted, now that she was headed to the Summer Ball.

Chapter 23

June 1902

A clock in the Club tolled eight as Miss Rose and Miss Annie alighted from the carriage that had been especially hired for the evening. The brick building was aglow with brilliantly sparkling lanterns. Small dinner tables, lined with whitewashed linens and dimly illuminated by candles set in floral arrangements, were scattered all over the porch, the same porch where Reva had stood not too long ago. The hypnotic scent of night blooming jasmine hung in the air like an invisible blanket. Overflowing from planters were delicate vines studded with shiny red fruit. The last of the *serbeti*.

Miss Annie had prepared her for the sight she was about to see, but that did not stop Reva's heart from sinking with awe and dread as she took in the scene playing in the main salon. All the English visitors, the summer residents of the hills, dressed in the most elegant and stylish fashions, were under one roof. Satins, velvets, and brocades were beginning to fill up the main salon. Men in dazzling whites and intimidating blacks stood attentively in the midst of all the beauties. A live band played in one corner of the main salon and a flimsy curtain of cigar smoke separated the newly arrived guests from the party that was getting underway.

Reva watched Miss Annie gracefully lift the full skirt of her pink silk gown and step lightly on the steps. Reva proceeded to do the same. As her mind made sense of the chatter around her, she sternly reminded herself, yet again, that she was prepared for this evening.

"Very kind…"

"…Magnificent sunset…"

"…These peculiar natives…

"How do you do?"

"Oh dear"

The words flowed through the doorway and lapped Reva as she paused to catch her breath at the top of the stairs.

"Annie dear, is that you?" a women's shrill voice called out. Miss Annie paused and smiled.

"Delighted to see you here. I wanted to look you up when I came to the hills this summer, but you know how busy it gets with the entertaining. I never had a chance," the woman said. She was dressed in a shameless gown, and her words were sugary sweet and unconvincing.

"How are you, dear Clara?" Miss Annie responded as they walked into the main salon, "So lovely to see you again. You know how my work at the sanatorium keeps me busy and away from this part of the world."

Miss Annie's ease and confidence impressed Reva, especially given their circumstances that evening.

"I can never understand why you prefer to work with those natives when our doctors would just about give an arm and a leg to have you work at our English sanatorium. I could never imagine being around those dirty scoundrels the whole day."

Reva was taken aback. While words like 'scoundrel' still tripped her, she gathered the overall meaning by the grimace on Clara's face. What could this woman have against the nice people of the village?

Miss Annie quickly interjected. "Clara, this is my friend Rose. She is visiting me from the Northwest Province. She is actually more of a patient now—recovering from a very bad throat infection caught on the way up the hills, you know. Rose, this is Clara. She is a regular summer visitor from Poona."

Reva forced a smile in Clara's direction.

"Oh you poor dear," Clara remarked, "that's our lot here. If it's not this illness, it'll be something else. It's the natives, you know. The bearers of all kinds of diseases...I see Eleanor... Eleanor!" Clara shouted as she waved to another woman in the crowd. "Excuse me ladies, won't you?"

Reva decided that she disliked Clara immensely, but she chose to turn a deaf ear to her ignorant chatter. Reva was on a mission, and she did not want any distractions. She inspected the crowd closely, seeking the gray-blue eyes, the dark face, and the tall frame amidst this sea of white. It had been six weeks since Reva had last seen Avi.

Some of the guests had now formed groups in the porch to catch the remnants of the warm summer air. Reva felt uneasy. She had not bothered to confirm that Avi would even be at this gathering. She had assumed he would. If he had other plans tonight, all the conspiring and lying would be a waste. She nudged Miss Annie towards the door on the opposite side of the salon that led to the back porch.

A few people greeted Miss Annie as she walked by. Many stared at Reva, their eyes openly displaying a mix of curiosity and, to her satisfaction, even admiration. Reva floated across the floor, chin up, cheeks flushed, eyes alert with anticipation and some apprehension. The corners of her mouth were turned permanently upwards. Rehearsing repeatedly in full disguise had not only strengthened her nerves but also tamed some of the discomfort Reva felt in the revealing clothing. Perhaps it was the string of pearls with the matching teardrop earrings, borrowed from Miss Annie, that had removed the last trace of the local Reva and transformed her into the elegant English Rose. With each step forward, Reva's confidence grew. She was in the midst of beautiful people. They had much to offer. She had much to learn.

Reva surveyed the small slice of life on display around her that the English had built for themselves in this corner of the world. She watched the native servants in starched white uniforms weaving through the guests trying to be invisible as they refilled drinks and monitored the food buffet. The sparkly silver pots full of steaming chicken, mutton, and vegetable curries and the soups perfectly adjusted to delight and satisfy the homesick English palate spoke of a slew of imaginative Indian cooks toiling in the kitchen. She recalled the advice Miss Annie had received from the villagers about the local weather, the vegetation, and the sicknesses. They had helped her adjust and live in these hills and carry out the work that she loved. Reva concluded that the English could not have done it on their own. Yes, they were different, but the people of the hills had much to offer and much to teach as well.

Reva's eyes were then drawn to the buffet table where tiny pyramids of shiny red berries were peeking out of dainty silver bowls. *Serbeti*. Reva approached the table, her fingers itching to reach out and pop into her mouth this little temptation that her Appa had loved ... and that had started the turmoil in her peaceful village. She remembered in the nick of time how Avi had eaten his fruit at the breakfast table. Scanning the food tray, she noticed the tiny fruit forks resting alongside each bowl. She carefully picked up a bowl and cupped her hand around it with an intensity that betrayed her excitement of eating a *serbeti* again, this time in all its delectable splendor.

As she bit into the fruit, her face soured a trifle. Miss Annie, who had miraculously appeared at her side, smiled and picked up her own bowl. Then Miss Annie reached for a slender creamer on the buffet. Reva watched as Miss Annie drizzled thick luscious cream all over the strawberries and then proceeded to eat her creation. Reva followed Miss Annie's example, attempting to sort out her feelings for this little fruit. Once again, the taste had not lived up to the promise made by its enticing color and shine. In fact, she would most definitely call the fruit a bit tart; it had made her mouth pucker yet again. Perhaps it was an acquired taste. But why would she care to acquire the taste of such a troublemaking berry? She found her answer the instant she put a cream covered strawberry in her mouth. The perfectly complementing tastes and textures of the strawberries drenched in the fresh sweet cream made Reva's heart sing. Strawberries and cream. Reva offered a silent prayer of gratitude to the Tarapore cows for salvaging her strawberry tasting.

"Oh Nash!" a woman's voice shrieked in mock disapproval from somewhere outside the salon.

Reva was about to step onto the porch. She hesitated. She was reasonably sure that the Nash being addressed was the one person she was looking for. An English officer had referenced Avi by the name before. She moved closer to a salon window that overlooked the porch to discreetly observe the group of people outside. Almost immediately, her eyes locked on Avi.

He stood with a group of women—some remarkably young, others, most likely, their mothers, aunts, or chaperones. He wore stylishly cut pants with a white shirt and jacket as black as the night of *amavasya*, new moon. His hair was oiled back like the other gentleman, revealing his face. Reva sucked in her breath. Avi was smiling. His smile reached all the way to his eyes and seemed to breathe life into every person it touched. The women were obviously entranced, but so was the one gentleman who seemed to be listening to Avi intently and laughing at his words.

"Nash, you wicked man!" the same voice sang as the woman it belonged to leaned closer to Avi, placing a hand on his chest pretending to push him back while linking her other arm around his to hold him close. Reva's cheeks burned with shame. She wanted to yank the woman's hands away from Avi and permanently seal them across her chest.

"I hope we don't run you out of Tarapore, Nash. What would we do without you here?" The woman's eyes spoke the words that her lips left unsaid.

"What we have always done on the hill stations. Pretend we are home. Away from the natives. *All* natives." Reva glanced at the new addition to the group and recognized the officer. His tone puzzled Reva. It was almost bitter.

"I don't have plans of going anywhere. I intend to live the rest of my life in the hills. With you," Avi answered smoothly, returning the woman's glance for a few seconds before sweeping it around the gathered circle.

"Then you better keep me happy, boy." The older gentleman slapped Avi's back in a friendly camaraderie and attempted to hand him his empty glass. "Don't make Mr. Jones wait for his drink."

"Beware, my dear father," the young woman replied. "Mother says Nash's work in the hills is being praised in far-off places. Perhaps, one day soon, it will be you who will have to keep him happy." She moved closer to Avi. Reva willed Avi to take a step away. But he just laughed comfortably.

"Rest assured that will never happen," Mr. Jones answered, unperturbed. "He may be the best officer, but my dear, under all that finery beats a native heart that cannot, by law and by our God given right I would say, rule an English mind. My job is assured. Now, what were we saying about keeping me happy?" Mr. Jones smiled suggestively to another woman in the group as they all indulged in more teasing.

Reva reeled under the shock and confusion of what she was hearing. The impropriety of the conversation with the young woman burned in her ears. Avi was flirting openly and with practiced ease. Were these the kind of meetings he had been attending every evening?

Most troubling and mind boggling to Reva was Avi's quiet acceptance, support even, of Mr. Jones derogatory comments about the Indians, including Avi himself. Which of the multitude of deities that she knew had given the English any rights over the Indians? If Avi was the best in the company, why should he not rise to Mr. Jones's position? Or even higher? The Avi who never admitted to being second best in things as trivial as a game of marbles was at peace with being denied his rightful title and responsibilities in his work? Where was the self-respect?

Reva looked around for Miss Annie, but she was caught up in a conversation. Reva needed her help to sort out her emotions before she presented herself to Avi. She motioned with her eyes for Miss Annie to join her near the window.

"I would've remembered this angelic face if I had seen it before." A gentleman walked towards Reva, swaying slightly on his feet.

Reva's heart beat faster. What was she to say? It sounded like a compliment.

"Thank you," she mumbled, bowing her head in acknowledgement.

"How positively charming!" the man boomed, now at an arm's length from Reva. "Allow me to introduce myself. I am Major Burns, and I am in charge of the English sanatorium here. And you are...?"

Reva blushed with the attention that was as scary as it was flattering.

"I am Miss Rose," she replied, barely hearing the words herself.

"Rose. As enchanting as the flower itself. Delighted. Do I detect a local upbringing, most likely under the care of a Christian *ayah*, nanny? Am I right?"

"You are right, Major," Miss Annie replied, stepping up from behind. "This is my friend. She has spent most of her life in the north, and right now she is my patient. She has strict orders to refrain from speaking to give her throat a rest. You understand, Major?" Miss Annie spoke with a smile but her words betrayed her authority as she led Reva away from the Major and out the door that led to the backside of the porch. They could now view the edge of the strawberry fields that Reva had seen during her last visit. The fruit was gone and the plants were resting to begin another season of fruiting. In the moonlit darkness, Reva told Miss Annie what she had heard. She could not bring herself to talk about Avi's flirting with the woman.

"Reva, I can see how these conversations are distressing, but remember, you are here to talk to Avi and get some answers. Answers that can help your family and the villagers. So stay focused on what you have set out to do. Don't lose this chance."

Miss Annie was right. She must focus on her task. She did not have much time. She had to be back at the sanatorium and dressed as Reva again in less than an hour.

A shattering sound pierced through the evening, followed by loud swearing on the front porch. The two friends hurried back through the salon towards the front porch.

A servant was scrambling to collect broken pieces of glass from the floor while the guests clicked their tongue with distaste at the man's fumbling.

"Bloody Indians! You cannot live with them, you cannot live without them!" the Major remarked loudly.

After a pregnant pause, another gentleman replied, "Hold your horses, Major! We are taking care of that problem. Aren't we, Mr. Jones?"

Mr. Jones replied, "That we are! Nash and I have been very busy. You know that, Major."

The crowd had started getting back into their little cliques. Reva was heading towards Avi, who stood with another gentleman on the side, watching the scene unfold. Both Annie and Reva stopped in their tracks at the mention of Avi's name.

"Mr. Jones, that was a brilliant idea to stop the natives from buying and using the land around the hills. That's the only way we can keep these hills pristine, if you know what I mean," the Major said.

"I say drive all the remaining villagers out too. They come to the house, filthy and stinking, bringing their sickness and clumsiness and heathen ways," said the woman still clinging to Avi's arm.

"Then who will cater to your every wish and demand?" Avi inquired smoothly.

Reva froze. The callousness of the English was just beginning to register in her mind. But it was Avi's cold, calculated reply that made her body tingle with an anger rising out of a growing sense of betrayal. She felt Annie's grip tighten on her wrist, holding her back.

"Who will work the fields to produce the feast you see before you? Strawberries do not grow by themselves you know," Avi remarked casually. "You need the locals."

For Avi, the villagers were nothing more than a means to an end.

"When I go to the bazaar, the few times that I do, I cannot bear to be accosted by those little ragged boys and girls running half naked and staring at me as if I were a ghost. They are too tiresome, and I cannot bear it," another older woman appealed to Mr. Jones.

"Don't worry, my dearest Mrs. Jones. Yours truly and his protege are taking care of that problem too," Mr. Jones, eyes red and hands shaking, announced with an exaggerated bow.

"What ever do you mean?" Miss Annie exclaimed innocently, stepping into the porch. The group looked in her direction.

"My dear Annie, it's an ingenious plan. Along with the wages to work at the house, we offer rooms, accommodation, only for one person in the family, so the wife and children have to live elsewhere. The poor buggers won't have a place to keep them here in our hills. No wife, then no children. We will have the workers we need, but they will never be able to put their roots down here. Problem solved. Ingenious plan. Mark my words, this boy will rise to the greatest heights a native can in the Raj," Mr. Jones raised his glass to Avi, who finished his drink with one gulp.

Reva heard every word that Mr. Jones had uttered. She shuddered when he dared to refer to the hills as 'our hills.' Her blood boiled. Avi was a traitor. He was selling out his own people, his own land. As Reva's angry glare locked on Avi again, she realized with a start that he had seen her and recognized her instantly. He could stare all he wanted, but today he could not stare her down. She had the knowledge and the indignation to meet his gaze with confidence and even defiance. None of her transgressions were as scandalous or as devastating as Avi's deception and betrayal.

Hurriedly, Reva stepped back into the salon as thoughts rushed through her mind like raging river currents in the peak of the monsoons. The English people looked down on the Indians. They detested them. They did not regard them as being worthy of this heavenly landscape even though the natives had lived on the hills and nurtured them for generations before the arrival of the foreigners. The British never intended to live amicably with the Indian population in the hills. The land reservation for strawberry cultivation was just an excuse. The dark reality was that the English wanted the Indians gone. And from every indication, Avi shared their disgust and distrust in his own people. Was this his way of seeking revenge on the simple villagers for Appa's death?

Stranger still was the fact that Avi seemed to believe that he was not a local.

So engrossed was Reva in forming her conclusions that she failed to notice that Avi had followed her into the salon. She failed to notice Rich staring at her from across the room. He now approached her and said, "Pardon me, I don't think we have been introduced. I am Richard, but everyone calls me Rich."

Reva's mouth went dry. She could not tell if Rich had recognized her as Avi's wife.

"Pleased to meet you. My name is Rose," she muttered. She could feel Avi's eyes fixed on her and tuned into the conversation.

"The pleasure is mine. But I feel I have had this pleasure before. I can't quite place it..."

Reva held her breath.

"Perhaps you have spent some time in the north. That's where you might have met my dear friend Rose," Miss Annie jumped into the conversation. "But you simply must excuse her. She is suffering from an inflamed throat and has strict instructions from me to be seen and not heard."

Rich smiled graciously at Miss Annie before continuing, "I am sure I'll remember it when the time is right. I could never forgive myself if my incompetent mind failed to recall the memory of an angel." With a bow towards the ladies, he headed inside the salon where the music had reached a crescendo and the dancing feet of the guests resembled the tongues of their audience—fast and loose.

If Rich had not glanced at Avi as he made his exit, Reva might have breathed a little easier and entertained the possibility that Rich had not remembered who she was. But he had. Reva was quite certain that her cat was out of the bag. And from the conversations she had just heard, she was fairly confident that Rich would not be an ally. Exactly what he would do was the sword that now dangled over Reva's head. Suddenly, the air felt hot and heavy and the cream in her neglected bowl seemed to have curdled from the heat and the acidity in the strawberries. She set her bowl down with disgust. It was almost three quarters past eight.

The dinner bell tinkled. As if in slow motion, the guests made their way to the porch to be seated at the tables.

Reva and Avi remained rooted in the salon. Seizing this opportunity for the couple to talk, Miss Annie pretended to accompany some of the guests out.

"Nash, aren't you coming?" The young woman who had been buzzing around Avi the whole evening pouted at Reva, unable to hide her dislike for this newcomer who was claiming her suitor's attention.

Without skipping a beat, Avi smiled and said, "I will be with you and Mr. Jones in a moment. You go ahead." Feeling partly reassured, she left the room but only after stealing another backward glance at Avi.

Avi's face was grim, his eyes dark as they took in every inch of Reva. Reva felt a fluttering sensation in her stomach as she realized that Avi was looking at her, really looking at her for the first time. His eyes took in the pearl studded pins that held her lustrous hair together, they acknowledged the fury in her hazel eyes, and noticed the heightened rosiness in her cheeks. They rested for a brief moment on her lips before they traveled lower and took in the luster of her string of pearls, the heated rise and fall of her breathing, and the reluctant unclenching of her fist as his ardent gaze released the steam building inside of her for the last hour.

Just then the Major, now clearly drunk, stumbled into the room again, followed by a flustered Miss Annie. "Miss Rose, may I have the honor of sitting beside you tonight? You don't have to say a word. Your beauty says it all." He grinned at Reva in a way that made her want to cross her arms across her chest again. But she would not embarrass herself in front of Avi.

Calmly she replied, "You are too kind, Major. But I am feeling very tired. It is time for me to go home and rest."

If her transformed appearance had ignited a spark in Avi's countenance, her response in flawless English lit the fire, a fire that promised to consume with every passing second.

"Major, your table is waiting for you," Avi addressed the intoxicated man, who was oblivious to the charged currents in the room.

"Charming, charming I say!" The Major complimented Reva again. "Miss Annie you must bring Miss Rose again. Sooner than later." He winked at Reva.

Reva cast a worried look at the clock.

"Major, would you be so kind as to walk us to our carriage?" The words tumbled out of Reva's mouth before she could stop them. Miss Annie's eyes widened.

"Delighted," the Major answered, genuinely happy at being given this opportunity.

"Go on then, Avi. I will see you at dinner." Reclaiming some authority, the Major dismissed Avi, who was forced to comply.

In the salon, now deserted, Reva let out a shaky breath. Without saying a word to Avi, she had gathered the information she needed. Feeling the last of her energy draining, Reva took the arm extended by the Major as they headed outdoors. Walking alongside her, Reva noted a quickness in Miss Annie's step that was unusual for her calm disposition. Even though it seemed that their plan had been successful, it had come dangerously close to unraveling beyond Miss Annie's control.

Chapter 24

Miss Annie and Reva rode to the sanatorium in silence. Reva was slumped against the seat but her mind was buzzing. She had all the answers she wanted and more. The problem was that she did not like anything that she had learned. She hated every bit. The Avi that she had idolized—educated, handsome, cultured, and blessed by the English—was also a traitor and a puppet in their hands. How she hated each and every one of the *firangi*!

She regretted the thought as soon as it passed through her mind. Stealing a glance at Miss Annie, her heart softened. Miss Annie, like Miss Tytler, had never made Reva feel ashamed of who she was. They had inspired her to become a better person, a stronger person. Having tasted the English way of thinking, Reva could appreciate the sacrifice and the hardship that both the women had endured in order to participate in the local life. Because of Miss Annie, the villagers learned about good hygiene and healthy living. They looked at her as if she were a God, and she did not take advantage of them. How could she be the product of the same culture that produced Mr. and Mrs. Jones? Was she really the exception and not the rule?

The contradiction made her think of Avi once again. The son of Appa, who lived his life and lost it pursuing better conditions for his people. The son of Mai, an epitome of tradition and family values. The brother of Viraj, who was beginning to follow Appa's footsteps. The Avi that she saw today had nothing in common with the people and the place that brought him in this world. This was not the Avi she had pieced together with so much anticipation, admiration, even love. She had lost the Avi she never had. This feeling of losing something precious was becoming more and more familiar to her now. It brought no tears, only a sense of hopelessness and emptiness for the years that lay ahead.

As they approached the sanatorium, Reva recognized Maadhu Kaka's cart waiting to take her home. Mai must have sent them earlier than planned. She strained her eyes to see if Viraj was inside. She could not wait to spill her heart out to him and share the devastating conversations she had heard at the Ball. She wondered if Viraj knew all along the hidden intentions of the English that Reva had been too blind, too stubborn to see. They needed to do something to protect their hills, to stop their home from being destroyed.

"The nurses have left the candle burning in the office again!" Miss Annie said exasperated, breaking the silence in the carriage. Reva knew the nurses would get an earful tomorrow for wasting their supplies. As their carriage passed Maadhu Kaka's cart, Reva saw him wake up with a startled look in their direction. Not seeing any face of interest, he settled back into his temporary sleep. Reva smiled. Poor Maadhu Kaka. Living a life of honest work and loyalty. Just like Gopi's family or even Hirkani. They deserved to see their families thrive on their hard earned and fiercely loved land.

Reva hurried out of the cart to change and get ready for the ride home. Viraj was probably taking a walk around the property while he waited. Maybe he was meeting with Sumi. Although that would not be appropriate, Reva hoped that were true.

Reva and Annie were surprised to see the two nurses sitting on the floor in the main office when they should have retired for the night. The dinner should have been served, and the patients should have been settled in their quarters by now. They would only call for the nurses if needed.

The nurses scrambled to their feet when they saw Miss Annie walk in. Reva hastily slipped into Miss Annie's quarters before they had a chance to figure out who Miss Annie's companion was. Five minutes later, Miss Annie burst into the room where Reva was undressing. She talked fast as she helped Reva out of her gown. Reva struggled to understand the jumble of words that rushed out of Miss Annie's mouth.

"Reva, Sumi ran away! Sumi ran away! The nurses think it had something to do with the two policemen from Satara who came to talk to a new patient. Sumi saw them in the garden looking for this patient. That's when Sumi started shaking and shivering as though she had seen a ghost. She pushed past the nurse who was bringing her a cup of tea. Then she broke into a run. The nurses tried to call her back, but she would not listen. They ran after her but lost her as she entered the forest behind the sanatorium. The nurses did not know what to do. They are scared for her, and frankly so am I. The trees are dense in that part of the hills and there have been sightings of big cats and coyotes and hyenas and snakes. Oh, Reva I am so afraid for Sumi!"

Reva had felt that the night could not get any worse. She was proven wrong yet again.

"Viraj," the name escaped from Reva's mouth.

"He is out looking for her right now. The nurses told him what had happened as soon as he came with the cart to get you. He sent the janitor to fetch some more villagers for the search party. There was no point notifying the village police since their appearance started this whole nightmare in the first place. Oh Reva! I blame myself. I should've done more for Sumi and her ailing mind."

For the first time since Reva had met her, she saw Miss Annie loose her composure. The same Miss Annie that was exchanging pleasant greetings with her white compatriots was beating herself over the fate of a native.

"Miss Annie, Sumi could not be in better hands. You are doing all you can," Reva reassured her.

"I am going to take Maadhu Kaka and search for Sumi myself. If she is hiding near the sanatorium, maybe she will recognize my voice and come back."

In that moment, Reva felt no fear from the dangers that lurked in the hilly darkness. Her walks with Viraj and explorations with Gopi had taught her all she needed to know about the trails around the sanatorium. Madhu Kaka could hold two burning torches while she beat two metal plates. The fire and the noise would keep the animals away. She was convinced that the animals would leave them alone—they would smell no fear today. There was no place for fear at home.

"No, no!" Miss Annie was vehement in her opposition to Reva's idea. "Viraj has left strict instructions for you to go back home with Maadhu Kaka. Mai is waiting for you. You must go home. On no account must she be worried about you or him."

Viraj's instructions, although contrary to Reva's need for action, had a wisdom that resonated with Reva. Mai had trusted her, and she must not break the trust. Reva also knew that Viraj would turn the mountains over to help Sumi. He would not rest until she was found. If Sumi was Reva's cherished past, she was Viraj's chosen future.

"I will send Viraj straight home once Sumi is back in the safety of the sanatorium," Miss Annie promised Reva. "Now I must go back to the nurses and threaten to pull their tongues out with my forceps if they gossip about what happened today." Miss Annie picked herself up and walked back into her office, her calm restored and her mind alert. It was going to be a long night.

As Reva slipped into the house, she noticed the candlelight filtering from under Mai's door.

"Is that you, Viraj? Reva?" Mai called out from her room. "I was starting to get worried. You are late."

"It is me Reva, I am back from the sanatorium," Reva replied, peeking into Mai's room and deciding not to volunteer more information than necessary, if she could help it.

"Then I can sleep restfully now," Mai said. "Tell Viraj to close the side door before he goes to his room. I don't want to find a stray in my kitchen tomorrow morning."

Reva waited in the dark *divankholi* for five more minutes. Then, as Viraj was likely to do, she closed the side door noisily, and hurried upstairs, relieved that Mai had not asked any more questions about her evening. It was further proof of the trust Mai had started to place in her.

In the safety and security of her room and family, Reva sensed Sumi's fear and loneliness acutely. Had Reva failed her cousin? Wrapped in her own world of English excitement and family entrapments, had she been distracted from following Sumi's health closely? She had let herself believe that Sumi was well enough. So why did Sumi react so violently when she saw the policemen? What had happened in her past that would not let her have a peaceful future?

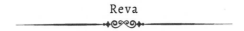
Reva sat on the windowsill watching the path that led up to the house. Viraj would need to enter the house unnoticed. Reva would stay awake to let him in. Reva would stay awake until she knew Sumi was safe.

Chapter 25

Viraj failed to return home that night. Instead, the next morning, as Reva woke up, tired and stiff on the windowsill, a solemn Gopi brought in two letters. A village urchin had stopped Gopi on her way to the house early that morning to hand over the letters with strict instructions to deliver them to Reva. Reva recognized Viraj's handwriting. One was addressed to her, the other to Mai.

As soon as Gopi had left the room, Reva tore open her envelope. Viraj's precise, uniform handwriting established a sense of calm in Reva which seemed beyond her reach a moment ago. Taking a deep breath and preparing herself for the worst, Reva read the letter.

> *Reva,*
> *We found Sumi hiding in the jungle last night, and she is*
> *safe with me, for the moment.*

Relief flooded through Reva's body like the first rain on the dry plains. Life saving and full of hope.

...She was hiding not far from the sanatorium, but she had refused to answer the call of the nurses out of fear and suspicion. She came out of her hiding place the moment she heard me call out her name. She trusts me, Reva. She trusts me. And, God help me, after seeing Sumi, who I thought I had lost forever, I cannot leave her side again.

Dear dear Viraj...Reva said a prayer of gratitude for her brother-in-law.

I have taken her to Gopi's village where the people know me. They have promised to help and be discreet about it. I have been trying to piece Sumi's story together from the incoherent words that rush out of her mouth in between her sobs. She has not stopped crying since I found her, and it breaks my heart. From what I gather, after her husband died, she was mistreated by her family. Her brother-in-law made some advances towards her which she refused. But he did not listen. Something happened one night ... she hit him over and over again with a rolling pin and ran away from the house—traumatized and hurt in the process of fighting off that demon. How she ended up in our village I still have not figured out.

Here the handwriting lost its steady rhythm. Reva could sense Viraj's agitation and anger as Sumi's past had finally come to light.

From her story, the only reasonable explanation I can draw is that she is fearful the police are looking for her on account of what she did, and worse, that she may have to go back to the family if they find her. Reva, I cannot begin to describe to you the fear and madness in her eyes when I found her. As long as I am alive, she will never have to relive those moments.

Here is what I have decided to do. I have written to Mai that I am going to Satara for land related work as I usually do. Sumi is sleeping right now. Miss Annie has given her some medicine to calm her down. When she wakes up I am going to ask her to marry me. If she agrees, I am going with her to the temple tomorrow to do the needful. As my lawful wife, she will never have to return to that evil family again.

The words were now tiny and squeezed together as Viraj ran out of space on the paper. But they expanded rapidly in Reva's heart until it was ready to burst. Viraj was going to marry Sumi!

Reva noticed another piece of paper inside the envelope. There was more. The handwriting on this scrap had regained its steadiness. Viraj must have added this part of the letter at a later time.

Reva, the village priest, Appa's loyal follower and friend, believes that Appa would have supported such a step. He is willing to marry us. I am not happy about deceiving Mai, Tai-Aaji, and even Dada, but I cannot take the chance that they may not permit this marriage given the circumstance and what people might say. Once we are married, they will have to accept it. But I know, Reva, you will understand the urgency of the situation and agree to this plan. I suspect you have known how I felt all along.

Yes. Reva had known all along. She laughed through her tears. Viraj was probably right about keeping his decision a secret from the family. Marrying a widow was not condoned by most, although Appa and his followers had worked tirelessly to change the people's mindset. Viraj would carry forward Appa's work through his own example. This was the happy ending that Reva had wanted for Sumi. For an instant, the image of Avi flashed before her eyes. She felt a tinge of sadness. Avi had Appa's name. Viraj had also inherited his spirit.

Reva had nothing to fear now. She would do all that she could to help him. Mai and Tai-Aaji would take some time to adjust to the idea of a widow as their daughter-in-law. If Reva needed to, she would remind Mai that Appa would've welcomed Sumi—sweet, kind, loving Sumi. And if Mai and Tai-Aaji would not support an unfortunate widow, then who else?

Her eyes quickly scanned the last few sentences on the letter.

> *Come to the sanatorium in the morning today, as you had planned. I will meet you there. We will proceed to the temple together. I take this step knowing that I may forever be cast out by my family and perhaps the community. But I also know Appa would have approved. I am waiting for you.*
> *Viraj*

The last lines spurred Reva into action. It was going to be a busy day.

Reva dressed with care. She hoped to attend a wedding that afternoon. She prayed that Sumi would accept Viraj's proposal. She packed the necklace and bracelets, that Mai had gifted her after her own marriage, to wear at the temple. Mai would question the occasion if she saw Reva decked up for breakfast that morning. Reva also took her treasured idol of *Krishna* as a gift for Sumi. After all, Reva was going to represent the groom's family and was obliged to gift the bride. She quickly scanned her cupboard for a new sari for Sumi. Tradition called for the wedding sari to be yellow, the color of *haldi*, turmeric. Orange was her only choice that day. She would make it work. Some traditions needed to be flexible. Some deserved to be broken. Reva longed to see Sumi dressed in color. She had endured a dull existence for too long.

As the downstairs clock struck eight, Reva grabbed her bag and hurried out of the room. Halfway down the stairs, Reva realized that Viraj's letters still lay on her bed. She rushed back to her room, slipped the letter addressed to her in her chest of drawers, and proceeded downstairs with the letter addressed to Mai. Reva composed herself as she waited for Mai, noting with some guilt how masterfully she was fabricating stories.

"Are you off to the sanatorium again, Reva?" Mai's sharp voice greeted her as she entered the dining room. Reva remembered her early days of living with Mai when the voice had arrested all the words in her mouth. It had made her miss Aai. Now she only heard Mai's concern in the same tone. It still reminded her of Aai.

"Yes, Mai. I must. Miss Annie needs me there today," Reva replied with genuine enthusiasm.

"But you were helping till late last night. You need to think about looking after this house too," Mai said.

Very soon, Mai ... you will never have to worry about the house again ... with Sumi under your roof, Reva thought.

"Is Viraj down yet?" Mai asked.

"Mai, Gopi handed me this letter just now. It's addressed to you. It's from Viraj."

Mai read the letter and called out to the new cook, "Rukhma, Viraj is not going to be home for the next few days. Don't account for him at lunch and dinner."

"Mai, I have rested well. I can be of help to Miss Annie at the sanatorium. Rukhma and Gopi can easily take care of everything around the house. If you need me to cook anything, I will be back in time to do that before dinner."

Mai shook her head as if giving up an imaginary battle and said, "Who can tell you are not Appa's very own daughter?"

Reva's heart soared. If Mai was comparing her to Appa, she must like her. Possibly even love her. Mai was proving to be like the seed inside the dried apricots that Reva had loved to crack when she was a child. Inside the hard cover, she would find the most perfect heart-shaped nut.

At the sanatorium, Reva peeked into Miss Annie's office, but she wasn't in. Neither was Viraj. Reva prepared to wait. They needed to be on their way to the temple so Reva would not be late for dinner. After a few minutes of nervous pacing and fidgeting, she decided to check in on some patients to reduce Miss Annie's work and inject some sliver of truth in the lies she had spun for Mai that morning. Thirty minutes later, as she headed back to the office, Reva heard voices coming from that direction. The nurse. A man—Viraj. Now they could get moving on their plan.

Reva burst into the room, a million questions for Viraj spinning in her mind, and stopped short. In front of her, like the rigid mountain visible through the window, stood Avi. His face was expressionless, but Reva knew how to read it. Avi was displeased, perhaps even angry.

Sumi's sudden disappearance had temporarily pushed the troublesome memories of the Ball in a remote place Reva did not wish to go if she had a choice. But here was Avi, ten feet away, in Miss Annie's office. A confrontation seemed inevitable. She collected herself and dismissed the nurse.

"You may be young. But you have the cunning of a woman twice your age," Avi fired first.

Reva had assumed that Avi had come to apologize for his behavior at the Ball, or for his disengagement from the family after Appa's death. Or to explain it. Or at the very least to discuss it. This attack left her speechless.

"You must understand. I was merely trying to get your attention with the disguise..." Reva began.

"What a humiliating way to get attention," Avi cut her off.

"No one recognized me." Reva attempted to pacify Avi. There were more important matters to be discussed.

"You are wrong. Rich. Richard. He recognized you immediately. I cannot imagine how! After you left, he made it a point to enlighten Mr. Jones that I was married. That you were practically just a child—that I am guilty of a practice that is barbaric and heathen and ignorant and everything that the English detest about the locals," Avi retorted angrily. "What little respect and approval I had earned in the company was dangerously close to being destroyed by your foolishness. It was only when I explained to Mr. Jones how I could not ignore my father's wishes and the unfair circumstance surrounding the marriage that their outrage was pacified... then they applauded me for being an honor-bound, loyal son instead... much to Rich's chagrin." Avi sounded amused at the end.

"Why is Mr. Rich so interested in your personal affairs?" Reva wondered aloud.

"It bothers Rich that I, an Indian, am the one favored by the officers higher up in the chain. He has lost sleep looking for an opportunity to pull me down. And you, with your childish thinking, offered him the sword to strike me, and that too on a silver platter." Avi's words were bitter and harsh. Reva stiffened.

"I am not a child," she argued.

"That you certainly are not. You proved that yesterday." His voice softened ever so slightly. "You proved that to me and my company." As momentarily as it had appeared, the softness in Avi's voice disappeared. "And it won't be long before the whole village will find out. And I will be the laughingstock. Our family name and reputation will be ruined."

Was Avi completely out of touch with reality to know that their family name was already compromised on account of his hand in the land reservation?

Reva glanced at the clock. Viraj was late.

"I cannot expect loyalty from you Reva, but Viraj? How could he do this to me?" Avi sat down with his head in his hands.

Avi's words hurt. He expected nothing from her. One expects nothing from a stranger.

At the mention of Viraj's name, Reva pulled up all her defenses. Avi could say whatever he wanted about her, but Viraj was a saint, and it would be ludicrous if he was faulted by Avi.

"What does Viraj have to do with this? I hatched the whole plan on my own," Reva defended her brother-in-law.

"It takes two to do the shameful thing you are planning to do."

Miss Annie could possibly be considered the second person, but what was he talking about? What was she planning to do? She had already done what was needed, as far as Avi was concerned.

"I don't understand what you are saying," she replied, genuinely puzzled.

"Looks like speaking English has made you forget your mother tongue?" Avi taunted.

Tears were beginning to form somewhere at the bottom of Reva's stomach, but her anger rose against the implications of Avi's words.

"You are accusing me of forgetting my mother tongue?" Reva asked in disbelief. "... when you have forgotten your own mother in all senses? Mai has spent hours by the window waiting for your return. Her anger is justified, and yet she cannot forget that you are her son. You have betrayed Appa by scheming with your English friends against your own people and against the place you called home. Just for the pleasure of being invited into a society of small-minded people, you have sold out your own conscience. And you accuse me of forgetting my mother tongue?" Reva was shaking out of indignation.

"Yes, I have learnt to speak English," Reva disclosed, pausing briefly for the enormity of the achievement to sink in her own mind. "And I am proud of it. Now I understand them better. All of them. The wicked Mr. Rich and the tyrant Mr. Jones and that pathetic white *memsaheb*, woman, hanging on to you. My appreciation of Miss Annie has increased ten-fold—I can see now that she is an exception rather than the rule in the white society. You, Avi, have used your knowledge of the English language and the people merely as a feather in your cap, to fan your pride, to pretend that you are not one of the locals, so you will be accepted by the white men, the very same men who detest our kind and consider us inferior. You believe in their lie. You have allowed that lie to shatter the peace in these hills."

Reva knew not from where she got the strength to fight Avi, but she could not ignore the thoughts that she had subdued all these days in order to excuse, even justify, Avi's behavior.

Avi stared at Reva as though she were speaking in a language that was neither English nor Marathi.

"All that the English want is a private enclave for a few months when they can recuperate from the hard life outside the hills. A place that reminds them of home. By now you should know they are not used to the weather, the food, the customs, and most importantly, the people here. Is that so hard to understand? ... Given all the good work they have done for our land and our people," Avi shouted.

Reva could not believe she was hearing him correctly. Avi was ready to destroy the lives of the locals so that the English could enjoy a few months away from the very people who made their fancy living possible. What kind of twisted selfish thinking was this? She attempted to reason with him again.

"Look at Miss Annie. She lives around the locals and works with them. She cares for them. There is no doubt that because of her, the villagers are better off. But she has built her world together with the people here, not by stepping on them...She recognizes the value that locals bring to her life too...So I want to know—why does my knowing English have to replace my Marathi? Why can't I use both to my advantage? One is not superior to the other—it is just different."

Reva paused. The plight of the locals had inspired her to examine her own beliefs in the loftiness of the English race. Standing in front of Avi, as her thoughts materialized into concrete words, she allowed them to erase some of her own misguided beliefs about the nobility of the colonists.

"Avi, you grew up in the hills. You talk about spending your old age in this paradise. Think for a moment. You are not alone here. There are other people who have the same dream. They may not be as rich and powerful as you. But that does not mean that their dreams are any less important. Our own Gopi and Sita—look at them now. Their dreams have turned to dust. Will you build your future on their sorrow? If you can, then you are worse off than I imagined." Reva threw every word out with conviction.

Avi shook his head. "What were we before the English introduced this village to a better way of living—good sanitation, roads that make travel to Satara faster, not to mention the choices in education? You cannot deny that their ways are better. Without the ideas of the English, Tai-Aaji's, and now Mai's, life would be worse." Avi's voice quavered, and Reva sensed his vulnerability.

"Yes, the English helped in stopping some barbaric practices, but does that give them the right to walk all over us? Is our gratitude and admiration an admission of our inferiority? The villagers don't think so. Their anger against the white people and their resistance to the preposterous scheming are evidence enough. On the other hand, your actions scream self-loathing—why else would you silently accept an idea that an Indian officer will never rise above an English officer no matter how good he is at his work? You may distance yourself from us locals all you want, but it is very clear—inferiority is not a condition borne by us locals, it is a disease that thrives in your mind and colors your vision. So no matter what language you speak and what clothes you wear, you will always feel unequal, inferior, to all those people you spend your days...and nights with." Reva could not resist the last addition. She had not forgotten the woman with her hands all over Avi the night of the Ball.

"So you are going to teach me a lesson on who I should spend my days and nights with? You, the woman who violates every image of propriety and engages with her brother-in-law behind the family's back?"

Avi's accusations rained on Reva like debilitating punches. The tears she'd held back now streaked down her cheeks. She watched stunned as a tear dropped on the floor. Avi's cruelty knew no bounds. What was he saying?

Interpreting her tears as an admission of guilt, Avi pressed, "What were you thinking Reva? That the world would not find out?"

A rustling sound forced Reva to raise her eyes. She saw Avi waving a piece of paper in the air. She recognized the paper that he held in a death grip. It was Viraj's letter. The second half of the letter.

Avi read each word aloud, making no attempt to hide the disgust in his voice ...

> *Reva, the village priest, who was Appa's loyal follower and friend, believes that Appa would have supported such a step. He is willing to marry us. I am not happy about deceiving Mai, Tai-Aaji, and even Dada, but I cannot take the chance that they may refuse given the circumstance and what people might say. Once we are married, they will have to accept it. But I know, Reva, you will understand the urgency of the situation and agree to this plan. You have known how I felt all along.*

Avi's finding Viraj's letter addressed to Reva could only mean one thing. "You searched through my room," she whispered.

"No, I did not," Avi spat out, as if it was preposterous to suggest that a person who betrayed his own people would ever search a room in his own house.

"I went to look for you at the house after that little drama you pulled at the Club. I went to find you in your room. And it was lying on the floor. But is that really important how I found out? So now you are out to shatter the family completely?"

Avi was accusing *her* of breaking the family? How could he be so blinded to not notice that it wasn't her but his English friends who were sowing the seeds of anger and distrust amongst the people in the hills? How could he be so heartless and suspicious of his own family? Appa's family. Her family.

"I am ashamed to even think of how you have taken advantage of

Appa and of the privileges given to you," Avi lashed out.

Reva's legs felt like water, soft and fluid. Avi was relentless in his attack. And Reva was exhausted. This nightmare needed to end. She had do it herself.

"Avi, you are accusing me of having a shameful relationship. I shudder to even think of it, let alone indulge in it. But let me tell you this—it is your flirting and shameful behavior in the English company that is leading you to look at the world around you with the same lens. It is your guilty conscience that is making a suspect of all the people around you. As you say, the world will find out one day. For now, I have to go and so do you. If someone sees you with us natives, you will have an embarrassing time answering questions at your Club."

Before Avi had a chance to say a word, Reva walked out of the room, holding her head up, and forcing her legs to solidify like the ice she felt in her heart.

Chapter 26

September 1902

It had been weeks since Reva's heated exchange with Avi. For a few days following their confrontation, she had hoped against hopes that Avi would regret the wrongful accusations he had hurled. That he would regret the pain he had inflicted. That he would take some responsibility for the events that had shaken the foundation of their life.

For some brief but sweet moments at the Ball, Reva had seen something ignite within Avi. A desire. He had listened to her words. He had followed her movements. He had explored every inch of her body with his eyes. And she had let him. He had seen her as a woman for the first time. And he had wanted her. He had glared at the Major like the mountain lion marking its territory. The memory made Reva shiver until she realized that was all it would ever be—a memory. Reva knew she could make Avi happy. Since the night of the Ball, Reva had begun to look at herself in much the same way as she saw Rose—strong and confident. Yes, she would make Avi very happy. But Reva was no longer sure if Avi could make her happy in return.

The day Reva had exchanged words with Avi had also been the day that Sumi had refused to marry Viraj ... until the time her past was settled so that it did not come to haunt her over and over again. Until then, Sumi had informed a disappointed Viraj, she would know no peace, and she could offer no peace.

Snippet by painful snippet, Sumi had revealed the horrendous events that had forced her to flee her husband's home after his death. As a widow, Sumi had been a victim of her brother-in-law's corrupt intentions. One evening, when the rest of the family was attending a wedding, he had entered Sumi's room where she sat, with her long hair oiled and loosely braided, sewing her mother-in-law's *loogduh*. An angry Sumi had ordered him out of the room. He had laughed and refused as she threatened to call for help. Both knew there was no help around.

The evil man had eyed Sumi lecherously and faulted her beautiful hair for tormenting him during the day and depriving him of his sleep every night. He told Sumi that it was he who had ordered that her hair not be shaved after her husband's death. Her hair belonged to him. He said her hair had led him that evening to find his peace in her room once and for all. He had advanced, and in a moment of panic, Sumi had picked up the pair of scissors lying close to her and in a few rough strokes had shorn off her long tresses. She had flung them in his stunned face and ran out of her room.

Recovering, he had followed her to the kitchen. But the few seconds of head start had given Sumi the time to get her hands on a rolling pin. And as he had walked through the door, she had whacked the pin on his head making him crumble to his knees in pain. Then she had aimed a few blows at his knees and shins, shocked at her own strength and viciousness as she registered his howls with a perverse satisfaction. Once she was certain that he was in no position to pursue her, she had run out of the house screaming. The last memory she had of that terrifying day was the crowd of people that had lined the village streets as she fled.

Propelled to action after hearing Sumi's story, Viraj had sent a letter home to Mai informing that he was going to be detained in Satara for two weeks awaiting a delivery of seeds. He was determined to help Sumi settle her past. His plan was to travel to the village where she had lived and check on her brother-in-law to assure Sumi that she was not a wanted fugitive. The idea of sweet tender Sumi being a criminal was unfathomable, but Sumi had been vehement. She needed to know.

Her next condition had made Viraj furious, but Miss Annie had stopped him from trying to change her mind, which at that time was fragile and unpredictable. Viraj, Reva, and Miss Annie had to keep Viraj's involvement with Sumi a secret. If there were any consequences she had to face for her past actions, Viraj's prospects would be spoiled forever—who would offer a daughter to the boy who wanted to marry a widow, a criminal, but was rejected? The situation was messy, complex, and volatile. What was constant and heartwarming and true was the love that Sumi and Viraj had for each other.

Therefore, the day Reva had exchanged words with Avi, Viraj had not turned up at the sanatorium to escort Reva to the temple as planned. After waiting for Miss Annie and Viraj, a worried Reva was about to return home a little after lunch time when she saw Maadhu Kaka's cart make its way slowly up to the entrance.

Mai must've sent it for me, Reva thought gratefully. The cart drew to a halt, and Reva saw Maadhu Kaka alight from his seat in front and unload a trunk. Reva recognized the trunk. It was hers. Head lowered, without a word, he handed Reva a note and proceeded to carry her trunk into the main building where he set it down and walked back to the cart. Reva watched Maadhu Kaka settle into the cart again as if he were preparing to wait.

Reva glanced at the letter. The handwriting was unfamiliar, the words a slap in the face. There was only one person who could inflict harm without touching a hair on her person. Reva was still recovering from his lashing that morning.

> *Reva,*
>
> *Mai is now aware of the shameful behavior you have indulged in while pretending to be a dutiful daughter-in-law. There is no place for you in this house anymore. You have ruined our family, and your continued association with this house will destroy whatever little chance we have to salvage our reputation in the hills. You have done enough damage. Viraj has also behaved in a thoughtless and irresponsible manner. If this decision is not acceptable to him, he can stay away from the house as well. Gopi has packed all your belongings in the trunk. Some of the family jewels are missing. If you have not sold them already, the last and only decent thing you can do now is to return them with Maadhu Kaka. We trust him more than we will ever trust you.*
>
> *Avi*

In a daze, Reva had retrieved the sari and Mai's jewels that she had chosen for Sumi and herself to wear at the wedding, wrapped them up in an old cheesecloth and handed them to Maadhu Kaka, whose eyes were bright with tears.

And so it turned out that Mai had heard it all—Reva's attendance at the Ball, Reva's shameful disguise and her inappropriate interactions with the English gentlemen, and Reva's alleged role in Viraj's sudden disappearance from home.

As Reva had reread Avi's letter, her cheeks had burned with shame for lying. Her good intentions had done little to ease her disgrace. Breaking

Mai's trust had turned out to be just as painful no matter her reason, no matter the color of the lie. Mai had every right to be angry at Reva.

But after the first waves of remorse and regret had subsided, her own anger had seeped into the cracks in her heart. At the injustice of it all—at her wrong portrayal as a characterless woman and at being denied any opportunity to explain or defend herself. Mai had pronounced her guilty of an unspeakable crime without listening to her side of the story. Reva had tried her best to be a respectful caring daughter-in-law and to keep her family together. She had neglected her own dream to attend school so that she could be the person Mai wanted her to be. She had followed every instruction, respected every whim, and truly loved every person in the family. But none of that had mattered. Mai had believed Avi's misguided words in a blink of an eye.

"What do you mean you were thrown out of the house?" Miss Annie had demanded when she had finally returned to the sanatorium at tea time, delayed on the way by a sudden spell of rain. She had just finished narrating Sumi's story and Viraj's plan to Reva when she saw the trunk in her office. Wordlessly, Reva had handed Avi's letter to Miss Annie.

"They do not realize what a gem they are casting away," Miss Annie had fumed after reading it. "I ought to march there and give that husband of yours a piece of my mind. Pandering to the wrong people, he is."

But Reva had stopped her.

"Miss Annie, what could we possibly say to Mai? Until Viraj comes back, we have promised to keep their love a secret. How can I explain the letter Avi found in my room without disclosing who the bride and groom in it were?"

The truth was that Reva had lost her spirit to fight. She wasn't sure what it was that she was fighting for anymore.

"Miss Annie, I have nowhere to go. Can I stay here and work to earn my boarding while I think of what to do?"

Miss Annie's fierce hug was the only answer Reva had needed. The thought of being out of her home again had unnerved Reva, but she had survived it before. She would turn seventeen years old on *Kojagiri*, the night of the October full moon. She was no longer that impressionable young girl who had come to the hills two monsoons ago. She would manage. She just needed to rest a little. And dream a little again. Wasn't the sanatorium, locked on all sides by the magical hills the best place to recuperate?

After spending two weeks in Gopi's village recovering, Sumi returned to the sanatorium, the lightness of her step matching her heart, now that she had unburdened and shared her story with her friends. Sumi was distraught to learn that Reva had been abandoned by her family for lying about her visit to the Ball, but as agreed upon by Miss Annie and Reva, she was left in the dark about the humiliating accusations that Reva had silently borne. Miss Annie and Reva had decided to share just half of the story with Sumi in order to keep her boat steady and afloat while Viraj was away.

Reva had listened to Sumi as she talked about her life with her husband after she had left Uruli.

"Sumi, when things were so unbearable after your husband died, why didn't you just tell Kaka and Kaku and go back home to Uruli?" Reva had wondered aloud one day.

"They came to visit me after I became a widow. I tried telling them how the family had changed, how that brother-in-law had overnight become a demon. My mother simply scolded me for thinking impure thoughts. My father accused me of maligning a good person. I knew then that the door to my parents' house was closed to me forever," Sumi stated with a sigh.

Reva couldn't think which was worse—her own Aai being suddenly snatched from her or Kaku intentionally walking away from her own child. The end result was the same. They both had ended up alone. Often Miss Annie would walk into the room and find the cousins hugging and consoling each other. Often Miss Annie would join in and share the hardships of her life in England, her journey to India, and her arrival in Tarapore. Each in turn would be grateful for having found a peaceful corner in the hills that they could call home.

In the days that followed Reva immersed herself in the work at the sanatorium. She checked in the patients. She translated their complaints to Miss Annie. She supervised the nurses. She assisted Miss Annie and the visiting doctor in treating the patients. Miss Annie called her Florence Nightingale, after an English nurse who had worked tirelessly treating and comforting wounded soldiers during wartime. The logic was simple for Reva—the harder she worked during the day, the better the chances were that she would sleep at night.

Before Reva could register the passage of the season, it was time to mark the arrival of the elephant-headed God, Ganapati. The year of mourning for the family was still ongoing. Reva could not help but recall the pomp and splendor of the last festival celebration that Viraj had planned when Appa was alive. Now Viraj's continued absence had cast a worrisome cloud over the sanatorium. Cryptic telegrams of his whereabouts from time to time were beginning to raise more questions in Reva's mind than answers.

As the morning fog turned thicker and the chill in the air made its way to the bones, Reva's mood became subdued and reflective. The monsoons had washed away most of the hurt and the anger, but she was still in the dark as far as what lay ahead. It was on one such morning that Reva had the urge to visit the Krishnali temple. She longed for the silence of the solid walls, the coolness of the black stone and gurgling reassurance of the flowing water. A brisk walk in the cool September air also promised to sprout ideas for her future that the back breaking work at the sanatorium had not. Reva declined Miss Annie's offer to call a carriage. Physical labor was her penance for betraying the hearts of the people she had cared about.

In the shadows of the temple, seated beside Gau, as she lovingly referred to the water spout, Reva laid out her options. She could continue to work as a nurse and a helper with Miss Annie, a position she had been offered unconditionally. But the proximity to Avi and the family would never let her recover completely from her own misfortune. Also, once married, Viraj and Sumi would be accepted into the family sooner or later. Even Mai would not be able to resist the gentle goodness of Sumi's heart. For Reva, it would be painful to live so close and yet not be able to see Sumi, as Mai would most surely forbid any association. Viraj would continue to fight for Reva, and the family would suffer under that constant strain.

Reva needed to get out of Tarapore, a thought that was heartbreaking—she may not have grown up on the hills, but they had grown on her in the two short years that she had called them home. Perhaps Reva could go back to Uruli ... but would her own village accept her? She was now a woman shunned by her husband, a fate worse than being a widow.

Staring her in the face was only one solution, one way out. It had been at her fingertips all along. The more she thought about it, the more she realized that it was what she had always wanted. It was what Aai had wanted for her. And so had Appa. She had to pursue her dream of going to school once again. Without a proper education, she had little power to stop the Mr. Jones' of the English world from taking advantage of the simple minded locals. With neither an education nor a family, she had no power to help herself. If only she had heeded Hirkani's warnings.

Reva had depended on other people for her happiness for far too long—Aai, Appa, Mai, Viraj, and even Avi. Some willing to help but unable by circumstance, others able but unwilling at heart. It was time to depend on herself, time to stand on her own two feet. Reva had shoved her dreams in the back recesses of her life for too many reasons. Now, she decided, she must test the strength of her willpower and the reality of her dream. She had nothing to lose anymore. She resolved to ask Miss Annie about the school in Panchgar village that Appa had mentioned. A small smile started to form on Reva's face as she realized Panchgar was very much a part of the majestic mountain range where Reva had made herself at home. She would still be a part of the hills.

In that instant, Reva felt her heart lifting ever so slightly. For the first time in months, she felt happy, even liberated as she contemplated the first step she needed to take. She wished she had brought Sumi along with her to share in this moment of joy, of relief. She looked around the temple with hopeful eyes. Then, turning her head towards the entrance of the inner sanctum, Reva called out softly, "Hirkani. Hirkani. Are you there?"

Silence. Reva chuckled to herself. Hirkani had missed her chance to hear Reva declare that her bow was restrung and her arrow was aimed, ready to launch. Reva was back on the path to school. A path from which she never should have strayed.

As Reva entered the gates of the sanatorium, a nurse ran towards her.

"Viraj *dada* is back! Viraj *dada* is back!"

Reva rushed into the main building to find Sumi in Miss Annie's office, beaming, next to a drawn, bearded, but smiling Viraj.

"Well!" Miss Annie exclaimed, "isn't this just lovely! All my favorite people back together again. The Lord be praised! ... But I am going to have to leave you to catch up with each other for a while." Casting a kindly glance towards Reva, she added, "...and plan a wedding while I go check in on my patients."

Overjoyed at Miss Annie's implication, Reva squeezed Sumi's hand.

"So tell us what happened when you went to Sumi's village," Reva entreated Viraj. She wanted a solid assurance that nothing and no one could spoil Sumi's happiness now.

Viraj laughed softly and drew in a long, slow breath.

"When I reached the village, the neighbors informed me that the family had moved shortly following that evening when a distraught daughter-in-law had stood in the village square shouting accusations and screaming for help. The family couldn't face their friends and neighbors after such humiliation. So they moved to their ancestral home in Konkan along the coast. It was not easy to locate the family since the information I was given was wrong, as I later realized. But once I had located them, I hatched a plan. I approached the family seeking information about a woman, Sumi, residing in a city shelter, who had run away from home. At first the brother-in-law rose up like a lion, claiming that it was a private family affair and nobody else's business. He coldly demanded the location of the shelter without a hint of interest in the well-being of the woman. My initial plan was to confirm with my own eyes that the man was alive and that he had not succumbed to his injuries. But his arrogance and depravity infuriated me. So I pretended to be an officer of the court sent, on the request of the woman's new husband, to investigate and arrest the culprit. The coward! He had the strength to fight a lone woman, but it vanished the moment I mentioned a husband and the police. He became a petrified mouse eating out my hand, and I fed him a lesson he'll never forget. I think I scratched Sumi's name out of his filthy mind forever." Viraj spoke fiercely before stealing a glance at Sumi.

Reva hugged Sumi close and whispered, "You are going to be so happy, Sumi."

"And what about you, Reva?" Viraj probed. "Miss Annie told me the preposterous things that have happened. I was so caught up in my own happiness that I failed you, Reva. Forgive me. Never would I have imagined that Avi would stoop to such a level or that Mai would be so easily swayed by him. Why didn't you just tell them the truth about the letter?"

"That's my fault," Sumi interrupted. "I am just as guilty of thinking selfishly. If Reva would've explained the letter, she would've broken the promise she made to me about keeping our feelings a secret. I was doing it to protect you Viraj, but I fed my cousin to the lions in the process. How could I have been so blind? How could I have thought of building my family on Reva's back?" Sumi teared up.

Reva silenced them both. Now that Sumi knew the whole story, Reva was concerned that she would suffer a relapse if she thought too much about Reva's bleak future and her own contribution to it. More importantly, Reva's visit to the temple had cleared more than a few cobwebs in her mind. She was determined to transform her misfortune into an opportunity.

"Maybe things would have been different if I had been honest with Mai," Reva admitted. "But relationships are tested by difficult times. Viraj, you took the time to know me, to teach me, and even to protect me. Appa may have laid the foundation to our relationship, but we nurtured it together. I could not have asked for a better brother. But I have realized now that Appa was the only real connection between me and Mai and Avi. With Appa gone, that relationship evaporated like the mountain fog. The last few weeks have helped me see who my real family is."

Reva meant every word. Miss Annie, Viraj, and Sumi were her family. Even Hirkani. She was not alone.

"I know that once you go back to the house, we may not be able to meet again. But you will always be my brother, and Sumi you were always my sister," Reva continued. "Miss Annie has been like an anchor in my stormy sea. She will never turn her back on me—I know it. I'll be happy, Viraj. In fact, I already am. I have made some decisions of my own that I will share with you shortly. Go on now. Go meet Mai and tell her everything. Despite her anger, she must be very anxious to see you and ensure you are well. Go introduce your bride-to-be to Mai and Tai-Aaji. I am honestly very glad that I am not going to be on the receiving end of that lashing," Reva added with an impish smile. It was a moment to rejoice, and she found the grim faces around her offensive.

Viraj prepared to take leave of the women promising Sumi that he would come for her first thing in the morning. As he was about to step out of the room, Reva said, "Viraj, your place was always elevated in my eyes. With your cherishing Sumi, you have risen even higher."

Chapter 27

September 1902

To Reva's immense relief, Viraj returned to the sanatorium early next morning as promised. He recounted what had transpired in the house, and Reva listened, silent and thoughtful. Mai and Tai-Aa-ji had been shocked to see Viraj and his physical condition, and then balked on hearing Viraj's news. At first, they did not register the significance of his marrying a widowed Sumi, as the horror of the accusations they had laid on Reva dawned on them. They had turned away a daughter-in-law when her only crime had been to strive for the happiness of their family, albeit in a misguided and immature way. Viraj's harsh words of admonishment and disbelief had further intensified their regret. Mai had wanted to rush to the sanatorium right away, but Viraj, sensing Reva's raw wounds, had stopped her. He had warned Mai to give Reva time to come to terms with this change of heart and to be prepared for the worst. Mai had then ordered Viraj to send word to Avi to come home, but Viraj, still reeling from the storm that Avi's pride and white-worship had unleashed, had refused to comply with her wishes.

Finally, Mai had asked Viraj, "So, who is this girl Sumi?"

"Mai has changed," Viraj informed his audience at the sanatorium. "She should've been furious with me for not consulting her before choosing my wife. But she only remarked that having misjudged Reva, she must question her own skills of judging a person's character and intentions." Reva felt a trifle vindicated.

Viraj had shared with Mai and Tai-Aaji all the details about Sumi, including her controversial but now settled past. His tone had suggested that there was no room for discussion or rejection. And the women had listened. Mai had taken some time to warm up to the idea of Sumi becoming her daughter-in-law, but surprisingly it was Tai-Aaji who had broken down with joy as she sang praises of her grandson's chivalry for not holding Sumi's widowhood against her. Mai was only now realizing first-hand that harsh reality. Tai-Aaji had not known an existence without it.

"When can we meet her, Viraj?" Mai had asked.

And just like that Viraj and Sumi's happiness had been sealed and blessed.

The marriage was to take place in two weeks—a small affair in the house. But Viraj wanted to invite the villagers for the lunch as an act of goodwill to relieve the tension in the community and restart the work of resisting the English atrocities in the hills. He also wanted the villagers to see that he was proud of his bride, a widow, a woman he loved and respected. He expected everyone to do the same. An image of Appa in his younger days flashed before Reva's eyes as she heard every word and read every emotion in Viraj's plan.

Viraj and Sumi were to be married. Mai and Tai-Aaji knew the truth and appeared to have forgiven Reva. This was as much happiness she could expect for now. She had Sumi at the sanatorium for two weeks all to herself. She would teach Sumi how Mai liked her table set, how to cook the stuffed brinjals that Viraj loved, and how not to mess with Tai-Aaji's prayer room. She would caution Sumi to stay out of Avi's way should any circumstance arise.

Day by day, Sumi blossomed under the care and attention that was showered on her. Reva had never heard her talk with as much hope and excitement about the future. She wished Sumi would not suppress her feelings in front of her. One day, as Sumi described, with a dullness, a new sari that Mai had bought for her, Reva had given her a fine scolding.

"If you are going to behave like it's my funeral instead of your wedding, I am going to leave the village right away and never come back. I am happy for you, dear Sumi. Don't worry about me, or feel guilty. I am grateful that Mai has forgiven me. Avi and I were never meant to be. I am not sad. I truly am content. Don't hide your happiness from me. It breaks my heart."

So Sumi had confessed everything—how Mai and Tai-Aaji had welcomed and pampered her. She counted the saris they had ordered and described the jewelry they had chosen for her. She talked about the lanterns being dusted and hung in the house for the wedding and the extra rooms that were being readied for the out-of-town guests. Some of Appa's friends and business partners from Satara were coming. She blushed while sharing how Viraj had chosen for her a beautiful nose ring from the family jewels. Hesitantly, she had mentioned her meeting with Avi—brief and awkward. The two brothers had barely exchanged a few words and Avi had left soon after. He was still living at the Club. Sumi shared how Mai's heart broke a little each time to see her two sons so distant and indifferent.

As Reva listened, she had a strange sense that the events of the past two years had been building to this moment—Reva had been destined to enter the family and pave the way for Sumi. Suddenly, her trials seemed worth the pain.

"Reva, Mai keeps asking to meet you," Sumi ventured tentatively, a week before the wedding. "Viraj has told her that the decision is up to you, when you are ready ... if you are ready."

"Sumi, really, I have no more anger or ill will against any of them. Even Avi. But the hurt still lingers, and my resolve still wavers. My healing will come when I explore the path I have chosen for myself. I need time," Reva replied honestly.

"I was hoping you would come to the house for the wedding at least," Sumi said softly.

Reva had considered this request. She had seen it in Sumi's eyes constantly.

"I really don't know what to do, Sumi. I do not want tears or sad thoughts to cloud your happy day. My mind tells me that I should stay away. And yet my heart demands that I be with my dearest cousin on her special day."

"Reva, you and Miss Annie are the only family I have. And Miss Annie won't understand half the things going on."

Both Sumi and Reva giggled as they pictured a bewildered Miss Annie without Viraj or Reva to help her understand and translate the proceedings. Miss Annie would also need protection from Tai-Aaji's glare as she tried to annihilate the foreign body polluting the auspicious ceremony.

Reva voiced a nagging worry. "Sumi, there is still the possibility of an ugly scene if Avi sees me at the wedding. He despises me, and I cannot forget how he has betrayed the villagers..."

Sumi shook her head.

So Reva implored, "Sumi, you did not witness the disgust with which he talked to me in Miss Annie's office. He could not control his anger. What if he does the same on your wedding day? I am still not convinced I should come."

"Reva, I don't think he hates you," Sumi voiced her disagreement firmly. "He will be at the ceremony briefly. The villagers detest him, and he knows it. He may not even stay for the lunch—how can he when he is the reason this ill will grew and spread in the village. If he dares to say anything hurtful to you, I will personally tell him to leave," Sumi said fiercely, bringing a smile to Reva's lips.

Pondering the future scene was exhausting. "What should I do, Sumi? I cannot think any more. I am tired," Reva sighed and slumped on the floor.

"Then let me take care of you for a little while, my dear," Sumi said gently, squatting next to Reva, "... and at least listen to what I say."

Reva relaxed her head on Sumi's shoulder while Sumi spoke. Reva observed silently how their roles had suddenly changed.

Two days later, Reva found herself hesitating on the doorstep of the very house that had been her home a few short months ago. Sumi and Viraj had already proceeded inside, taking with them whatever little confidence Reva felt at carrying out Sumi's plan. Sumi had convinced Reva to meet Mai and Tai-Aaji before the wedding day, so they had an opportunity to talk and share and forgive in the privacy of their home rather than in a crowded marriage house. Reva had agreed. She needed to close this chapter of her life in order to open the next.

Reva glanced back uncertainly in the direction of the cart and saw Maadhu Kaka motion with his wrinkled hands and wise eyes to step forward. As she turned to face the door again, she realized the decision was made for her. Mai stood in the doorway. Sumi and Viraj stood right behind, beaming. She even saw Tai-Aaji smiling in a way she had never seen before. In that poignant moment, she expected Appa to appear in his armchair that was still in its place on the front porch. Mai stood in the doorway, a lighted lamp in hand, ready to perform the ritual meant to welcome a loved one home after a long absence. Reva's tears were flowing and so were Mai's.

Meeting with Mai and Tai-Aaji was as satisfying as Sumi had promised. It was also heartwrenching when Reva informed the women that returning home was not in her destiny for now. In that moment, as she knowingly turned down the safety and security of the home she had strived to belong, Reva silently prayed that the confidence she had built on the basis of a childhood dream and an uncertain plan would continue to forge the way forward for her.

When the sun made its way south that evening, Mai wistfully bade Reva goodbye. She ran her hand over Reva's head in blessing and said, "Whatever decision you take Reva, remember you are a daughter of this house. This door will always remain open for you. It is our loss that we did not see this diamond in the rough."

The night before the wedding was the October full moon, the night of *Kojagiri*. Reva turned seventeen. As Reva got ready to sleep, her last night with Sumi, she gasped. On the bed lay the most gorgeous sari—a deep silky blue, like the Krishna river, delicately embroidered with silver thread that made the fabric resemble a resplendent night sky. A set of pearls that matched the splendor of the sari lay right beside it. Reva also noticed another bundle wrapped in a familiar cheesecloth. She did not need to open it. She knew it was the necklace and bracelets that Mai had accused her of stealing on a sad day not too long ago. It was Mai apologizing yet again.

"These are gifts from Mai. And Tai-Aaji. You are still a daughter-in-law of the house, and you have to look that part tomorrow. But, if you ask me Reva, you don't need this sari or any of Miss Annie's gowns to dazzle. You shine from within," Sumi said, hugging Reva to her heart.

Reva drifted off into a restful sleep soon dreaming of another *Kojagiri* night when she and Aai had shared the excitement of the moonlight together. At first, Reva did not recognize the young woman sitting shoulder to shoulder beside Aai. From behind, her back was straight, her chin was up, and as she turned to glance over her shoulder, Reva saw that her hazel eyes were like the fire that fueled the full moon and her fair skin was tinged with a delicate red of the mountain strawberries. That special night, if the Goddess came calling, "Who is awake?", she would know in a heartbeat that Reva was most certainly awake.

Chapter 28

October 1902

Reva stepped back to admire her handiwork. She was more than satisfied. One look at his ravishing bride and Viraj was going to wish he had not insisted on inviting a crowd for lunch following the marriage rites. Long braided hair studded with fresh fragrant *mogra*, dark eyes lined with charcoal black *kajal*, a nose ring over rose-tinged smiling lips set in a radiant complexion, Sumi was ready to mesmerize the guests. Gone was the young girl, the forlorn widow, the helpless patient. In her place stood a blushing bride, smitten by her love. Reva dabbed some *kajal* behind Sumi's ear to ward off the evil eye.

Maadhu Kaka was waiting with the cart to take Miss Annie and Sumi to the house for the early morning rituals. Miss Annie was pretending to be the mother of the bride, and judging from the number of times she had teared up that morning, she really seemed to believe she was.

After seeing Sumi off with a promise to reach Appa's house as soon as possible, Reva surveyed her room—Sumi's belongings made their absence felt. Forcing herself out of the melancholy, Reva hummed as she got ready for the festivities. She remembered the last time she had taken as much care on her appearance. It had been the evening of the

Summer Ball that had rolled her life downhill. The girl in the elegant English gown had been exciting but a stranger nevertheless. Her reflection today was familiar, comforting. The girl in the gown had taught her that she could be whoever and whatever she wanted to be. The sari-clad woman in the mirror today had decided who she wanted to be and knew what she needed to do.

A knock on the door caught Reva by surprise. She was not expecting Maadhu Kaka to return so quickly. It had barely been an hour. She had not even had a chance to put up her hair or wear her jewels. Maadhu Kaka would just have to wait.

"There is someone to see you, Reva *tai*," the nurse announced from outside.

"If it's a new patient, sister, you know how to check in. I'll do the paperwork later. We talked about this yesterday," Reva said, slightly annoyed.

"No, Reva *tai*. It's not that. The man says he is your husband."

Reva froze. The public acknowledgement of a relationship that she had sought to nurture, fought to save, and then been forced to cast away made her momentarily question her own sanity. She recalled the scene at the Club that summer when she had waited patiently, her heart in her mouth, for Avi to meet with her. She recalled the embarrassment and frustration when he had not even bothered to come out of his quarters.

"Tell him that I am getting ready for an important marriage. I cannot be disturbed." The words came out before Reva had a chance to weigh the consequence. She heard the shuffle of the nurse's feet, the exchange of muddled words, and then silence.

Had she regressed in her life, wanting to exact a childish revenge for a past humiliation, or was she genuinely concerned that she would be late for Sumi's wedding? She convinced herself that she would've responded in a similar manner if it had been any other person. And in reality, over the past few months, Avi had made it clear that he was just another person.

The cawing of the crow right outside her window broke her train of thoughts. She had to get going, or else Sumi would never forgive her.

Reva walked into the house as the marriage rites were in full swing. Sumi cast a grateful glance in her direction. Miss Annie, seated behind Sumi, was trying her best to understand what the priest was saying. Tai-Aaji would probably come down from her room at lunch time. Viraj looked handsome, dressed in a *bundhgala* and *dhoti*. Standing right behind him was Avi, in an attire similar to the groom. Their eyes met. Reva held his glance briefly, then looked away. She had promised herself that she would not have downcast eyes—she had nothing to be ashamed of, nor did she feel shy around him anymore.

Reva found a corner in the room where the view was clear and the air relaxed.

"Appa would've been so happy today," a voice beside her remarked. "Two strapping sons and two enchanting daughters-in-law adding to the magic of his beloved hills."

Reva remembered him. He was Appa's friend, Damoo Kaka, who had planned to retire in Tarapore.

She respectfully touched his feet for his blessings and replied, "It would've been even more wonderful if you had a home here as well. Then our family would have been truly complete."

"What are you saying, child? Didn't Avi tell you? He has talked his office into reconsidering some of the land transactions that were rejected a few months ago. He has the charm of a magician, that boy." He smiled and winked at Reva. "I am moving to Tarapore as soon as the winter is over. My new house is on the way to the Krishnali temple. I will remind Avi that you young people should pay us a visit. It will give us some vitality." Chuckling at his own comment, Appa's friend moved to find a seat and watch the ceremony.

Partly confused, Reva's eyes flew to where Avi had been standing. He had disappeared. Her eyes skimmed over the crowd that had started to filter in but failed to spot the face they sought. Just then, she felt Mai's hand tug her in the direction of the lunch area. The villagers were beginning to seat themselves and as Sumi had predicted, it seemed that Avi had left. Reva thought about her behavior that morning when Avi had tried to meet her. She struggled with the information that Damoo Kaka had shared. She acknowledged that she had let her pride ruin whatever little hope there was of having a courteous relationship with Avi. For Viraj and Sumi's sake.

It was almost four hours later, after the last guest had left, that Reva, with a heavy heart, began to take leave of the family. Mai motioned for Reva to follow her to her room.

Closing the door behind her, she bade Reva to sit down beside her. This was the Mai, Reva knew and loved—commanding and direct.

"Reva, you know your room is still waiting for you here. You don't have to go back to the sanatorium. I know there is much to sort out between you and Avi, but this is your home while you do that..." Mai said, "... or even if you don't."

"Mai, if I stay here, I cannot move on. And neither can Avi. So much has happened. I need time and space to think. Please don't make this harder for me than it already is. You are like my mother, and I will always be a daughter whenever you need one."

Mai's hands slumped to her sides.

"I am indeed an unfortunate mother. With one hand I welcome a daughter, and with another I bid a daughter goodbye," she sighed. "But what can I do? Everything is changing. You have minds of your own, and I don't have the energy or the wit to fight it all. But there is something that I can and want to do. I know Appa wanted it too. It's a gift. After all, a marriage in the house and no gift for my oldest daughter-in-law?"

Mai reached under the bed to pull out Reva's gift. Reva gasped as Appa's briefcase came into view.

"It's yours. Appa had told me once how much you liked it. I think he would've wanted you to have it," Mai said tenderly. "I think you are going to need it."

Reva looked at Mai, puzzled.

"Open it," Mai instructed. "My gift is inside."

Reva clicked the clasp open. Inside lay an envelope.

"Open that when you get to the sanatorium. Miss Annie can explain everything. You are not the only one that can keep secrets," Mai said attempting to lighten the mood. "Now go. Maadhu Kaka is waiting. It has been a long day for him too." With a wave of goodbye, Mai dismissed Reva.

Reva's first inclination was to refuse the envelope, assuming it contained a cash gift as was customary. Her pride wished to decline any help. But the truth was that she needed money now to pursue her dream and refusing would have hurt an already vulnerable Mai. So, Reva quietly accepted the envelope, touched Mai's feet, and headed outside to find Maadhu Kaka.

As the cart rattled along the dirt road, Reva opened the envelope. There was no money inside. Only a letter. In it, Mai had gifted Reva her dream.

It would be another fifteen minutes before they reached the sanatorium. But Reva could've crossed that distance in five, so hard was her heart racing. Reva now had a definite plan for the following day and the day after and the weeks and months ahead. She could not wait to talk to Miss Annie as Mai had instructed. Mai had given her the gift of a third life. How happy Sumi would be to hear that Reva was also making a fresh start.

The cart began to slow down. Reva grimaced. Was there a problem? The sun would be setting soon and finding help at that hour would be difficult. She frowned as the cart came to a complete standstill.

"Maadhu Kaka, you can turn back and go home now. We are going to walk the rest of the way," a crisp voice commanded. Reva watched Maadhu Kaka's head bobbing up and down in agreement, getting ready to coax the animals around while waiting for Reva to alight from the cart.

Reva's mind replayed an old memory of Avi and her visiting the Krishnali temple. Avi was still issuing orders.

"Did you understand what I said, or should I say it in English, Miss Rose?" Avi demanded. He had come around the side of the cart. There was a hint of humor and a threat of action in his voice.

Standing alone on the dusty road, Avi did not look as composed and confident as Reva remembered him. He appeared a trifle distraught, uncertain even.

Not wishing to create a scene in front of Maadhu Kaka and still a little ashamed of her rude behavior that morning, Reva stepped down. Avi and Reva both waited for Maadhu Kaka to turn the cart around. Reva watched the cart disappear in the distance. She felt herself completely unprepared for this moment.

"I don't bite you know," Avi said, studying her face closely. "At least I won't today." He smiled.

Reva blushed. Damoo Kaka was right—Avi could ooze charm. But Reva knew the danger of succumbing. Taking in a deep breath, she met his gaze and asked, "What do you want to talk to me about?" She started walking in the direction of the sanatorium.

"Can't you guess?" Avi stepped in front of Reva, stopping her in her tracks. "I want to apologize for the pain I have caused you. You are just a girl and I should have..." But Reva cut him off sharply.

"I am not just a girl anymore, Avi. So you need not worry."

His name had rolled comfortably off her tongue without neither a pause nor a stutter.

Reva tried to walk past him, but Avi put his arm across to hold her back.

"On the contrary, I have so much more to worry about now," his voice trembled, and he came dangerously close to Reva whose legs matched his voice.

Reva noticed that Avi's lower lip had a deeper cleft than his upper lip. The intimacy of the discovery made her step back. She stumbled, and Avi reached out for her, pulling her closer to him this time.

Ignoring the blood rushing into her head and desperately commanding her legs to stiffen, Reva looked around to see if anyone was watching.

"What are you afraid of, Reva? You have a right to be here with me. You are my wife," Avi said.

The words that would have turned her life to gold a few months ago snapped Reva out of her dark fantasy. She loosened her arm from his grip.

"If I don't want to be seen with you, it's because I don't want any of the villagers to consider me your ally, let alone your wife. I shudder to think of all the evil scheming that I witnessed at the Ball. You pander to the white people who will never give you the kind of respect you deserve on account of the color of your skin or the place of your birth. That's where we are different... I may be your wife on paper, but our thoughts are at odds. Such a marriage is doomed even before it starts." Reva paused for a breath and Avi seized his chance to explain.

"What you say is true, Reva... I cannot deny it ... I have learnt some bitter lessons myself. The moment Mr. Jones realized that the villagers wanted nothing to do with me, that they would not listen to my word as they used to, he turned his attention and granted favors to Rich, never wasting an opportunity to remind me of my compromised position. Overnight they had no use for me. I became a wretched local who must be tolerated. I realized then how foolish I had been. For the last few weeks, I have been speaking out against the land reservation, trying to tame the demon that I helped create. It is true that the English want to create their own private enclave in the hills. But they are also aware that doing so may fuel the fire in the freedom struggle gaining momentum in the rest of the country. They are experimenting with the idea in Tarapore to test its viability and to judge the strength of the people's resistance to it. If it is successful here, it will be enforced in the bigger hill stations as well. So far, they haven't had much success. The locals are refusing to work for wages preferring to leave the village instead and finding other farms to toil. Some are resorting to trade. There aren't enough workers to cook, clean, and entertain the white people anymore. Before long, the English are going to realize that the land reservation is just as dangerous to their continued presence as it is disastrous to our people."

Seeing that Reva was listening to him intently, Avi continued to plead his case.

"I am speaking up against it to the officers higher up in the Raj. Our people have taught me an important lesson about self-respect ... I can go on Reva, but what I am trying to show you is that I am already repenting for the decisions and choices I have made in the past. Every accusation you have made is true. But by doing so, my dear Reva, don't you see? You have proved that you are the best choice for me. You are my *ardhangini*, my better half. Please forgive me and give me a chance to show how I have changed… how knowing you has changed me."

Avi moved closer. His voice dropped to a whisper, "Let's start our life together as Appa had wanted us to. Come home, Reva."

Reva closed her eyes. She imagined Appa himself waiting expectantly for her answer. Avi sounded like a different person, but only time would prove the truth in his claim. After all, it was only the passage of time that had made Reva the person she was today. On the other hand, Avi had called her 'dear Reva'. How sweet it sounded to her ears. How easy it would be to give in to his charm. How delicious would be the consequences of that surrender!

Mai's letter that Reva had clutched in her hand all this time fluttered to the ground. The whiteness of the envelope lying in the red dirt reminded Reva of the huge contrast in what she had planned to do just a few minutes ago and what she was about to do now.

Gently, she pulled her hands out of his warm grasp. She smiled, willing God to give her the strength she needed.

"If you truly love me, then you will let me go," she said, handing Avi the letter.

Reva had read and reread the letter so many times in the cart that she could recite every line as Avi's eyes quickly took in the contents.

> *Dear Miss Revati Tambay,*
> *We are delighted to inform you that you have been admitted into St. Joseph's Convent School, Panchgar for the school years 1903 - 1904. Given the breaks in your course of study on account of your unfortunate life circumstance, you will work*

*with a private tutor until matriculation. In return, you will
provide tutoring services for the younger students and help in
the office, as needed. Your room and board has been paid for
the entire period by the family of Appasaheb Tambay.
Welcome to St. Joseph's Convent School. We look forward to
your arrival in January of the new calendar year. God bless.
Sister Maria
Daughters of the Cross*

"I am going to school, Avi," Reva whispered gently, as she retrieved the letter from his still hands. The words felt right as soon as they emerged from her mouth.

"Ever since I can remember I have wanted to study. I want to become a doctor and cure poor villagers, or perhaps be a leader like Appa or Viraj, or even a lawyer to fight for the rights of our people, to be their voice. I want to see who Reva is and who she can become. I need time. If you truly love me, you will wait for me just like I did for you."

Then Reva started to walk down the trail, the softest of chimes ringing in her ears. At the entrance to the sanatorium, she turned back towards Avi and waved. It was time to go to school.

EPILOGUE

Uruli, August 1908
6 years later

R eva had traveled to Uruli as soon as the monsoon ended. Her birthplace, where the seed of learning had been sowed in her earliest memories, seemed like the best place to visit after earning her law degree from the Bombay University. After all, in the smallest room of the farthest corner in the *vaada*, Aai and Reva had planted and nurtured the lofty dream of a little girl going to school.

The visit, however, had been a disappointment. The room that Reva had shared with her mother had been converted into a storeroom with mounds of dust and a family of lizards amidst a jumble of things that were unloved and forgotten. Reva felt foolish for believing that she could relive her time with Aai in a place where they had last been together. She now sat morosely and watched the dirt track unfolding and stretching away from the *vaada*.

Reva would have completely succumbed to her melancholy, if it hadn't been for the *buggywala*, carriage driver, encouraging Reva to taste the sugarcane grown in Uruli before continuing the journey towards Tarapore. Reva was amused that the *buggywala* was treating her like a newcomer to this village. If only he knew that seven years ago she could've have pointed to the precise plot of land that produced the sweetest fruit. But she merely nodded and instructed him to head towards the market.

Soon the cart came to a halt in the village market that Reva remembered so well. Her eyes spotted the *halvai*, sweet shop. She made a note to tell Sumi how the owner had moved all the sweet displays inside—probably to hide them from the good-for-nothing children who swiped them when his back was turned. Reva stifled a giggle as she remembered how she and Sumi had outrun the boys one afternoon many years ago.

"*Agga bai!* Oh my goodness! Are my eyes playing tricks on me? Is that my little Reva all grown up? It must be! Who else in this village has skin as white as the moon, and a smile as radiant as the sun itself!"

Reva's head jerked up in the direction of the shop where the *buggy-wala* was buying the sugarcane. Amidst baskets of brinjals, potatoes, cabbage heads and bananas sat Hirkani with four children buzzing around her.

"Hirkani? HIRKANI! Is that really you? I looked all over for you!" Reva ran to Hirkani's side. Impulsively, she reached for Hirkani's hand and gave it a squeeze as if convincing herself that she was not hallucinating. No longer did she care for social norms that kept her away from the people she loved. As a newly appointed lawyer, she would take to task anyone who bothered Hirkani about it too.

"Why? I have been right here. Where would I go?" Hirkani replied, still recovering from her shock. "It's true I don't visit houses anymore to sell my produce since we bought this little store. And to tell you the truth, I don't miss those long days in the sun one bit!"

"I knew it! I had a feeling you must have returned to Uruli! I was away from Tarapore too—in Panchgar village. So even if you had visited the temple, I had no chance to run into you," Reva rambled, reveling in the joy of seeing her friend again. "Hirkani! You will be the happiest to know that I went back to school just like you kept telling me to ... in the temple. Remember? Not only that, after matriculation, I went to college and got a degree from the University, Hirkani! I am a lawyer now!" Reva was ecstatic that she could share her news with Hirkani.

"Reva, my dear girl! What are you talking about? What temple? And where is this Panchgar? And tell me, how can I return to the village as you said when I have not left it even for a day? God promise. Ask my children ... But let that be. What is that other thing you said? You are all smart and learned now. I always knew you would go places. And look at you—you did!" Hirkani stopped only when her attention was claimed by an impatient customer.

It was just as well, for Reva was dumbfounded. Hirkani's words had put her mind in a spin. Reva had not only seen Hirkani at the temple in Tarapore, but Reva had unburdened herself to Hirkani each time and found a sliver of peace in her advice. Hirkani had been her lighthouse in the stormy years, helping her find her way out to safety each time. And yet ... and yet Hirkani claimed that she had never left Uruli!

All through Hirkani's subsequent chatter about Reva's success, Avi's good fortune, and their match made in heaven, Reva wrestled with what she had learned in Uruli that day. As the carriage began its uphill journey into the mountains early the next morning, Reva concluded that there was only one possible explanation. And it made her home in the hills even more magical.

Acknowledgements

Most special thanks to Aai-Baba for believing in me and my make-believe. When you threatened to take my manuscript to the publishers yourselves, it was motivation enough for me to get cracking on the nitty-gritty of bringing a book into this world.

Special thanks to my husband Ashish for keeping the wine cellar stocked and for pairing each pour with sincere appreciation, spot-on critiques, and barely any unsolicited opinions. You kept this project and me above water right from the Prologue (there used to be one) to the Epilogue.

Special thanks to my daughter Arohi for reacquainting me with the exciting world of dreams … and then making me want to achieve mine. Reva was bound to follow.

Special thanks to my extended family for being my memory holders, my storytellers, and my unconditional cheerleaders. You bring out my best self. Both real and imagined.

Special thanks to my multi-talented writing buddy Alice for diligently reading by shitty first drafts and adding immensely to the plotting and pantsing that followed. Your creativity and drive inspire me beyond words.

Special thanks to my editors Julie Mosow and Julie Tibbott for keeping their eyes on the pesky details that eluded mine. Your efforts made my story richer and my writing stronger.

Special thanks to my Gal Pals - the title says it all. I may have written the words to this story, but as daughters, wives, mothers, and friends, you have just as much ink in it as me. You have added to the interest, emotion, depth, and perspective of my story by sharing with me your own.

And a 190-degrees-extra-hot tall thanks to my dedicated coffee-companions for being my pop-up sounding-boards and for keeping my Starbucks office afloat. Nothing like a jittery muse to fire the imagination!

Made in the USA
Middletown, DE
18 September 2020